Hot Summer Nights

Books by Joan Elizabeth Lloyd

THE PRICE OF PLEASURE

NEVER ENOUGH

CLUB FANTASY

NIGHT AFTER NIGHT

THE SECRET LIVES OF HOUSEWIVES

NAUGHTIER BEDTIME STORIES

HOT SUMMER NIGHTS

Hot Summer Nights

JOAN ELIZABETH LLOYD

KENSINGTON BOOKS

KENSINGTON BOOKS are published by

Kensington Publishing Corp.
850 Third Avenue
New York, NY 10022

ISBN-13: 978-0-7394-8390-9

Printed in the United States of America

Hot Summer Nights

Chapter
1

Burned out, Leslie thought. What a ridiculous concept. She loved her job—most of the time—was phenomenally well paid for it, and everyone who did business with her told her how wonderful and talented she was. How could she be burned out? Well, she sighed, as she drove east through Connecticut on Route 95, maybe this vacation would help her sort through her feelings. She wasn't about to give up her job, and yet she wasn't looking forward to her eventual return to business either.

When had she started thinking burnout?

It had begun several weeks before with a favorite client, Bob Rowan. She had been using the motel room in Club Fantasy, a simple room that could be rearranged to become a photo studio, a hooker's room, or, as it had been that evening, an elegant bedroom in a mansion in the suburbs. That evening, dressed in a sheer peach-colored nightgown and red silk robe, Leslie had been sitting at the dressing table brushing her shoulder-length ash-blond hair when she heard someone in the closet. Heartbeat speeding as it always did when something like the action of that evening began, she kept taking long strokes through the strands and glanced into the mirror at the door to the closet, where she knew Bob was hiding.

They'd played this fantasy so many times that she knew exactly what was going to happen but still she threw herself into her role and played innocent. As the closet door slowly opened, she whipped around. "What's that . . . ?"

Despite the warm late spring weather outside, Bob was dressed in a black turtleneck, black jeans with black socks, and tennis shoes. Black leather gloves covered his hands and a black watch cap hid his salt-and-pepper crew cut. "Say nothing, do nothing, and everything will be fine," he growled.

"What the hell are you doing here? Get out of my house!" She spoke softly, yet forcefully.

"I'm here for you," Bob said. In only two strides he was behind her, holding her hair twisted in his fist, pulling her head back.

"You're hurting me," she said, knowing that the slight pain he caused was all part of this playlet and helped keep her in character.

"Only a little," he said, a slight grin causing creases to form around his deep brown eyes.

She remained silent although she could have screamed or protested. She knew he wouldn't stop unless she used the safe word they'd agreed on.

He pulled harder, forcing her to stand to ease the pressure on her scalp. "I didn't think you'd be home so early," he said.

"I'm sure you didn't," she said, her eyes narrowing, her pulse pounding.

"But you know," he continued, "this might be an added bonus. I get to steal your jewels and have you too."

"My jewelry. Of course. Listen," she said, sounding as reasonable as she could, "take my jewels and then just leave. I promise I won't tell anyone."

"I know you won't tell anyone and we're going to have some fun together before I leave." He dragged her toward the bed and tossed her onto it, throwing her robe open, revealing her peach-colored satin nightgown beneath. His eyes roamed her body as if he'd never seen it before. "Lovely. Truly lovely."

Her eyes widened. "What are you going to do?"

His laugh was genuine. "As if you didn't know."

It was all she could do not to giggle; it was so theatrical, but in its own way delicious too. She sighed, heaving her ample bosom, pulling herself back into character. Tightening her grip on herself she said, "Please. Don't hurt me."

Bob opened the bedside table drawer and pulled out several strips of fabric lined with thick fur that she'd put there for him. With little fuss despite her struggles, he tied Leslie's wrists to the bedposts, the bindings secure and pulled just tight enough to stretch her arms wide without undue discomfort.

She kicked and twisted, careful not to injure him or herself, yet with ease he grabbed one ankle and fastened a strip around it, then attached it to one of the bed legs. Then he made quick work of the other. She was wet, her nipples tight, her belly throbbing. Leslie was always surprised at how hot it all made her despite the fact that she was playing a part. Bob ran a gloved finger through her vaginal folds and laughed. "This really turns you on, doesn't it?"

"Yes," she answered, both for her character and for herself.

"Good. I'm glad." He grabbed the front of her gown and pulled, ripping it easily down the front along seams that had been carefully loosened. "Because you're mine and I intend to take you. Slowly."

"Please," she whimpered, "don't. I don't want you."

"Your body says different," Bob said, rubbing his dampened fingers together. "I hope you're not going to scream. If you do I'll have to gag you too."

She shook her head violently and whispered, "I'll be quiet."

He cupped her chin and leaned over, pressing his mouth against her, his tongue pushing its way into her cavern. Leslie loved the way he kissed, molding his lips against hers, drawing out all the pleasures within her. She felt her body relaxing, but that wasn't the way the fantasy was supposed to play out. Reminding herself of her role, she twisted her head. "Don't do that!"

He raised an eyebrow and his smile was sardonic. "I'll do anything I please. After all, you're in no position to argue." He knelt beside the bed and took one erect nipple in his mouth while he pinched the other between his fingers. She arched her back and gasped at the sudden onslaught. God she loved what he did to her body every time they acted out his fantasy.

Finally, after what seemed like hours of playing with her breasts, he stood and removed his clothing, leaving only his black, butter-soft leather gloves on. Several months ago he'd added them to his attire and later he'd said how much that increased his pleasure. Leslie didn't know why, nor did she care. The only important thing was that he enjoyed himself to the utmost. She looked at him, slightly paunchy, with heavy thighs and a chest covered with whorls of straight hair. She was delighted to see that his erection was full and hard.

He grabbed her hair and twisted her face to the side and, knowing his next move, she opened her mouth so he could ram his engorged cock into it. "Be a good little girl," he said, "and suck me good."

She did, using everything she knew about the way he liked it. She flicked the tip with her tongue, then licked the length of him as he dictated the rhythm. She sucked and lapped at him until she knew he was getting close. She wanted to fondle him, but her hands were still tied, so she used her lips and tongue to bring him closer and closer to orgasm.

Finally she heard the deep catch in his breath and he spurted into her mouth. She swallowed as fast as she could, milking the last of his orgasm from him. When he was fully satisfied, he untied one of her wrists and dropped into a chair to catch his breath. "Satisfy yourself while I watch," he snapped, and she quickly moved her hand to her crotch, easily finding her erect clit and rubbing. His eyes were fixed on her fingers as she pleasured herself. His actions had so aroused her that it took only moments for her to climax, her small moan the only sign.

Minutes later he untied the remaining restraints and quickly put on his clothing. "That was wonderful," he said with a deep sigh, "as always. By the way, I'll be away for August, but I'll call and make an appointment for September."

She slowly sat up. "I'll look forward to it." That was when it had first hit her. Would she look forward to it? Although the sex was satisfying, and of course the fifteen-hundred-dollar charge to his credit card, a thousand of which would find its way into her bank account, was wonderful, she was restless and bored, tired of all the things she had to do to maintain herself as one of the highest paid "entertainers" in Manhattan.

Bob closed the bedroom door quietly behind him. It was almost midnight and she knew she was the only one left upstairs in the brownstone that housed Club Fantasy, one of the most exclusive and well-attended brothels in the city. So after Bob left the building, gloriously naked except for the wide-open robe and clutching the torn nightgown to keep from tripping, Leslie crossed to the bathroom. She knew the club's bodyguard was downstairs locking up, but he wouldn't disturb her. "Good night, Rock," she called and after a moment heard his answering, "Good night, Leslie. I'm going to set the alarm so remember to disarm and reset it when you leave."

"Will do." She heard his door close as she stripped off her robe and tossed the shreds of her nightgown into the trash. Just part of the expense of doing business, she thought as she turned on the hot water in the shower.

Bob would be away for August. How delightful. Quite a few of her regular clients would also be gone so that month should prove to be a very quiet one. *God*, she thought, *I could use some quiet*. Some peace and quiet. Suddenly, as she stood beneath the spray and soaped her tired body, she realized that she wanted, no desperately needed, some time away.

Was she suffering from burnout? Who cared what name you called it. In a flash of understanding, she realized that she hadn't been enjoying her job for months. Yes, she got sexual pleasure out of her encounters, and emotional pleasure out of pleasing her clients, but where was the fun, the adventure, the newness of satisfying a client for the first time, of watching his, or even her, face as they found something they had so long sought? It had been so great in the beginning; now it was just routine. Where had that explosive fire gone?

As the days passed, Leslie realized that as exciting as the fantasy games were for her clients, it had all become boring for her. What a joke. Great sex with rich and powerful men had become almost tedious. Boring. She'd been able to satisfy all her clients but she knew that it was only a matter of time before they'd start to become bored with her. And that must never happen.

She'd been working for the owners of Club Fantasy, where dreams were fulfilled for a hefty fee, for almost nine years. She worked five evenings a week and frequently made several thousand dollars each night. She played roles as varied as a harem dancer, a maid captured by a pirate, a female prison guard, and a young teenaged girl. She also had dinners with the movers and shakers, with hanky-panky afterward. It was wonderful fun, but it was also lots of work. In order to be able to converse with them, she read the *New York Times* every day, and *People*, a news weekly, and at least one sports magazine each week.

She wasn't ashamed of what she did at all. She entertained, gave pleasure, and was well paid for it. She saw nothing immoral about any of it. Illegal? Maybe, but the New York City police left her and Club Fantasy pretty much alone. Maybe that was because the owners of the Club knew a little more about some government officials than they wanted publicized.

Maybe because it was hard to fault a business that gave plea-sure and harmed no one. There were no drugs allowed, every-one was of legal age, and everything was strictly honest and aboveboard. Dangerous? Not really. The clients were thor-oughly vetted and Rock, 220 pounds of bodybuilder and black belt martial arts expert, was always in residence, although his bouncer skills had never been needed. For whatever reason, she felt no compunctions about what she did.

As she drove through the early August heat, Leslie thought about it all. She hadn't had a truly filling meal except with a client since she put on several pounds while cruising on a yacht with a wealthy stockbroker the previous winter. One of her regulars had actually mentioned that she looked a little "softer" as he'd put it. Since then, dieting had become a way of life, as well as weekly trips to the hairstylist and the nail salon and a strict regimen at the gym.

Several weeks earlier she'd called a real estate agency that specialized in vacation rentals. "It's already July, Ms. Mor-gan," a motherly woman named Janice had said. "It's going to be really tough to find something for August, but we do occa-sionally have cancellations. Let me see what I can come up with."

A few days later, the agent had called back, suggesting a cottage in Sound's End, Connecticut, right on the water. "The guy who rented it had a minor family emergency. His youngest broke her leg in a bicycle accident. Anyway, he's cancelling out on this lovely little place he rented for August. It's really part of a hotel but it's a freestanding house, one of several they own adjacent to the main building, and it's got all the ameni-ties. They treat it like any other hotel room, maid service and such, but it's more private. There's a full kitchen, if you want to cook, and if not, there's a dining room at the hotel. You can have it from August first through to Labor Day, if you like. My client will be delighted to have his deposit back." She men-tioned a substantial price but it had taken Leslie only a moment's thought. Salt air, relaxing all day and going to bed alone each night. It had sounded like heaven. "Done." Now it was August third and she had finally been able to get away so she was on the way there.

She'd memorized the directions and now took the exit east of Old Saybrook and drove toward the tiny town of Sound's End, so named, she'd learned when she looked it up on the Internet, because the town was located directly opposite the eastern-most tip of Long Island so it was technically at the intersection of the Long Island Sound and the Atlantic Ocean. As she slowed to thirty miles per hour on the main street she looked around. The town appeared to be typical of the small New England towns she'd seen on the Net, white buildings with black shutters surrounding a large town square with a veterans' memorial, all basking in afternoon sunshine. On one side stood three banks, a couple of gas stations, a post office, and a row of small, one-story, boutiquey stores, including two that sold T-shirts and other tourist items, one that seemed to specialize in photography, and a few that had FOR LEASE signs in the window.

The main shopping area on the other side of the main street consisted of a florist, a small market, and a ladies' clothing shop. Interspersed were several restaurants: a diner, an American-style family restaurant specializing in seafood called the Wayfarer, a Chinese sit-down place and one that specialized in takeout, an Italian restaurant called Victorio's, and a pizzeria. *I guess I'm not the only one who doesn't cook*, Leslie thought. Since it was midafternoon, many were now closed with OPEN FOR FAMILY DINNER AT 5 P.M. signs hanging on the doors.

She pulled into the parking area in front of what appeared to be a small convenience store. A sign over the front door read MARTINELLI'S MARKET—ITALIAN SPECIALTIES and she climbed out of the car. The air here in Sound's End was completely different from the hot, muggy stuff they called air during the summer in Manhattan. Here it was a bit cooler and clearer, but the sun was intense and there was the hint of salt in the air. She inhaled deeply, then turned her face to the sun and stood there, listening to the sounds of kids running around the playground in the little park area between the town library and the market. She didn't try to control the wide grin that split her face.

The market had looked unimpressive from the outside but inside it was filled with unusual Italian delicacies. One case was filled with sausage, much of it homemade. She read a few labels: veal and Parmesan; pork, oregano, and mozzarella; sweet sausage with dill. She pushed her cart toward another glass-fronted display case filled with delicatessen goodies: meats and cheeses of all kinds, homemade salads, and antipasti. This small, seemingly unassuming market would put even the high-priced Korean grocery around the corner from her apartment to shame.

She spent almost an hour filling her shopping cart with things she'd need for at least a couple of days. Since she seldom ate at home she kept little in her Manhattan apartment. Buying food was an adventure. She poked around, lifting cans and reading ingredients and nutritional information, selecting those with low saturated fat, sugar, and calories. Then, with a little thrill and a shrug, she threw several fattening, totally bad for her items in her cart. Grinning over a jar of chunky peanut butter and a can of pork and beans, another of ravioli, and a third of deviled ham, she headed for the checkout counter. She'd have to investigate the goodies in the cases another day. She considered that she might actually try cooking somewhere along the line but for now she'd just open cans. Cooking. That was a good idea. Something different and totally out of character for her. Maybe she'd prowl the Net and find recipes she could attempt. According to the agent, the house came with a completely equipped kitchen. Cooking. What a concept.

As she unloaded her purchases she actually felt herself unwind further. With a deep sigh, she watched a portly, middle-aged man check prices on cans and boxes and ring up the items on an old-fashioned cash register. "Welcome to the neighborhood," he said, his voice light and cheery, with a slight New England twang. After her equally cheerful thanks, he continued, "You're new here. Going to be here for awhile?"

"I'm here until Labor Day and I am really looking forward to it."

"Where are you staying?" he asked as he rang up her jar of peanut butter.

"Someplace called the Rogers Cottage. It's part of the Atlantic Beach Hotel."

The man put the jar down and reached out a large, beefy hand. "We'll be neighbors," he said. "My wife, the kids, and I live just across the street. I'm Joe Martinelli and my wife's Marie. Welcome to the neighborhood."

Well, this certainly wasn't New York City. "I'm Leslie Morgan." She took his hand and enjoyed his firm grip. It was novel for a man to be friendly around her without wanting any part of her body. Leslie knew she was attractive, and she'd been told that she seemed to exude an air of sensuality from every pore. This "friendly thing" was really wonderful. "Nice to meet you."

"Listen," Joe said, picking up a loaf of whole-grain bread and checking the price, "we have a cookout the first Friday evening of every month right beside the beach. It will be kind of in your side yard. I want you to be sure to come. It's tomorrow evening around six, and bring your appetite."

Tomorrow evening. It was a temptation. Being around real people, just because. No one to impress. But . . . "Thanks for the invitation, but I couldn't impose."

"It's no imposition. Marie loves to cook; we always have lots of folks from the houses around, so one more person won't even make a dent." He winked. "Actually, the hotel foots part of the bill and lots of their guests come, too. And, of course, you'll get to meet all the neighbors." He chuckled. "You'll have already met Suze. She makes sure to get all the dope on all the new folks, quickly and efficiently."

"Suze?"

"It's really Susan Murdock but no one's called her Susan in forever. It's just Suze. She's the mayor of Sound's End and she feels that she has to know everything about everyone. She's up for reelection in the fall this year and now she campaigns all the time. Although you won't be here to vote, of course, you might have the opportunity to influence someone who does, so she'll be all over you." He sighed. "She means well, though. Anyway, we'd love to have you. The hotel will pay for your attendance, but, if it would make you feel better, you can bring something to eat, or put a little money in the coffee can on the grill. I'll look forward to seeing you there."

It sounded so comfortable that Leslie knew she wouldn't be able to resist and making a contribution would make it feel less like an imposition. "I'd love to."

Joe grabbed a paper chart from beside the register. "You'll need a tide table. Lots of what goes on here depends on the tides." He stuffed it into one of her plastic bags. "Did you get plenty of sunblock?" he added.

"I've got a tube of number 45 in my car."

"Good, use it. Sorry. There I go sounding like your father."

Leslie winked. "You're not nearly old enough to be my father, and anyway, my father never treated me this well."

"Okay, older brother."

Her grin widening still further, she winked and said, "Agreed, bro."

Leslie paid for her groceries, feeling lighter than she had in a long time. She hadn't even seen her cottage and already she'd made a friend in the neighborhood. She hadn't realized how uneasy this trip had made her. It had seemed like such a good idea when she made her plans, but she was a city girl at heart. What would she find to do for a month in a small beach community with rural people and no subways? Now she felt a bit better. This would be just what she needed. Anyway, she could always go back to her apartment.

Chapter

2

In the hot parking lot, Leslie put her grocery bags into the trunk of her rental car and reflexively checked the directions. About five hundred yards down the main street she took the turn onto Atlantic Beach Road and headed toward the ocean She drove carefully since she so seldom got behind the wheel. Taxis and limousines were her usual method of transportation but she quickly found that she enjoyed the freedom of being in control of her own car.

The road wound southward, toward the water, between small, older homes with large yards and hundred-year-old trees. The sounds of children playing were everywhere. Wading pools and swing sets dotted the lawns and gravel driveways led up to flower-covered front porches. Dogs of all sizes and colors roamed at will. Families obviously flourished here.

As she headed toward the water, Leslie wondered what she was going to do all day, every day for a month. She hadn't had this much time for herself in many years. Time for herself. Amazing. She'd probably spend some time in the sun and the rest of her days as she usually did. A confirmed couch potato, she could certainly be content with cable TV, video rentals, and her computer, linked to the Internet. She also had a number of novels she'd wanted to read and a few relatives and friends to whom she would send e-mails. Friends. She had a few, women she'd become close to through her business. Certainly Jenna and Marcy, the twin owners of Club Fantasy, both now involved with their new babies. And Rock and Chloe, of course, "entertaining" and loving it. But real friends?

She thought back over the past few years. She'd had no time to make friends and no place. Where could she meet people who wanted to become friends with a thousand-dollar-an-hour prostitute? Well here no one would know who she was or what she did for a living.

She followed Atlantic Beach Road as it traveled south, then turned east paralleling the water. She'd been told that her cottage was the last one between the water and the roadway. She spotted it, similar to the houses around it, with well-weathered, grey shakes covering the two-story wood building, geraniums in flower boxes along the edge of the front porch and beneath the windows on the ground floor. Curtains fluttered in open windows, stirred by the ocean breeze. She pulled into the short sandy driveway and just sat and stared.

Hers was the last house on the ocean side of the road, but there were five more, almost identical houses facing the beach on the other side of the road before it dead-ended in a stretch of sand and low shrubs. She'd learned on the Net that each beach area had its own name, Middle Beach the next one east with Sea Grape to the west. Atlantic Beach Road had once connected to Middle Beach, an article explained, but a hurricane had washed it out twenty years earlier and it had never been rebuilt. Now you had to either walk along the sand or go back out to Route 1 and follow the signs.

Leslie turned and gazed at the ocean. The water was glass calm with tiny waves lapping at the flat, wet sand. Gulls wheeled overhead, screaming to each other and occasionally diving after fish. A pair of swans cruised low over the water, looking somehow out of place.

The Rogers Cottage bordered a small parking area that ended

in a seawall that paralleled the ocean and beyond lay several yards of flat beach where water had obviously been only hours before. She'd learned that the lack of full-time beach made this section of the Connecticut shore less desirable than others. Of course, Leslie thought. That's why the nice man in the market told her she'd need a tide chart. There was more beach area the lower the tide.

It was just after four o'clock and several women in bathing suits sat on the damp sand under a beach umbrella, supervising two young children who were paddling around in the shallow water. Colorful plastic toys littered the beach. Sandbars, interspersed with areas of flowing water, extended almost to the small rocky island about half a mile offshore. She'd read that it was called Short Island as a sort of joke, since the islet was opposite the eastern end of Long Island.

Finally, when the urge to put on a pair of shorts and wade in the water became overwhelming, Leslie got out of the car and walked past what she assumed were more rental cottages, toward the rambling, two-story building that sported the sign ATLANTIC BEACH HOTEL—ENTRANCE.

The lobby was uninspiring, but she'd been warned not to judge. Filled with white wicker and ferns, with sandy floors and whitewashed walls, it looked like something out of a photograph taken fifty years earlier. A tall, slender man in his early twenties with dark brown hair that he wore almost as long as hers and deep brown eyes stood behind a small desk. When she told him her name he tapped a few computer keys and found her reservation. As he handed her a card to sign and took an imprint of her credit card, he cast a few admiring looks her way. She ignored his appreciation. She was used to it and marveled that even a ponytail, baggy clothes over a sports bra that flattened her large breasts, and a complete lack of makeup couldn't conceal her natural sensuality. She knew it and had grown accustomed to it. She was pretty sure he'd watch her walk out and maybe find some reason to check with her later to make sure everything was "okay in the cottage." It was flattering of course, but it got old really quickly. She'd been dealing with it since junior high.

He explained the hotel's policies, described the location of the air conditioner's controls, and urged her to make full use of the kitchen or eat any or all her meals in the hotel's dining room. He also invited her to attend the cookout the following evening. "If there's anything I can do to make your stay more comfortable, please feel free to ask, either in person or by phone. Anything at all."

Several minutes later, key in hand, she walked back to her new "home," unlocked the front door, and carried her suitcases and groceries into the house. A light breeze wafted in through open windows and, although she could put on the air conditioner, she loved the smell and decided that she'd leave it off as much as possible. Resolved that she'd delay poking around the house that would be her home for the next month, she stuffed her perishables into the refrigerator then dug in a suitcase and found a pair of denim shorts and a loose-fitting, light blue T-shirt, slipped her feet into a pair of flip flops, and headed outside.

The strip of dark sand was slightly wider than it had been when she drove up and she saw that the seawall was about four feet high with sets of wooden steps at intervals leading up to the parking area. On the water side of her house and all the others to the west along the ocean was a concrete area with an outdoor table and chairs, then a long flower box to prevent you from accidentally falling off the edge of the seawall that bordered the beach.

The tide was obviously on its way out, and she wandered down to the water's edge, slipped off her flip flops, and waded in the surprisingly warm water. She remembered a trip she'd taken to Maine with a client one summer. The water was almost unswimmably frigid so she was delighted to realize that she'd be able to paddle around in the ocean without freezing her parts off.

"Hello," a woman's voice called as she waded slowly through the tiny waves. Leslie turned toward the sound and a woman waved, her smile wide beneath a pair of dark sunglasses. "Come over and sit with us when you're tired of the water."

Leslie saw the three women she'd noticed earlier sitting in the shadow of a large beach umbrella. She wasn't sure she wanted to visit and she didn't quite know how she was going to answer their inevitable questions but she walked over and crouched beside a forty-something woman with piercing blue eyes and neatly cut auburn hair. "Hi. I'm Suze Murdock." She indicated the two other women and listed their names too quickly for even Leslie, who prided herself on her ability to remember names, to catch. She leaned forward with a forced intimacy when she spoke.

"I'm Leslie. Leslie Morgan," she said. "You must be the mayor," she said, remembering Joe's comments in the market. Suze. What a weird name for a mature woman, she thought.

Slightly surprised, the woman said, "How did you know that?"

"I stopped at the market in town and the guy there mentioned that we'd be neighbors."

"Oh," a matronly, black-haired woman said, suddenly beaming, "you must have met my husband."

"I guess I did," Leslie answered, settling herself on the corner of Suze's blanket. "You must be Marie."

The woman extended her hand and Leslie shook it. "I am, and it's nice to meet you. We noticed you come out of the Rogers Cottage. Are you staying there?"

"I took it for the month of August." She had resolved to answer questions as briefly as she could. She certainly didn't want to get into what she did for a living.

"It's a wonderful place to get away," Suze said. "The greatest. And you summer folks are so good for our economy." She pulled a camera from the pocket of her shorts and snapped a picture of Leslie. "That's for my scrapbook. I keep pictures of most of the things that go on around town." The whole idea of having her picture in Suze's album made her a little uncomfortable, but, after all, she'd been photographed many times before in more *interesting* settings.

"Mark and Tammy, you're getting too far away!" a tiny, slightly frowsy woman called. Leslie glanced down the beach and saw two young children running back up the beach. "Sorry to attempt to deafen you," the woman said, looking apologetic. "I'm Abby Croft and those two wild animals are Tammy and Mark." She brightened and her chin lifted when she talked about her children.

"Nice to meet you. Are you all visiting for the summer, too?"

"No, indeed," Suze said. "Marie and I are permanent." She said it with a bit of pride, like summer visitors weren't quite as good. "Abby is here for the summer like you, though. Her husband, Damian, commutes here on weekends from Hartford. You married, Leslie?"

There was obviously no block in front of Suze's mouth. "Nope. Never have been."

"From the city?"

"Manhattan born and bred."

Marie chuckled. "We think of the city as Hartford, since it's so much closer. Manhattan. Joe and I used to get to the Big Apple a few times a year, for shows and such, but we haven't had a chance to in many years. Too much to do here, and too many kids."

"Oh?" Leslie said, glad to detour the interrogation for a few moments. "How many do you have?"

Marie's eyes twinkled. "Six. Joe's very"—she paused as if searching for the right word—"active."

"Bravo," Leslie said with a chuckle. "I'll vote for active over disinterested any day." She saw Abby duck her head, then stare at her children.

"This just vacation for you?" Suze said.

"Stop the third degree," Marie said, "and let the woman catch her breath." She turned to Leslie. "She's the mayor of Sound's End and feels that gives her the right to pry into everyone's life." Her light tone took most of the sting out of the rebuke.

"Not right, but responsibility," Suze said. "This is a nice little town and I just want to keep it that way."

This isn't a woman to think kindly of a prostitute on a summer holiday, Leslie thought. A car drove slowly into the driveway diagonally across from the Rogers Cottage, and a collective sigh went up from the three women. As a tall, nicely built man climbed out, leaned into the backseat, and pulled out a plastic bag, Suze said, "That's Brad DeVane. Isn't that a wonderful name? Sounds like a western hero. We don't know much about him except that he's a New York City cop who's here for a few weeks. I think he's getting over some kind of trauma and he's pretty evasive about it. He's been here since Monday. He works out, I understand, and spends most of the rest of the day closeted in that cottage, coming out in the late afternoon to swim. I think he's really sad about something. Maybe he lost his wife or his partner was shot in a gang war."

"Suze, cut it out. You've romanticized him into something bigger than life—the stereotypical brooding hero," Marie said. "To me he just looks sad all the time."

Tongue in cheek, Leslie said, "You haven't been able to check out his résumé, Suze?"

Suze looked a bit embarrassed. "Okay, I guess I do pry a bit, but I'm just being protective. What if he shot some big-time gangster and someone's after him?"

"Oh Lord, Suze," Marie said. "Get real."

Leslie watched Brad go into the house. He really was well built, with great shoulders and a nice looking butt. She couldn't see his face, however, and great bodies didn't mean much. She'd certainly seen enough of them. "Is that his house?"

"That's part of the same hotel you're in. The Whitsons moved out about two years ago and the hotel bought it. He's only here for a few weeks I gather."

Leslie pointed to the house next to Brad's, the second of the five that faced the ocean. "And that one?"

"That's me," Suze said, "and Marie and Joe are two houses down. The one in the middle belongs to Vicki Farrar and her daughter Trish, who just graduated from high school." Suze sighed. "They're a strange pair." Leslie glanced at the grey-shingled house with the little silver sports car in the driveway. Cute car.

Marie chimed in. "Vicki is a predatory female if I ever saw one. She hits on every man between the ages of eighteen and fifty. Actually we don't get many men over fifty but I think she'd hit on them, too. She's been trying with Brad but getting nowhere." She grinned. "It must frustrate the hell out of her. She's in her thirties; tall, gorgeous, and stacked; and loves to show off her figure in tight shorts and bikini tops."

Leslie quickly calculated. *If Vicki's in her thirties with a daughter already graduated, she must have had her really young.*

"We're all just a little jealous I think," Abby added.

Marie continued, "Trish, on the other hand, is just ordinary looking. She's eighteen but still gangly like a young teenager, all knees and elbows."

"And flat chested, which makes Vicki furious," Suze said. "Like it's her fault. They make quite a pair. The lion and the mouse."

The women chuckled. "I'm on the end," Abby said. "The house belongs to one of my husband Damian's friends and we've come here for the last three summers. The kids love it." Leslie noted something almost defensive about the way Abby spoke.

"So, let's get back to you, Leslie," Suze said. "What do you do in the big city?"

Leslie had thought about how she'd answer that inevitable question. "I'm part of a small business. We deal in remodeling." She did, in a way. They remodeled the rooms in Club Fantasy frequently, to suit the wishes of their clients.

"You mean interior decoration?" Suze said. "I could use some help with my living room."

"Enough," Marie said. "Leslie's on vacation. Stop trying to get free advice."

"Actually," Leslie said, "we deal more with professional space." She groaned inwardly, worried she'd forget what story she'd told.

"Oh, of course. Like doctors' offices."

Leslie said nothing. She didn't want to lie, but she'd let these women jump to their own conclusions.

Abby glanced at her watch. "I've got to get going. It's getting time for me to make dinner. Mark and Tammy! Come on over and get ready to go inside for dinner!" she called as she stood, shook out, and folded the towel she had been sitting on and began to put sand toys into a large, yellow plastic pail. When the two children ran up, she introduced Tammy, aged seven and Mark, eight.

With perfect manners, Mark thrust out his hand. "Nice to meet you, Ms. Morgan."

She shook. "Nice to meet you, too."

"Do you have any kids here?" he asked.

"I'm afraid not," she said.

"I'm sure the Martinellis will be home soon," Abby said to the slightly lonely looking little boy.

Maria glanced at her watch. "Absolutely. Phillip and Stacy should be getting home from their friend's house within the next half hour. I'm sure they'll be out and about a little while later."

"Can we go out after dinner?" Mark whined. "Please, Mom."

"You can go back outside after you finish eating," Abby said. "I'll sit on the porch and you can go only as far as you can see me clearly." Mark's face brightened.

"Me too?" Tammy said, putting her shovel and strainer into the bucket.

"You, too."

Marie turned to Leslie. "Phillip's ten and Stacy's nine but they all seem to play together despite their different ages."

"And your other children?" Leslie asked.

"Joey and Paul are gone now, both working upstate. Actually Joey's engaged. Melissa's seventeen and since she got her own car I only see her when she comes home to sleep. She does hair at the salon in the mall and works about a zillion hours a week. You'll have to give her a try. She's very talented. Tony's fifteen. He's working in construction with a friend in Rhode Island for the summer."

"I'll never keep them straight," Leslie said, smiling ruefully.

"That's okay, Joe and I sometimes get them tangled."

"Kevin and I just have two," Suze said. "Kevin Jr., he wants to be called KJ right now, is seventeen and a bit of a handful as you can imagine, and Eliza is fifteen and a typical teenaged girl." Motherly pride filled her voice as she talked about her children. "They're both around town somewhere. They'll be working soon enough so my husband, Kevin, and I agreed that they could enjoy this summer without having to work."

"Okay, kids, let's get going," Abby said and she, Mark, and Tammy plodded across the sand toward one of the wooden staircases that led up to the top of the seawall.

"She's quite a case," Suze said, checking to see that Abby was out of earshot. "Her husband parks her here so he can be free to do whatever he pleases during the week."

"You don't know that," Marie said, shaking her head.

"Come on," Suze responded. "It's obvious if you know Damian."

Leslie looked up at the sound of a door slamming, precluding Marie's answer. "Here he comes," Suze said. "Mr. Jock."

Indeed, Brad DeVane had reappeared, dressed in a pair of knee-length swimming trunks with a towel around his neck. Not bad, Leslie thought. Not bad at all. He crossed the seawall a few houses down the beach, dropped his towel on the sand, and headed into the water. He waded out into deeper water and began to swim parallel to the beach. As the women watched he swam smoothly and efficiently until he was almost out of sight then reversed course and swam back. "He does that at least once a day. I would guess," Marie said as he turned and retraced his previous course, "that he swims several miles every time. It exhausts me to watch."

"It's really good exercise," Leslie said, wishing she were a better swimmer so she could work out that way, too. It looked so invigorating.

"I've got to get going," Marie said, getting to her feet. "Joe will be home soon and it's time for me to get dinner started."

"Me too," Suze said. "Kevin won't be home until later—he teaches high school in town, and he's doing some tutoring for the summer—but I've got a few things to do and some phone calls I have to make, then I've got a council meeting tonight."

"I think I'll just sit here for a little while longer," Leslie said, shifting onto the hard packed sand so Suze could pick up her blanket. "It's so peaceful." She gazed at the water and the sun, still high in the painfully blue sky.

"I don't know whether Joe told you but we have a cookout the first Friday evening of each month during the summer and there's one tomorrow night," Marie said as she picked up her beach tote and stuffed her towel inside. "You can either bring something or contribute to the kitty. I'd love it if you'd join us."

"Joe did tell me, and I'll be there. I'm afraid I'm hopeless in the kitchen so I'll just feed the kitty."

"Great. We'll probably see you before that," Suze said. "We

who live in these houses are sort of a family and, since you're our nearest neighbor, you're adopted."

Leslie viewed this as a mixed blessing but she smiled and watched the two women make their way toward the stairs. Normal people. While not friends yet, certainly comfortable acquaintances. How wonderful.

Chapter

3

"She seems nice," Marie said to Suze as they climbed the steps.

"Yeah, she does."

"Her voice is so low and sexy, and she's absolutely gorgeous even without makeup. I really should hate her but it's difficult not to take to her."

"I know. Strange, though, it seems like she's trying to downplay her looks. I'll bet she's got quite a shape but with that chest-flattening thing she was wearing, she's quite, well, flat."

"Suze, you're amazing. You notice the oddest things."

"I guess, but being mayor and all I need to be observant."

"Right. See you tomorrow."

As neighbors for the seven years since she first moved to Sound's End, Suze and Marie had become good friends. Well, Suze thought, maybe not *good* friends. After all, Marie had only a high school education and wasn't much for reading good literature. While Suze spent considerable time watching public broadcasting, Marie was always up on the latest TV shows. She could give you the background of each of the *Desperate Housewives* in great detail and she had a strict "do not ever call during *Lost*" rule.

As Suze climbed the stairs to her front porch, she heard the loud roar of an approaching motorcycle. With a long sigh she thought, KJ's home. The roar stopped with a screech of brakes and a scream of rubber as she stepped into the living room and only moments later footsteps pounded up the back porch stairs. "KJ?"

"Yeah, who else?"

"Wipe your feet."

She sensed rather than heard his long sigh. At that moment she heard a car door slam then the motor roar away. Mingled with the heavy boot steps, she heard lighter ones. "Eliza? That you?"

"Of course, Mom."

"Right." Suze walked to the rear of the house and into the kitchen where the two siblings had their heads stuck in the refrigerator. "Dinner's in less than an hour so don't eat."

Totally ignoring her, as they usually did, they each reached inside. Suze barely noticed her son's jeans-covered behind, but she couldn't overlook her daughter's tiny shorts and the wide expanse of skin between the lowered waistband and her tiny tank top. "I thought I said no belly shirts, young lady. Is that new? I don't remember buying it for you."

Eliza pulled back and stood, a can of soda and small container of leftover Chinese food in hand. "Oh, come on, Mother. Everyone's wearing these and I just got it. Nothing interesting is showing."

Suze gazed at her fifteen-year-old daughter who looked only one step from a hooker. Her lovely chestnut brown hair currently had a bright blue patch over one temple and she wore heavy blue eyeshadow on her blue eyes and deep red lipstick. Suze got a better look at her daughter's tiny black shorts that barely covered her pubis and cropped red tank top with sparkly white letters that said *No, wait. I AM the center of the universe* across the front and barely covered her well-developed breasts. The expanse of tan skin below was lean and taut as only a teenager's could be. "You're not. Put something decent on before your father comes home."

"He doesn't care what I wear."

"Change."

"Oh please," Eliza said.

"Eliza!" Suze said, her voice rising.

Without a backward glance Eliza, soda, food, and a small plastic shopping bag in hand, headed for the stairs.

"You really shouldn't eat so close to dinner."

Totally ignoring her, Eliza reached the top of the stairs and, only a moment later, slammed her door. Suze could hear as she turned on her stereo.

"You too, KJ," she said as he pulled a container of orange juice from the fridge and drank several long swallows from the spout. "And don't drink out of the container!" Suze looked at her son. When had he gotten to be a man? she wondered. He was already taller than his father with a well-developed body, a cap of curly brown hair and his father's deep brown, almost bedroom eyes. *Where had her children gone?*

"Come on, Suze, I'm a big boy now. Lay off." He took another long drink.

"You've really got to get the muffler fixed on your motorcycle. It makes a terrible racket. Isn't that much noise against the traffic laws?"

"I sort of like the noise and none of your cops would ever give me a ticket."

"They're not *my* cops."

"Same thing. Whenever they stop me, once they realize who I am, they let me off with a warning."

"Whenever they stop you? When have you been stopped by the cops?" Suze asked, horrified.

"Every now and then," KJ said, exasperation accenting every line of his body and every note in his voice.

"For what?"

"Oh, you know, routine kid stuff. Going a little too fast,

going through the stupid stop sign at the intersection of Route 1 and Atlantic Beach Road. It's so bogus. You can see for a mile in every direction so sometimes I just blow through it. You do too, Suze, I've seen you."

"I do not." Actually she frequently glanced both ways then went through the light but she certainly didn't do it when anyone was watching. "It's the law, even if it is in a dumb place. We've been trying to get it changed to a yield for years but the state DOT won't hear of it. Anyway, stop changing the subject. I don't want you getting stopped by the police. It doesn't reflect well on me as mayor."

"Don't sweat it. It's all bullshit."

"And don't use that kind of language either."

"Right," he said with deep sarcasm. "Call me when dinner's ready." His motorcycle boots made loud clunks on the wooden stairs as he climbed to his room.

He's certainly a handful, Suze thought with mixed emotions, *but he does well at school and so what if he wants to play on his bike? Kids should be allowed to be young. God knows I don't remember ever being that young. And when did he start calling me Suze?*

The phone rang and Suze answered it. It couldn't be for either of her children since they each had a cell phone. "Hi, Suze, it's me," her husband, Kevin, said. "I'm going to be a little late. I ran into George Parissi. You remember him, the guidance counselor? Anyway . . ."

"That's fine, dear," Suze said, mentally rearranging what she had been going to make for dinner.

"I assume you've got work to do so I thought George and I would just grab a bite together in town and catch up. He wanted my opinion on . . ."

She did have a stack of town paperwork to look over and the local newspaper to read thoroughly before her council meeting. "That's great. Then I'll see you later."

After a slight hesitation he said, "Fine."

*　　*　　*

Kevin hung up the phone and looked around for his friend George. Suze didn't seem to care whether he came home at all. She'd already been mayor for two three-year terms and was going to run for yet another. He didn't begrudge her her career but it would be nice if she paid a little attention to him once in a while. They hardly ever talked, well maybe about the kids, and they hadn't had more than weekly, perfunctory sex in forever. Maybe he wanted more. He glanced toward the bar and noticed a statuesque redhead sitting, nursing a drink. He wondered what would happen if he sat down next to her and struck up a conversation. Nope, he wasn't desperate enough to go outside his marriage. Not yet.

He could tell George that he'd changed his mind and approach the redhead. It would never occur to Suze to consider that he was seeing another woman, and he secretly wondered whether she'd care. As long as he was discrete and no one knew, and as long as "the other woman" kept him out of his wife's hair, he thought, she'd probably be grateful. He sighed, then plastered his usual big smile on his face and caught George's eye. As he passed the redhead he paused, then kept walking.

Eliza closed her door, put the food container and soda on her desk, and turned on her computer. She put the bag containing her new designer jeans on her bed, propped a chair under the doorknob, and, when the computer asked, entered the password that protected all her files and mail.

She'd been out all day with Angel. Angel wasn't really a friend, but she was old enough to have a car so a bunch of them had driven to a large, upscale mall where she'd spent most of her very generous allowance on a pair of skin-tight, low-rise jeans. Her mother would pitch a fit, of course, but that hardly mattered. All the girls had told her how really great they made her look, thin and grown up. She'd wear them the first day of school. Stop thinking about school, she told herself. She had many weeks until then.

She clicked on the icon to bring up the list of her incoming mail and let out the breath she'd been holding when she saw that there was a letter from Dennis.

Hi Eliza—such a pretty name,
   Sorry I couldn't write sooner. You understand how busy life gets sometimes in the advertising business. It's just work, work and more work to meet deadlines. I got the picture you sent and it's even better than the posed one on the site. You're so beautiful that I can't believe that you're only fifteen. Wow, you look so mature I'd have assumed you were in college. I'll send you my picture soon. Oh, and I'll be online after nine tonight so, if you're on, IM me. I can't wait to talk with you.
Bye, gorgeous,
Dennis

Would she be online? Of course she would. She looked at her watch. Less than four hours to go. She could live until then, just barely. She leaned back and daydreamed about the handsome, mature man who thought she was beautiful.

She'd first gotten mail from Dennis three weeks before, only about a month after she'd posted her school picture on the "Friends" Web site. He'd told her a little about himself, that he was thirty-two, not too tall, with green eyes and black hair, lonely, eager to make friends with someone so youthful and vibrant. They'd exchanged letters, then she'd sent him a snapshot one of her friends had scanned in for her. She couldn't wait to get a photo of him.

Next door to the Murdocks, Vicki Farrar heard the roar of KJ's motorcycle as she sat on the sofa, her pink polished toes tucked beneath her, poring over a pile of legal papers. God, she thought, reading all this is going to be a nightmare. Marty Simonetti, the real estate attorney who was both helping her with her current project and sleeping with her when his wife, a sales rep for a pharmaceutical firm, was out of town, had insisted that she couldn't sign anything without reading it at least once.

She picked up the first stapled stack but got a sudden reprieve when she heard the front door slam. "Trish, that you?"

"No, Mom, it's a burglar."

"Ha, ha. Very cute. Where have you been?"

Trish entered the living room, dressed in a loose-fitting T-shirt and lightweight jeans. "Around."

Vicki gazed at her eighteen-year-old daughter. How in the world could someone as special as she was have such an ordinary daughter? She's such a stick: limp mousey brown hair, a sallow complexion, and no breasts at all. She had great eyes, or she would if she ever wore makeup. Well, with the right guidance, she'd straighten out and understand that this life was all about good looks, and men. She ran her fingers through her thick, honey-blond hair. It would just take a little time. "Right. Around. With KJ?" When her daughter remained silent, Vicki said, "I just heard his motorcycle. Why in the world do you ride on that death trap? You know what they call people who ride motorcycles without helmets? Organ donors." She thought about the silver Z4 convertible sitting in the driveway. A much better way to travel indeed.

"Mom, we always wear helmets and anyway, KJ's always careful."

"You know that Suze hates it when he hangs around with you." She reflexively adjusted her tiny bikini top over her large, silicon-assisted breasts. "She thinks I'm a bad influence on you and thus on him."

"He's my best friend," Trish whined. "Anyway, Suze won't know anything. She never notices what KJ does. She thinks he's still ten years old. Just in case, however, since it's low tide KJ dropped me at Middle Beach and I walked here along the sand."

"You're right about that. She hasn't noticed that he's turning out to be quite a hunk."

With an exasperated sigh, she said, "Please, Mom. Enough." She spotted the stack of papers and raised a curious eyebrow.

Vicki patted the sofa beside her with her long, graceful fingers, tipped by perfectly manicured bubblegum-pink nails. It was time to tell her daughter all the wonderful plans she'd made. "It's business stuff but it's got to do with you, too. I've actually got a surprise. I know you've been looking for a job since graduation, but I'm taking care of that for you. I'm opening a business in town and you'll be able to work for me. It should pay off quite well. I've made several business plans and my accountant has helped me with cash flow projections and one-year forecasts. I've even gotten a small amount of bank financing." She'd had to put up the house as collateral for her small business loan but it would be worth it.

Trish picked up a sheaf of papers and flipped through them. "You don't know anything about business, Mom. What kind?"

"I know enough about this kind of business and Marty is helping me with all the legal stuff. I've gotten a license, lots of permits and stuff, and the only thing left now is to finalize the lease on the storefront." She was quite proud of herself. She'd only slept with Marty a few times before they started to talk about what she did to keep herself occupied. She'd done a few things over the years but she'd hated most of them.

"How do you support yourself?" Marty had asked.

"My folks were killed in a bus accident and the settlement with the transportation company left me quite a bit of money. I manage pretty well." Actually she managed with some astute financial guidance from a guy she'd slept with almost a year ago. He'd set up an account with his brokerage firm and since they'd split, a few comments from her about how his wife wouldn't want to find out about their "relationship" encouraged him to continue to manage her money. He'd been quite successful and her nest egg had kept her in relative comfort.

"You must be bored to death, especially with Trish ready to go out on her own," Marty had said. "You should really think about doing something more with your life."

She had thought about it and over several long dinners at an anonymous restaurant fifty miles from Sound's End, they had hatched the idea for her new venture.

Now Trish said, "So what kind of business are you thinking about?"

"I've done much more than think. We're opening an erotic boutique. Vicki's Erotic Emporium. We'll have lingerie and stuff in the front with a video rental and toy area in one back room. There will be computers linked to several sites on the Internet and, with my advice, we'll sell everything anyone might want to play with. This afternoon I poked around the building that used to be Sherman's Art Gallery before it closed. It's perfect and I've got the lease right here." She pawed through the papers. "Somewhere."

Trish's mouth dropped open. "In this town? You'll start a revolution. What makes you think there are women here who want that sort of thing?"

"Actually the lingerie in the front will attract lots of women, like the Victoria's Secret in the mall in Saybrook. I wandered through it several times and it's always crowded. The stuff in the back will have men coming in, too." Vicki giggled at her double entendre but her daughter's face remained grim.

"What about Suze? She's not your biggest fan, and once word gets out about the store she'll go ballistic."

"She thinks she's got clout, but Marty tells me she can't really do anything about it. All I have to do is sign these papers and it's a done deal."

Trish sighed with resignation. "Do whatever you want, Mom. You will no matter what I say, but I, for one, think it's a dumb idea."

Vicki looked down at the stack of documents. "I'm expecting you to work there with me, of course."

"Me? I don't think so, Mom. I've gotten several positive responses to my résumé, positions that might become careers in time. I want to get started on making my own life."

Nonsense. Trish would never get anywhere without the right guidance and her mother was just the person to show her exactly how to get what she wanted. "Don't be ridiculous. This is the opportunity of a lifetime. This store will be worth a mint but I can't run it by myself six days a week. I expect you to participate and that's that."

She watched her daughter's shoulders stiffen. "I don't think so, Mom." Trish would resist, and Vicki watched her jaw tighten but she was sure her daughter would come around. This was best for her, and the store would keep her close and under Vicki's tutelage. That was part of the attraction.

Another part of the lure of the store was the men it would attract. All kinds of guys, from lawyers to truckers, would hear about her store and its creative products and wander in. They'd never expect to find someone like her, gorgeous and willing. As she watched Trish walk into the kitchen, Vicki leaned back on the sofa and closed her eyes. She saw the store, colorful, exciting, all done in black and various shades of reds and pinks. There would be piles of silky panties, bras, and gowns, and she could pick and choose what she wanted to keep for herself, at wholesale.

Vicki wiggled down so she could rest her head on the back of the couch and pictured the scene. In her mind, a guy walked in and picked up a deep blue bustier. He had large hands and a jaw stubbled with five o'clock shadow. His long black hair flowed past his shoulders and his eyes, a deep, icy blue, seemed to see through her clothes. "You'd look good in this," he said, looking her over with obvious interest. "Wanna model it for me?"

Did she want to? Her pussy was already swelling and her panties were getting wet. "There's a dressing room in the back," she said in her dream, flipping the sign on the store's window to show it was closed, then leading him through a curtain to the try-on stalls beyond. She opened the door to the largest one and he followed. "I'm going to have to undress to put that on," she said, licking her lips to moisten her deep red lipstick. "Turn your back." She knew he'd turn, but with mirrors covering the walls and the back of the door he'd be able to see her anyway. She went along with the game though, slowly, sensuously removing her blouse and slacks as though she didn't know he was watching, then taking off her bra and panties. Gloriously naked she posed, sucking in her stomach and thrusting her large breasts forward.

She slithered into the bustier and slipped on the matching panties. "You can turn around now," she said, her voice breathy.

He turned and his grin showed white teeth. "I knew you'd look sensational in that," he growled. "You look sensational without it, too." He grabbed the top of the bra and pulled her close. "You're fabulous."

His kiss was deep and demanding, just the way she liked it. He cradled her head in his long fingers and pressed her lips against his mouth, his tongue plundering. He cupped her scantily clad buttocks and ground her pubis against his groin so she couldn't mistake the rigid rod beneath his zipper. With a single motion he scooped one breast from its cover and lowered his mouth to the rosy tip. As he sucked he made loud slurping noises, and she cradled his head against her. He loosened the other breast and licked its tip, then alternated between them.

He grabbed the back of her hair and pulled her face to his, covering her mouth with his, ramming his tongue into her dark cavern. God, she loved it this way, hard and hungry. Finally, he said, "I'll pay for the outfit," grasped the front of the panties, and pulled until the slender sides parted. He pushed his finger into her soaked depths and laughed. "Hot little bitch, aren't you?"

"Hot for you, lover."

"I've got what you want." He unzipped his fly, lifted her, and pulled her legs around his waist. He pushed her back against one mirrored wall so she could feel the cold against her skin then thrust into her, driving his thick cock deep. He lifted one breast and bit her erect nipple, hard, until she screamed with pleasure. She came from the combination of pleasure and pain and the rumble of his laughter reverberated through her body.

Several more thrusts and he came as well, filling her pussy with thick goo.

"Mom," Trish called from the kitchen, dragging Vicki from her fantasy, "when's dinner—or should I just fend for myself?"

Shit, Vicki thought. "Get whatever you want. I'm going upstairs." She dashed up the stairs and into her bedroom, found her vibrator, and pressed it between her legs. The buzz echoed through her body and brought her to orgasm quickly. *God, I can't wait until I set up the store.*

Chapter

4

Soon after the roar of KJ's bike stilled, Marie heard her husband, Joe, slam the back door. As he always did, he swept his wife up in a bear hug and as she always did, she said, "Stop it, you beast." With a giggle she added, "What about the children? They just got home."

"They'll see that their parents like to smooch." He planted a large, noisy kiss on his wife's mouth.

"You're incorrigible," she said with a laugh. "Kids!" she yelled. "Daddy's home and dinner's ready." She turned to him. "What brings you home so early?"

"It was pretty quiet at the market so I left Carl in charge and snuck out the back, Jack. Too many hours working makes me a dull boy." He hugged her tighter.

"Stop," she said and playfully slapped at his shoulder. "Did you bring anything home with you?"

"I had a bit of leftover potato salad and I brought some new kind of sausage Carl whipped up. Veal, basil, and sun-dried tomatoes. Sounds a bit bizarre, but I thought we could try it tomorrow night."

"And poison everyone at the cookout? Sounds really weird but then Carl seldom makes anything that isn't wonderful."

"He'll be here tomorrow evening so we can make him eat

some first." His embrace lifted his wife's feet off the ground but he put her down as Phillip and Stacy ran into the dining room.

"Dad," Phillip said, "cut it out. You two are supposed to be setting an example for us kids."

"I'm setting a great example. Family and love are great things, and should be shared. Now go wash up and then help your mother in the kitchen."

"I don't need any more help than yours, Joe," Marie said. "Kids, Daddy's right. Go wash up because dinner will be on the table in five minutes."

"What are we having?" Stacy said, reluctant to commit to anything until she understood all the parameters.

"Fried chicken and mac and cheese," Marie said. "Two of your favorites."

"And broccoli?" Stacy asked, ever suspicious.

"Yes, broccoli and you have to eat three bites. Now scoot."

The two children dashed toward the bathroom, each yelling dibs on being last to wash. Marie and Joe walked into the kitchen and busied themselves getting organized. "I met a really nice-looking blond lady today," Joe said.

"That was Leslie. We talked to her this afternoon on the beach and she told us that she'd met you. She seems really nice, levelheaded and able to deal with Suze pretty well."

"You're not jealous? She's quite a looker. And that sexy-as-hell voice . . ."

"She really is beautiful, and although she tries to downplay it, it doesn't work. And no, I'm not jealous. You're too stuck on me to be interested in anyone else."

"Right you are, woman," Joe said, slapping Marie's bottom as she bent to pull the casserole from the oven. She seldom made anything from packages, preferring to concoct her meals from scratch. "Oh, and I saw Vicki Farrar poking around the old Sherman Gallery property this afternoon. I wonder what that was all about. That place has been empty since last fall."

Marie looked up, knowing that the old Sherman place was across the street from the market. "What do you mean by poking around?"

"She and some guy in a suit had the key and checked inside and out for over an hour. I can't help but wonder what's up."

"If anything's up, Suze will know about it before long so I'll bet we won't have to wait long to find out."

"Yeah, she'll know everything, probably before Vicki does. Did you invite Leslie to the cookout? I did, but I want her to feel like she's really invited."

"You just want more of a look at her, but yes, I did invite her and she said she'd be there."

At the sound of the slamming bathroom door the two parents yelled simultaneously, "Don't slam the door!" And with that, dinner was served.

Despite the fact that there were two houses between hers and Suze's, Abby Croft heard the roar of KJ's motorcycle as she tidied up the living room before dinner. The children were upstairs, playing video games on the two computers that Damian had installed at the beginning of the summer. As if to conjure him up, the phone rang. "Hi, honey, it's me," he said, his voice loud and cheerful. "How are things going?"

"We had a pretty ordinary day here," she said, happy to hear her husband's voice. "How about you?"

They spent several minutes exchanging details of their days, then Abby said, "I'm really looking forward to seeing you tomorrow evening. It's been a long and boring week."

"You sounded busy."

"That's kid stuff. I miss having you home each evening."

"But hon, you know that I need . . ."

"I know," she interrupted. They had similar discussions often. Damian thought that having a beach and other children to play with was beneficial for Mark and Tammy while Abby would have been happier staying in their house in a suburb of

Hartford and letting the kids play in the neighborhood. She truly missed having Damian home each evening and she couldn't help being a little suspicious as well. Every time she suggested that she and the kids could return to Hartford for a couple of days so they could play with their friends, Damian argued strenuously against it. She couldn't help but wonder whether he was spending his evenings with someone else while she was neatly out of the way. "I love you and I miss you. Having only the children to talk to gets boring."

"You have all those neighbors to hang out with."

"Right." She paused, then continued, "There's a new neighbor, in the Rogers Cottage. Her name's Leslie and she's really beautiful. You'll probably meet her tomorrow evening at the cookout. I think you'll like her." He'd certainly like looking at her.

"Sounds great. Listen, I've got a business dinner in a few minutes so I've got to run. I'll be there tomorrow, although it might be a little later than usual. Office stuff."

"Okay. We'll be waiting. I love you."

Damian's "I love you back," was a bit too perfunctory for Abby's comfort, but she had no choice but to hang up the phone.

In Hartford, Damian snapped his cell phone shut and dropped it on the carpeted floor beside him, then lay on the bed, naked, while his latest liaison, a twenty-two-year-old brunette who dreamed of being a movie star, lay between his legs, his large cock in her mouth. "You've got to be more careful," he said, only half serious. "You almost made me lose my train of thought."

The brunette, he thought her name was Diane, licked the length of his erection. "Fuck trains of thought," she said. "Concentrate on this." She took most of the length of him into her mouth and he did, indeed, fuck his train of thought.

*   *   *

As the sound of KJ's motorcycle abated, Brad DeVane watched Leslie slowly rise from the sand, dust off the seat of her baggy shorts, slip her feet into a pair of flip flops, and turn toward her cottage. So, she'd finally arrived. He'd been waiting for her since Monday, knowing she had paid in advance for the entire month. What a stroke of luck it had been when the DA's office had found out about this vacation. Leslie, or Carolynne with an "e," her name in the trade, had chatted animatedly about it with another pro in a small restaurant and someone from the DA's office had accidentally overheard. He was asked to "encounter her" and see what he could find out about Club Fantasy, the infamous brothel in which she worked, and specifically its client list. Someone wanted the information badly enough to pay for the rental cottage he was in for a few weeks.

When he'd been approached to take the assignment, he'd balked. Although he'd been in limited duty because of his leg, he was his precinct's top computer investigator and he was working on several important cases. He certainly didn't want to take time sitting around some beachfront hotel waiting to connect with some prostitute. And how the hell was he supposed to find out information that she obviously didn't want to reveal. Romance her? Not a chance.

He'd wondered whether his boss, Mike Mitcham, had taken advantage of this bullshit assignment to give him some time off, time he'd been trying to convince Brad to take since . . . "You can take your computer," Mike had said, "and probably get more work done there, away from the precinct. She's important of course, but so's the East Coast Recycling matter and the background work for the Volkov investigation. We can be in touch whenever you want me and that way you can kill several birds with one stone."

Mike had known all the right buttons to push, so here he was, climbing out of the water, looking conspicuously macho while trying not to limp, in an effort to attract her. She was certainly worth attracting, despite all she'd done to play down her looks. All that incredible sandy blond hair was slicked back in a ponytail, she wore no makeup, and baggy shorts with that awful sports bra hid her sensuous body. He'd gazed at the pictures in her file and had to appreciate the package. She was a looker, all right, but that was a prerequisite for being a thousand-dollar-an-hour whore.

Tomorrow evening would provide the opening he'd been looking for, he realized. She'd be at the cookout, everyone at this end of Atlantic Beach Road would come, and he'd strike up an innocent conversation, slowly ingratiating himself and subtly pumping her for scraps of information. He'd find out quickly enough whether there was any reason to question her further, which he'd do over the next week. Then he could end this fluff and get back to the city and do his real job.

As he approached, Leslie was almost at the stairway over the seawall. He ran up and decided to "accidentally" bump into her. "Sorry," he said, panting, "lost my balance."

"That's okay," she said. "No harm done."

"I'm Brad DeVane."

"I know. Suze told me."

"God, Suze is a piece of work," Brad said, shaking his head. "She grilled me like a well-done steak yesterday. She's the mayor but should be chief of police. Or maybe an FBI interrogator."

Leslie's laugh was as deep and warm as her sexy voice. "She really does want to know everything about everyone. I got the same third degree. Nice to meet you. I'm Leslie Morgan."

Not using Carolynne. "Nice to meet you, too. Did you just arrive? I didn't see you here yesterday."

"Yeah. Late this afternoon. I'm here for the month. You?"

"For another week, anyway. A long overdue and, I'm afraid, much-needed vacation. And before Suze warns you off, I'm a cop."

He watched Leslie's expression and saw a tiny wariness

creep in around her eyes. "I'm not sure I've ever known a cop up close and personal. Where do you cop?"

"New York City. I hear a little Big Apple in your accent. You, too?"

"Guilty. Manhattan born and bred. What kind of cop are you?"

"You mean good cop or bad cop, like in the movies?"

"I'm sure you're a good cop." She looked him over thoroughly. "You'd never pull off 'bad cop' with your looks. I meant do you drive around in one of those marked cars or are you a detective?"

He didn't want to tell her that he was temporarily assigned to a desk so he slipped back into his previous job, the one he was trying to forget. "I'm a sergeant in the Chinatown area. What do you do?"

"I'm part of a small business in Midtown. We do remodeling."

He wanted to invite her to dinner and pump her for information immediately but he knew it was too soon. God, she was quite something as she gazed at him with those wide-set hazel eyes. Actually he wanted to ask her to dinner just to get to know her but that wasn't why he was here. "Did Suze tell you about the cookout tomorrow evening?"

"She did. I'll be there. You?"

"With bells on."

"Good, I'll see you then, if not before." She started up the stairs and Brad watched her behind, not as well concealed as she might think since the baggy shorts tightened over an A+ ass as she climbed. Yes, this assignment might just have delicious fringe benefits.

The apartment was dark, dingy, and smelled of stale whisky and garbage. A woman screamed at a man who leaned out an open window, a child held in front of him by one arm. Brad focused on the baby's red overalls and black shoes as the man dangled the boy high above the concrete. He tried to approach but with every step the man got farther away, the room longer and narrower. He tried to shut out the shrieks of the child but as hard as he tried the screams penetrated more deeply into his brain.

He knew his partner Pete was behind him, but when he swivelled his head all he could see was the screaming woman, her mouth wide, her face distorted. The man's fingers uncurled and the child fell from his grasp. Although he knew it was a physical impossibility, Brad dove to catch the toddler before he hit the ground and, in diving, he exposed his partner to the gunman's revolver.

His heart pounded, his breath came in short gasps as he watched the baby who kept falling and falling. He wanted to run back down the stairs but he knew that he wouldn't be in time to save the kid. "He'll kill him!" the mother cried. "Do something! Stop him!"

Then shots, flashes of light, pain, screams. Then terror and nothingness.

Brad awoke drenched in sweat as he always did, his tongue rubbing over his broken front tooth. It took a trip to the bathroom and a full glass of water before he finally stopped shaking. Damn, he swore, returning to his bed. This is so fucking stupid. You see it in the movies, but it doesn't happen in real life. Okay, the department shrink said he'd probably have nightmares but it just wasn't his thing. He didn't have post-traumatic stress. He wouldn't allow it. *Shit, I sound like a macho jerk.*

This was part of the reason the department had given him this assignment, paid two weeks of rent on this house to get him close to Leslie. He needed space, his boss had argued, a little time to deal with it all, and it wouldn't hurt to let his leg heal for a week or two more. And his brain.

He tried to get back to sleep but shards of the dream kept interfering so, after half an hour of fruitless attempts, he untangled the sheets from around his waist, dragged on a pair of trunks, grabbed a towel, and headed for the water. He knew it was foolhardy to swim alone but this seemed the best way to work off the dream.

Half an hour later, tired from his exhausting swim, he climbed back into bed and fell into a light, but refreshing sleep.

Earlier that evening, when she returned to the cottage, Leslie spent an hour prowling. Downstairs, the building had a spacious living room, furnished in contemporary comfortable: the sofa upholstered in a floral print with two generously stuffed chairs in coordinating fabrics, wicker coffee and end tables, brightly colored ginger-jar lamps, and several pieces of colorful pottery. The kitchen was large and, as the agent had said, completely equipped with dishes, pots and pans, and, surprisingly, a closet filled with condiments and spices, probably left by previous tenants. She found lots of closet space for her market purchases and checked on the perishables she'd put in the large refrigerator earlier.

The small dining area contained a light colored wooden table with four chairs with padded seats and a sideboard that held place mats and tablecloths. A pair of ceramic candle holders with matching salt and pepper shakers graced the center of the table. The downstairs bathroom was functional, with towels, floor mats, and lots of small bars of soap.

The upstairs bathroom was luxurious, with a Jacuzzi tub and French hand-held shower. Leslie glanced at the space on the floor between the toilet and the tub, then remembered that she'd left her scale at home. She'd use the zipper test. If her pants still closed, she'd forget dieting—well, sort of.

The three bedrooms were similar, each room in white with a different muted shade. She put her suitcases in the pink room, as she thought of it, because the drapes, spread, and cushions on the white rocker were all the same soft rose and beige stripe, with lamps and small dishes scattered around in coordinated shades of rose and tan. The four-poster bed was also white, as was the dresser and mirror. The other rooms were clones of the first, one done in moss green, the other in robin's egg blue.

There was a good-sized-screen TV in each room and when she snapped on the one on her dresser, she was delighted to see that she got more than a hundred channels. She could be happy here, she realized, at least for a month.

Back downstairs she set up her laptop computer on the dining room table and hooked the dial-up wire to a phone jack in the kitchen. Now she could check on her e-mail messages and work on her schedule for September. No! she told herself. She wouldn't think about September. Not for quite a while yet.

Unused to being home in the evening she made herself a peanut butter sandwich, settled in front of the giant screen TV in the living room, and channel surfed. She watched a few shows she'd talked about with clients but had never actually seen. She laughed with *Sex in the City* and pondered a case throughout *CSI* as she sipped a glass of reasonably decent Merlot she'd brought with her. At about ten, she wandered into the kitchen and took a bag of microwave popcorn from the closet where she'd put it, then, with an evil grin, put it back. Instead she grabbed a bag of sour cream and onion Ruffles and a can of Diet Coke—she couldn't get too frisky with the calories—and returned to the sofa for an episode of a show a client had recommended called *Without a Trace*. Not bad, she thought. I could get used to this.

Finally, well after Jay Leno and Conan O'Brien, she climbed the stairs and slept deeply until after ten the following morning. As she pulled up the blinds in her bedroom and opened the window wider, she was almost blinded by the reflection of the sun on the water. Like yesterday, the sea was like glass and the air hazy. The bedroom was beginning to heat up as the sun beat on the wide windows so she reclosed the blinds, hoping she could enjoy fresh air without the room getting like an oven.

She yawned and stretched, wondering what she would do all day. After a long, hot shower she pulled her hair back in a barrette, then put on a lightweight, slightly baggy T-shirt and a pair of lightweight denim slacks, noticing that the zipper slid up easily. Feeling hungry she decided to splurge and find someplace to go for breakfast, or, since it was now after eleven, lunch. Grabbing her car keys and purse, she drove into the town of Atlantic Beach and along the main drag. The town seemed comfortably busy. Several cars were parked in front of Joe Martinelli's Market and a little silver convertible that might be the one she'd seen in her neighbor Vicki's driveway sat across the street in front of a storefront with a for lease sign in the front window.

The Wayfarer, a family restaurant, tempted her growling stomach so she pulled into the parking lot and entered. The place was cool and bright, with beige and blue industrial carpeting and light colored tables and chairs. She was shown to a booth and handed an eight-page laminated menu.

"Hello again," a male voice said. She looked up and saw Brad, standing tall and handsome beside her table. He was gazing down at her with his deep brown eyes and wide smile. He had a small chip out of one of his front teeth and that tiny imperfection made the rest of his face look still more perfect: long slender nose, wide-set eyes, full lips, and a small brushy moustache over a sensual mouth. His hair was neatly trimmed and mahogany brown, with a deep wave that crossed the top of his head from the top of one ear to above the other.

"Hi." She wasn't sure she wanted the strain of making conversation with a good-looking hunk, so she kept the expression neutral.

"I've been here several times and I haven't made it through the menu yet. Want some company?" When she hesitated, he continued, "That's a yes or no question and you're certainly allowed to want some alone time." When she kept silent for another moment, he continued, "No sweat. I'll see you at the cookout tonight."

What the hell, Leslie thought. He's just a nice man. A nice man who's a cop. "Please. Join me. My brain is just a little slow this morning. I'm trying to switch into vacation mode." He was really gorgeous, in a rugged, uneven sort of way.

"Thanks," Brad said. "Glad you thought of it."

Chapter
5

Brad settled onto the bench seat opposite Leslie. She looked wonderful, even without makeup, her dark blond hair caught in a clip at the back of her neck. Before he'd seen her picture in the file he had expected a model-type with a perfect face and figure, maybe a bit too much makeup making her look brassy. Well, she had a perfect shape but her face wasn't quite beautiful. Her mouth was a little too large, her nose a little too long. Her eyes, on the other hand, were perfect, large, wide set and an odd combination of brown, green, and gold. The photos didn't begin to capture her vitality, her charm, and that drop-dead sexy voice.

When she said, "Do I pass inspection," he realized that he'd been staring.

"I'm so sorry. You're really a lovely looking woman and I guess I was just appreciating that."

"Okay, you saved yourself," she said, her smile warm and genuine. She really did have a sexy mouth. "What brings you out this morning? I thought I'd be the only one around at this odd hour."

"I'm on my way to the gym to work out. I tend to be a night person so, since I'm on vacation I allow myself to sleep in, then come here for breakfast before going to exercise. You?"

"Also a night owl. You've found a place to work out?"

"There a really nice place on Route 1 called The Fitness Club, an appropriate name if I ever heard one. I stopped into quite a few the day I got here and discovered that at this one you can get a monthly membership at a reasonable price so I joined. You look like a woman who works out."

"When I'm not on vacation I usually go to the gym several times a week. I don't know whether I'm going to continue while I'm here. I want to get as far away from my normal routine as possible."

"I'm with you, but I just can't let myself go."

"I guess since you're a cop you need to stay in shape."

He thought about the rehab he was continuing on his own. His leg was getting back to its preinjury condition but he didn't dare let the thing go. Anyway, had he been just a bit faster he might have avoided everything. "I like to stay in shape. If you want, you can get a day pass so you can come along sometime." He might as well try to get closer. To learn about her business, of course.

"Thanks. I might take you up on that."

It had been sheer chance that Brad had seen Leslie's rental car in front of the Wayfarer. He had thought he'd have to wait until the evening's cookout to get to know her better. "Are you having breakfast or lunch? I don't cook so I come here a lot and can give you an idea about what's edible on the menu." When she made a face, he added, "Most of the cooking is actually pretty good, but there are a few stinkers."

"Oh? What's terrible?"

"Their pancakes could be used as flagstones and no self-respecting bagel joint in Manhattan would dare serve what they call bagels. The rest of their menu is pretty decent."

He found Leslie's laugh warm and sort of comfortable. He wondered whether her charm was natural or practiced. After all, what was a high-class hooker if not a professionally charming woman? "Okay, there are two things I think I'll avoid."

A short, chunky woman in a singularly ugly ruffled pink apron approached. "I know, honey, coffee for you, black, hot, and strong," she said, grinning at Brad. "How about you, love?" she asked Leslie.

"I'll have decaf." Leslie looked at Brad. "I'm ready to order if you are."

"I'm ready."

"I'll split the difference between breakfast and lunch." She looked up at the waitress. "I'll have an egg salad on white toast and," she smiled broadly, "a side of very well done french fries. I'll need milk for my coffee, too."

"Sure, honey," the waitress said, her voice thickly sweet, "and you, Brad?"

"I'll have a western omelette with hash browns, and give me a large orange juice."

As the waitress walked away, Leslie said, "Brad? She knows your name?"

"She's the restaurant's equivalent of Suze. She'll know everything about you in two days."

"I'm not sure I want anyone knowing everything about me," she said, her eyes tightening.

He decided to push just a little. "Oh? Skeletons?"

"No, just private stuff. Don't you have some things you just don't want to talk about?"

Brad thought about The Incident, with a capital I, as he had taken to thinking of it. Sure, there were things he didn't want to talk about, even think about. "Yeah, you're right. Some things are private."

"Cop stuff?"

"Some of that, of course. I usually get to see the worst side of people." He thought a moment. "Sometimes the best, too, but I'm sure that you see mostly good stuff."

"Good stuff?"

"You know, people redecorating. Starting new." He'd let her stick with her cover story.

"Oh that. Right. I do professional space. It's really kind of boring. Tell me a little about police work. Do you carry a gun?"

"Not with me. I'm off duty and in another state. I have one hidden away at the cottage, however."

"I'll remember not to sneak up on you at home. So tell me, is being a cop in the city anything like the shows on TV?"

During their breakfast/lunch he told her a few of the less gory and more interesting stories about being a policeman in New York City, then they talked about a myriad of topics, jumping easily from one to another. Brad found he could understand why she commanded the kind of prices she did. She was undoubtedly great in the sack, but she obviously wasn't half bad over the dinner table either. A great conversationalist, and an intent listener. When he talked she looked at him as though what he had to say was the most important thing in the world. Usually the women he met had an agenda, and when you talked they either thought about what the proper response should be to get what they wanted or how to change the subject to something in which they were more interested.

They explored a few of his interests, the plight of the New York homeless, World War II movies, and Internet dating, at which he'd failed completely. He even told a few self-deprecating stories and she laughed in all the right places. She, in turn, was passionate about universal, quality education, antiques, although she didn't own many, and good Midtown restaurants. Quite a dame. Attractive in so many ways. Always remember though, he told himself, she's a hooker.

Although he hadn't found any way to nudge the conversation toward what he was here to learn, he decided that he'd pressed things as far as he dared on first meeting. And, in the back of his mind he wasn't quite as fixated on finding out what she knew as he had been. They agreed to split the check and walked out into the hot sunshine. "Well," he said, "I'm off to the gym. You?"

"I think I'm going to the beach and just veg with a book. I guess I'll see you tonight at the cookout. Is it really all right for me to just show up?"

"I haven't been here for one, but everyone's made it abundantly clear that we're welcome. We'll have to sit together and gossip about all the neighbors, which seems to be most of what the women do around here." He winked at her. "And just because I'm a guy doesn't mean I'm not interested in all the info."

With a chuckle she said, "I guess that's what makes you a good cop. Ear to the ground, always paying attention."

"Right you are. See you later."

He got in his car and headed for The Fitness Club. Step one, he said to himself. Not bad at all. If it takes a few days to find out what I need to so what? I'll just enjoy her company in the meantime.

He hadn't really considered how he would find out what the investigators wanted to know. What do you say? Oh, by the way, I understand that you're a hooker. My bosses want a copy of your client list. You wouldn't mind giving that to me, would you? Not a chance. Now that he'd met her he was quite sure that this whole thing would never work. Another one of the chief's bright ideas, or was it just Mike's way to get him to rest and try to recuperate, physically and mentally. Maybe they never thought he could be successful. He should call the whole thing off, but what would it hurt to stick around for another week? After all, he had the house and the time, and, if he were to admit it, he did need to decompress. When he returned to the city he'd merely tell everyone how hard he'd tried and how angry he was that he'd struck out.

What about Leslie? He knew exactly what she was, although she had surprised him with her comfortable manner and good conversation. She was a very highly paid hooker and thus she had to be a good listener and a good entertainer. She had gazed at him as he talked as though he was the only man in the world, and when she unconsciously licked her lips he pictured her tongue on his body.

No! Don't go there! She's a case, a source of information, and nothing more. And don't forget, he told himself again, *she's a whore.*

As Leslie climbed back into her car, she thought about the hour she'd spent with Brad. She'd slipped into entertainer mode with little thought, but had quickly found that she didn't have to make the effort. Like many of her clients, he was easy to talk to and readily held up his end of the conversation. Stop that! she told herself. She had to stop comparing everyone, well every man anyway, to her customers. Brad was just a nice man who happened to be staying across the street. But what was the little tug she felt? Cut it out. He's a cop. Tug or no tug, he's the last thing she needed.

She spent the next hour driving around the shore area. The town of Sound's End was a comfortable little hamlet with old-fashioned New England charm, but much of Route 1, the Boston Post Road, was so commercial that it had lost any of the old Connecticut ambiance it might once have had. Between the fast-food restaurants, T-shirt shops, boat rental establishments, and motels, it looked like any other tacky mass-vacation destination.

Back on Atlantic Beach Road, she felt like she'd come home. Thank heavens for that real estate lady, she thought. She might have ended up in a neon tourist trap but this was delightfully low key, exactly what she'd been looking for. And she was actually looking forward to the cookout that evening.

Leslie spent the remainder of the day sitting quietly on the beach slathered with number 45 sunblock, reading one of the many novels she'd brought with her. She hadn't read for pleasure in more time than she cared to remember and she'd actually forgotten how nice it was to really get into a book, just for fun, not so she could impress someone or make clever conversation.

During the afternoon, she idly noticed the comings and goings on Atlantic Beach Road. A woman she assumed was the infamous Vicki arrived back at her house somewhere around two in the little silver sports car she thought was the same one she'd noticed earlier in town. Abby and her children left just after lunch and returned around five, while Suze came and went several times, waving to her from a distance each time.

Brad also waved at her when he came back from his workout, then, around four-thirty, came out in a pair of cut-to-the-knees jeans and began to swim, long graceful strokes carrying him back and forth, parallel to the beach. At just after five, she watched a young man wheel a large tub-type grill out to a spot in the parking area behind the seawall, then pad back into Marie's house. She quickly glanced at her watch and realized that, if she was going to clean up and change for the evening's festivities, she ought to get moving. The afternoon had disappeared without her notice. How fabulous.

After a quick shower to remove the layers of sweat and sunscreen, she wondered what to wear. What did one put on for a cookout? She glanced out her side window and saw Joe and Marie setting up a large metal table between the two grills that now graced the lot. They were both wearing jeans so she selected a lightweight pair and added a yellow polo shirt, socks, and sneakers. She pulled her hair back in a plastic butterfly clip, put a ten-dollar bill into her pocket for the kitty and wandered out. As she closed the door behind herself she was delighted that she didn't feel the need to double lock it. This sure wasn't Manhattan.

In the few minutes since she'd glanced out the window, the crowd had grown and the area along this little stretch of parking lot and seawall was bustling. People were setting up folding chairs and tables while Joe poured charcoal briquettes into one of the grills from a large bag, poured lighter fluid on, and lit the fire, then loped back across the street and into the house. "What can I do to help?" Leslie asked as she approached Marie.

The woman's smile was wide and welcoming. "Glad you're joining us," she said, "and there's really nothing much to do. It's gotten pretty routine, especially since I've done it so many times. We wait until the charcoal is ready then plop stuff on and grill. Joe and Kevin, Suze's husband, do most of the actual barbecuing." She paused, then said, "If you want to fetch and carry, you can go around to our back door. Joe's gathering up stuff and you can help him bring plates and bowls out."

"Sure thing." She reached into her pocket and pulled out the bill. "For the kitty."

"Thanks," Marie said, closing Leslie's hand over the money and pushing it away, "but you needn't do that. The hotel takes care of you. We ask the residents to chip in a little so they don't feel like freeloaders. Making donations seems to make folks more willing to come since they think they're paying their way. This meal is practically free anyway. It's salads left over from the market and we often try out new things to get people's reactions. The hotel chips in for whichever of their guests, like you and Brad, eat here," she said, winking, "and then Joe deducts it all on his taxes. The hotel also supplies the beverages. There will be soft drinks, beer, and wine arriving in just a few minutes."

"It sounds like you've got this down to a science," Leslie said, putting the bill back into the pocket of her slacks. "If you don't need me here I'll just go and see whether I can give Joe a hand."

As she walked up the Martinellis' driveway, several young people bustled past, carrying chairs, paper plates, plastic glasses and utensils, and bowls of salads and chips. "Hi," a boy in his late teens said, his eyes roaming her body. "You must be Leslie."

"That's me," she said, a bit suspicious of the high school

aged boy's obvious interest in her body. "How come you know who I am?"

"You're new around here and Suze, my mom, said you were a knockout. I'm KJ Murdock."

So this was KJ. She quickly connected him with the racket the previous afternoon. "Right. You must be the one with the motorcycle."

"That Honda's mine all right. Isn't she a beauty?" He gave her body another long, assessing look, his intent all too obvious. "I'd love to take you for a ride sometime."

He was quite a piece of work, Leslie thought, at least a dozen years younger than she was and hitting on her. Ye Gods. She schooled her face to be cool, yet charming. She didn't want to make waves. "Thanks for the offer but I think I prefer a little more metal around me when I move at more than ten miles an hour."

"Your loss," he said, then took off with a large bowl of tortilla chips in his hands.

Leslie stared after him, then shook her head in disbelief. Several young people pushed past her as she approached the back door, some going in, others heading for the beach. She climbed the rear stairs and saw Joe through the screen door in the midst of a group of teens bustling around the kitchen. He was standing in front of an almost industrial-sized refrigerator pulling out bowls and plastic bags. "Hi there," she said through the door. "This seems like quite an operation. You've got everyone regimented."

"Hi, Leslie. I'm glad to see you decided to join us, and yes, everything is very well organized. I spent several years in the army. Learned the fine art of getting things done, and delegating."

He handed a large platter of hot dog and hamburger rolls to a middle-sized, not unattractive teen wearing form-fitting cotton jeans and a tight T-shirt that said *If I were humble I'd be perfect* on the front. "Take this out to Marie," he said, then pushed her toward the door. "Leslie, have you met Eliza, Suze's daughter?"

With a sour expression and a muttered "Hi," the girl pounded out the door and let it slam behind her. Leslie gazed after her, watching her strut like a stripper.

Turning back to Joe, she asked, "Were you an officer in the service?" He certainly gave orders like one, she thought as he handed people things to bring outside.

"Nope, but I saw how they got me to do stuff I didn't want to do so I just copied their approach." As she laughed, he ushered her into the large kitchen, efficient, clean, and shiny despite all the activity. At that instant it was also silent.

"What can I do to help?"

"Carl made deviled eggs today and we only sold about half, so they're up for grabs." He pointed to a tray on the counter. "Taste one, and if they pass muster, you can take the platter outside."

Leslie picked up the hard-boiled egg and remembered that, as a kid, she'd always hated eggs in any form, along with lamb, Mexican food, and all vegetables. Then she flashed back to one of her first clients. He had taken her to a sushi restaurant, and when he found out she'd never had raw fish— nor did she want to—he spent an hour introducing her to different kinds of raw fish and fish eggs and showing her how to eat them. She remembered being really squeamish at first, but she'd quickly decided that she'd have to change her picky-eater ways if she was going to dine with clients. Now she loved almost every kind of food, from Korean to Peruvian.

She looked at Joe, then took a bite of the yellow and white treat and was delighted. "This is wonderful. There's something just a little hot in the filling. It's surprising."

"Cayenne. Just a touch adds a little kick."

"It certainly does. Do you have the recipe?" She'd probably never cook them, but she might, and anyway it was a compliment to him to ask.

"Sure. I'll get Carl to write it out for you. There are quite a few ingredients but they're pretty easy to make."

As she chewed, she asked, "How many people usually show up at this shindig?"

"Quite a few of the hotel guests come, like you and Brad, and all the neighbors on this stretch of Atlantic Beach Road. It usually adds up to a couple of dozen adults." He contemplated. "We've had as many as thirty. Someone usually brings a CD player so there's music and dancing and occasionally someone brings fireworks. It's become quite the thing."

"Does Marie do all the cooking?" My God, thirty people. She was already feeling sorry for Joe's wife.

"Carl, my assistant at the market, does quite a bit. He's studying to be a chef. Kevin Murdock, Suze's husband, does most of the actual barbecuing and Suze and Abby bring casseroles and stuff. Then there's Vicki. Have you met her?"

"Not yet," Leslie answered, "but I've heard a lot about her."

"Yeah, she's quite a character. Anyway, she doesn't cook a lick so she usually goes to a wonderful little bakery in Saybrook and brings cake. Oh, and Steve Carpone, the local ice cream man, stops by and does quite a business while he snarfs down hot dogs and barbecued sausages." He gazed at her and must have seen a slight frown.

"Don't get that look, Leslie," Joe added. "Marie loves to do this and if I took it away from her she'd bitch loud and long. Talk to her, and if you get any hint of negative feelings, let me know and I'll put an end to it in a heartbeat. You'll tell me?"

Her heart lighter, Leslie said, "Sure, Joe. No problem. And these eggs are terrific. Maybe you should give out the recipe when folks buy them. That way, they'll like the eggs, decide they're too complicated to make themselves, and buy more."

Joe looked thoughtful. "I love a woman with a creative mind. That's actually an interesting idea. Let me give it some thought. Give out recipes that are too complicated. Hmm. I could do that with some of Carl's sausages, too. He's my store's secret weapon and you have to taste some of his creations tonight."

"Have you ever thought of going into the catering business? If you can pull off a dinner like this, catering a wedding would be a piece of cake."

"I've thought about it but I wouldn't want to get Marie involved in something like that. It's a tremendous amount of work and she's happy taking care of the kids."

"They're getting older." She snapped her mouth shut and tamped down her inherent buttinskyness. In her business she often gave advice to men about their sex lives and other personal issues. Sometimes she was the only one they could talk to.

Leslie popped the remainder of the egg into her mouth. After she swallowed, she said, "Well I, for one, am impressed with the food and the organization." Leslie could see that Joe's mind had wandered so she grabbed the egg platter. "Is this ready to go out?"

Joe nodded so she headed back out toward the food area that had become a beehive of activity. A large table had been set up to serve as a bar and now was covered with bottles of wine and alcohol, with a few sizes of plastic glasses. Several large coolers filled with ice sat beneath it, and she watched people reach inside to get cans of soda or bottles of beer, supplied, she assumed, by the hotel. Leslie put her bowl with others, then wandered over and grabbed a can of Diet Coke. She popped the top, then stood watching the interplay of small groups of people.

She'd become an expert at reading the subtle clues in people's body language. Several couples leaned close, talking and laughing lightly together, lovers on vacation, she thought with a smile. Several teens were sitting on the seawall talking companionably, arms draped over shoulders. Other people chatted comfortably in small groups while a number of singles strolled through the crowd looking to make connections. She was surprised at how many unattached people there were. Maybe this had become the once a month equivalent of a Manhattan singles bar.

"Hi, Leslie," a quiet voice behind her said and she turned to see Abby. "Nice to see you again."

Abby looked as though she'd made an effort with her wardrobe, wearing a becoming teal summer sweater and white slacks. She wore a touch of lipstick, something Leslie hadn't seen before, and had curled her short brown hair. Leslie was quick to notice the two-carat diamond studs she wore in her ears and the rock the size of a small cube of sugar she wore with her wedding ring. Right, Leslie remembered, Abby's husband was due to arrive from the city. Although no one seemed to get made up, she couldn't help but wonder what a touch of mascara and shadow would do for this slightly mousey-looking woman's toast-colored eyes. "Hi. Nice to see you again, too. Where are those wonderful children of yours?"

Abby pointed. "Over there with a bunch of their friends." It was amazing how women brightened when they talked about their children. It did wonders for Abby's looks. "It's so nice to know that all the neighbors will have their eyes on everyone's kids so I can be a little more relaxed."

The two women stood on the edge of the growing gathering and watched the crowd. "I'm surprised at the number of people who seem to be single," Leslie said. "I would think this would be sort of a couples thing."

"I hadn't focused on it but I guess it's happened gradually. Vicki attracts guys like a magnet and several of the employees of the hotel come over to try to get—well let's just say to get connected. She's got a very active social life. Once the guys arrived a few unattached women from the hotel started to come over and it sort of just developed. Sometimes people who were singles in June are part of a couple by August. You know, summer romances and all."

"An interesting dynamic," Leslie thought out loud. Then, turning her attention to Abby, she said, "I remember that you said your husband arrives on Friday evening. Is he here yet?"

Abby hesitated, then said, "Oh, he's often late. He works really hard." She unconsciously patted the small square bulge in the pocket of her slacks. "I've got my phone and he'll call when he's on the road." As if summoned, the phone rang. Abby clicked it on, then listened. "Great. I'll see you in about an hour." She turned away from Leslie and spoke softly into the phone, but Leslie couldn't help but hear her quiet, "I love you and miss you." She watched as Abby listened and then snapped the phone shut. "He's on his way," she said, with a slightly forced lightness. "He had to work late again."

"I'm looking forward to meeting him when he gets here."

Her voice filled with a kind of pride. "You'll like him. Everyone does. He's so handsome and charming."

"What does he do for a living?"

"He's a very well-known entertainment lawyer and agent."

"Really? Does he work with anyone I'd know?"

Abby named a few TV personalities Leslie had heard of, two of whom she'd entertained herself. "That must be exciting," she said. "Do you get to meet them?"

"Occasionally, but with the kids and all it's tough for me to get out. Damian's not big on babysitters."

Smoke from the grill began to drift upward. "Is one of the men doing the cooking Suze's husband?" Leslie asked, changing the subject.

Abby looked toward the grill. "The short, Hispanic guy is Carl Hernandez, Joe's assistant at the market, and the taller one with the spatula is Kevin. I wonder where Suze is." She looked around, spotted the mayor, and pointed. "There she is. She wouldn't miss this." She huffed out a breath. "She has to work the room. Some of these folks are voters."

Suze was wearing beige slacks with a short-sleeved shirt with wide bright red, navy, and tan stripes. Anything to stand out in a crowd, Leslie thought. "Right, I see her." Leslie decided to pump Abby for some local color. "Has she been mayor long?"

"Four or five years, I think. At least since I've been coming here." She huffed out a breath. "She's a bit difficult to take sometimes, but I think she's got a good heart. I'm not sure what a mayor of a small town like Sound's End does but she seems to be bustling around all the time. Meetings. Luncheons. Lord only knows."

"I've no idea," Leslie said with a shrug. She saw a small crowd gathered around a woman who seemed to be in her midthirties with a mane of blond hair that she seemed to flip with each turn of her head. "Is that the famous Vicki who makes Suze turn colors?"

Abby chuckled. "That's her. And over there," she pointed to a slender young woman sitting with the group of teens, "is Trish, her daughter. Vicki tells anyone who'll listen that she had her when she was only sixteen."

Leslie took several moments to study the two women. Vicki was a bit overblown, statuesque, with large breasts that she displayed beneath a Kelly green shirt with tails tied across her diaphragm. Tight white slacks emphasized her firm behind and, as opposed to the usual sneakers, she wore strappy white sandals. She was talking animatedly with several men, one of whom Leslie recognized as the guy who had checked her in at the hotel.

In contrast, her daughter wore jeans shorts and a polo shirt and sat talking to the young man who'd introduced himself as KJ, Suze's son. She glanced back at the man doing the cooking and saw that the two men looked quite a bit alike, tall, lean yet muscular, both with curly, brown hair. The man from the hotel turned away from Vicki, caught Leslie's eye then said something to another man that made him look her way, laugh, and give a thumbs-up sign. With a wide grin, he broke away from the group.

"Hello," he said as he walked over. "It's Leslie, isn't it?"

"Yes. I'm surprised you remember."

"We don't get many women as attractive as you are," he said, giving her a quick once-over.

Leslie kept her long sigh to herself. She was used to the effect she seemed to have on men, and it helped her no end in her job. In social situations, however, it became tiresome to constantly have to deflect come-ons. She turned. "You must know Abby."

"Of course," he said, his focus still on Leslie. "Nice to see you again."

"Hi, Gerry," she said, moving away. "I'm going to check on my kids." She all but ran, leaving Leslie with Gerry.

"This is quite a crowd," Leslie said, trying not to be too rude.

"It usually is." He lowered his voice. "I was hoping you'd be here."

She sipped her soda, then saw Brad leave his house and head for the grill. There it was, that little tingle of awareness. Shoving it to the back of her mind, she said, "I think I'll say hello to Suze. If you'll excuse me, Gerry."

"Sure," he said, looking deflated.

Leslie made a beeline for the mayor. "Hi, there. This is quite a party."

Chapter

6

"Hi, Leslie," Suze said as she approached. "I'm glad you could come. This is quite an event."

"I can see that. They have this every month?"

"We call it First Friday, and it's become a summer happening, the first Friday of each month from June to Labor Day."

She thought about Marie's efforts. "It's quite an undertaking."

"Every time someone mentions not having it, Marie pitches a fit. She and Joe just love doing it. Have you met everyone?"

"Not by a long shot."

Suze began a guided tour around the gathering, taking snapshots and filling Leslie in on the gossip about everyone in the neighborhood. As she prattled on, Leslie considered Gerry and KJ. She'd done her best to downplay her looks and had made no flirtatious remarks or gestures. What the hell was it about her that seemed to always lead guys on? What about Brad? They'd had a lovely meal together and he hadn't made a pass. She couldn't help but wonder why not.

Her innate sensuality was what made her so good at her job. She seldom had to make an effort to turn a customer on, and in the outside world, men seemed to find her irresistible. She smiled inwardly then glanced over at Vicki, who would probably find Leslie's problem a desirable condition. Leslie, on the other hand, just wanted this vacation to be easy and comfortable. She didn't want to have to fend guys off left and right.

She tuned in on Suze's monologue. "Those are the Johnsons," she said, indicating a nicely dressed black couple helping themselves from a bowl of chips. "They just moved into the new apartments on the far side of Route 1. I met them in town right after they moved in." There was a slight tightening in Suze's voice. "I think it's Dewayne and Tanisha. Where do those people get those names, anyway?" *Those people.* Leslie bristled at Suze's racist remark, although she had no idea whether Suze meant it to be offensive. "The cops patrol that area frequently." Then she quickly added, "Of course we welcome people of all colors and such." Okay, Leslie knew exactly what Suze was saying.

The couple walked over and the tension in Suze's expression quickly became a beaming smile. "Well hello," she said. "We were just saying how nice it is for you folks to come over to our little shindig."

"Thanks." The woman was lovely looking, with café au lait skin and tightly braided hair. "We saw Joe at the market a few days ago and he invited us. Of course we put money in the kitty."

"That's so kind of you," Suze said, the wide mayoral smile plastered on her face. "This is Leslie Morgan. She's renting for August. Leslie, this is Mr. and Mrs. Johnson."

"It's really Doctor and Ms.," the woman said, hugging her husband's arm against her. "Dewayne is in his first year of residency at Yale New Haven Medical Center. He works about a hundred hours a week but, believe it or not, he actually got this evening off, so here we are."

The pride in Tanisha's voice was obvious and Leslie enjoyed the slight look of surprise on Suze's face. "That's wonderful," Leslie said. "What kind of doctoring do you think you'll do, Dewayne?"

Dewayne's face lit up. "I'm interested in emergency care

and specifically in trauma. Yale New Haven is a Level I Trauma Center, you know."

Suze chimed in, "What in the world made you move here? That's quite a drive."

"It's less than an hour and since I put in my hours in such big blocks, and catch winks at the hospital, it isn't too bad. Actually Tanisha grew up in New London."

"I've always loved the shore," Tanisha said, "and when Dewayne got his residency, we just decided to find an area we could settle down in. He's in New Haven for three years, and maybe we'll decide to settle here permanently if he eventually gets a job somewhere close."

"Sort of long-term temporary," Leslie said. "So that's why the apartment, rather than buying a house?"

"Yeah, and it's convenient, with good schools and stuff. And not too expensive. I guess the doctor here," she cuffed her husband's arm, "will eventually earn a living wage, but that's still a ways off."

"And you, Ms. Johnson? I assume you work outside the home," Leslie said, rubbing Suze's nose in her neighbor's lives.

"It's Tanisha," she said with a wide smile, "and I was a floor broker on the stock exchange. It was incredibly high stress and I hated it but it was necessary while he was in med school and internship, both in the city. When Dewayne got his residency we had to move and I couldn't be happier to be somewhere calmer. I'm working in a small local brokerage firm right now and loving the calmer atmosphere."

"She'll take time off when the baby comes," Dewayne said, beaming.

"A baby. How wonderful," Suze said, her voice tight.

Leslie looked at Tanisha's slim figure. "No wonder you're interested in schools. You're not due for many months, I'd say."

She beamed. "I'm due in February but this guy here," she glared lovingly at her husband, "is treating me like some delicate flower even though he's a doctor and should know better. I'm strong as an ox, and I haven't been sick at all. I've read lots of books but I will admit that the whole thing's still a bit daunting."

"You should get to know Marie Martinelli," Suze said. "She's had six kids and should be an expert on being pregnant."

"Gee, that would be great," Tanisha said. "I'd love to meet her. I'm an only child and Dewayne has only one sister, and she's much younger. Both our mothers are gone so I don't have anyone to talk to except doctors and what the hell do they know about being on this side of the prescription pad."

Suze scanned the crowd until her gaze lit on Marie. "She's over there by the drink table. The one with the navy polo shirt and jeans."

"That's really kind of you," Dewayne said. "Thanks for everything."

The couple made their way through the crowd and Suze turned her attention to Leslie. "Have you met my husband, Kevin, yet?" She led Leslie over to the tall slender man wielding utensils over the grill. "Hey, hon," Suze said. "I told you about Leslie."

"You sure did. Nice to meet you." He stuck out his hand, then realized that he was wearing a large oven mitt. "Sorry," he said as he whipped it off and shook Leslie's hand.

"Nice to meet you, too," she said. "Whatever you're cooking smells great."

Kevin's expression was open and less predatory than many of the men she'd met. "Carl Hernandez, he works with Joe, is a whiz with these sausages. I never know what's in them, but each month he creates something better. I've been trying to convince Joe to start some kind of specialized sausage business. Anyway, if you don't like sausages, we've got burgers and dogs, with grilled vegetables and lots of fresh local corn."

"Sounds just fabulous."

"Why don't you grab a plate and I'll see what's ready."

Suze wandered off and Leslie returned to the grill with a heavyweight paper plate, napkins, and some plastic utensils. "Okay," Kevin said, his gaze warm, "what can I get you?"

She started to opt for the veggies, then reconsidered. "I'd love a small piece of the sausage and maybe a burger." To be able to eat whatever she wanted was an unparalleled treat.

Kevin used long-handled tongs to drop a piece of sausage onto her plate, then said, "That burger, with or without cheese? And how about a toasted bun?"

"Without cheese and with a bun, please," Leslie said.

"What would you like on it? We're a full-service operation here." In a sing-song voice he reeled off, "We've got onions, both raw and fried, lettuce, tomatoes, relish, ketchup, mustard, mayonnaise. . . ."

Leslie couldn't remember the last time she'd eaten raw onion. With a profession like hers, she couldn't risk garlic or onion breath. "I would love a slice of raw onion. Thanks, Kevin."

"You're very welcome," Kevin said, putting a slice of red onion on her burger. "Come back for seconds whenever you're ready, and help yourself to side stuff, too."

"Will do," she said as she moved over to the table loaded with salads. She gazed at the onion on her hamburger, then thought, To hell with everything. She served herself a spoonful of potato salad and one of macaroni salad, then added several black and green olives. Fuck calories. She saw Marie, Suze, and Abby wave her over so she dropped into an empty chair at their table. As she leaned over to take a bite of her burger, she felt a large hand in the middle of her back. "Evening, all," a male voice said.

Leslie could feel the warmth of his hand through her shirt. "Glad you could come, Brad," Marie said. "What do you think of our little gathering?"

"I never expected anything like this," he said. "There must be thirty people here."

Marie glanced at her watch. "It's still early. By seven all the tables will be full."

"I really admire you and Joe for doing all this," Brad said.

"My husband does most of the cooking," Suze said.

"I know and that's great." Brad let that thousand-watt smile land on Suze. "I got to talking to him earlier. Let me get some food and I'll join you if there's room."

"Sure," Marie said. "I'll find a chair."

"Don't bother," Brad said. "I'll just sit on someone's lap."

Marie and Suze giggled. Like kids, Leslie thought. He certainly is a charmer. Probably makes him a good interrogator, the good cop to someone else's bad cop. Brad motioned to Marie to stay where she was and quickly found an unoccupied chair and put it between Leslie and Suze. "Right back," he said.

A few minutes later he was sitting beside Leslie, devouring a sausage sandwich and radiating heat and testosterone. He's a cop, Leslie told herself. He might be attractive, but he's a cop and you're off all men, particularly cops, at least for the duration.

After they finished the meal and put all the debris into large garbage bags, Abby went in search of her children and Suze and Marie headed off to do who knows what. That left her with Brad at the table by themselves. "I can't believe that Marie and Joe actually think the Red Sox have a chance this year," Brad said, continuing the topic begun just before the group broke up. "Okay, they finally won it once, but in the time it took them to win one World Series, the Yankees did it twenty-six times."

"Hey, you're preaching to the choir. I've been a Jeter fan forever." Her enjoyment of baseball had begun early in her career. Many of her clients enjoyed the National Pastime and she'd begun to read up on it, then started to watch the occasional game. Eventually she began to enjoy it, then she'd become a Yankees fan. It had led to several heated arguments with clients but she decided to express her views, even if they went against those of her date.

"I didn't know you liked baseball," Brad said.

"I don't know too much about the finer points, but it's hard to be a New Yorker and not root for either the Mets or the Yankees and I like to root for a winner."

"Giving the Mets their due, they did win the National League pennant in 2000."

"Right, and lost to the Yankees in the series." This is too comfortable, Leslie thought. Damn.

"Hi, Brad," a melodic, female voice said from behind them.

Brad turned. "Hello, Vicki." He flashed his thousand-watt smile with the charming chipped tooth again. "Have you met Leslie?"

Leslie stood and extended her hand. "Leslie Morgan." She took a good look at the woman who seemed so out of place in such a small town. She was almost a caricature of a sex kitten, with large green eyes surrounded by long eyelashes that many women Leslie knew would kill for, a halo of fluffy blond hair that probably wasn't all its natural color, and full lips that added to the erotic look. She wore a bit too much makeup for a warm summer evening. *Phew*, Leslie thought, *I'm actually being bitchy. Cut it out!*

"Vicki Farrar." Her grip was quick and cool, her hands soft and delicate, her nails long and polished hot pink. Leslie glanced down at Vicki's strappy sandals and saw that her toes were polished the same bright pink. A total package. She'd been this woman in many fantasies, seductive, with an erotic combination of aggressiveness and reticent little girl. "I see you've met Brad," she said, her voice low and breathy. God, Leslie thought, does she know how obvious she is, and how much sexier she'd look if she toned it all down just a little? Obviously not. "He's a cop, you know. I just love a man in a uniform."

"I'm not a cop right now, Vicki, and it's nice to see you again."

Vicki dropped into a chair beside him. "I couldn't help but overhear. You were talking about baseball. I just love the game." She placed her hand on Brad's bare forearm. "There is a local team. They play Sunday afternoons. It's not the Red Sox, of course, but they have fun. Maybe we could go to a game sometime." She lowered her head so she had to look up at him through her lashes and snaked her tongue over her full lips. It was all Leslie could do not to laugh out loud. She'd played this scene often, the seducing, predatory female and the innocent man. It was a favorite of several of her regulars.

She recalled her most recent encounter, living out the fantasy of a man named Jonas and allowed her mind to drift while Brad and Vicki talked.

She sat at the crowded bar of a large, luxurious hotel in Midtown, wearing a slender black skirt, slit deeply up the side, her long legs crossed so her shapely thighs were visible above her four-inch, high-heeled black pumps. Her gauzy white blouse with its full, floating sleeves was unbuttoned to show a great deal of shadowy cleavage. She'd gotten there a few moments before, just enough time to slither onto a bar stool.

"I'll have a cosmopolitan," she said to the bartender who, although trying not to stare, gave her the once-over in the large mirrored wall behind the bottles as he mixed. He set her glass on a coaster and she reached for her wallet. As she pulled it out of her small black handbag, Jonas slid onto the only available bar stool, the one beside her, and ordered a beer. He was in his early forties and loved to play the innocent to Leslie's slut. He glanced over at her and they exchanged smiles.

"Hi," she said as the beer arrived. "I'm Carolynne." She used her usual pseudonym. "That's spelled with an 'e' at the end."

Jonas kept his head lowered. "Jonas," he said.

"Nice to meet you, Jonas." She sipped her drink. "What do you do?"

They made small talk and eventually he ordered them each another drink. As the second one arrived, she took his hand. "You've got great hands," she said, stroking his palm. "So soft." She rubbed his hand against her cheek. "I love a man with soft hands." The dialogue was really a bit over the top but she could see by the growing bulge in his slacks that Jonas didn't see it that way, and he was paying big bucks to have the fantasy go exactly as he wanted.

She used her index finger to raise his chin. "I'll bet your lips are soft, too." She kissed him lightly, brushing her mouth over his. He really was a great kisser, kissing like it was an end in itself, not a means to one. A man seated near them cleared his throat loudly, but they ignored him.

When Jonas pulled back, she took his hand and put it on her stocking-covered thigh, revealed by the split in her skirt. "I'm soft other places, too."

Despite the fact that this was a playlet that they'd acted out several times before, his breathing was uneven and his hands shook. "Well, I'm here from Boston and I've got a room upstairs." Actually he lived in Queens but being out of town was part of the illusion.

Her grin revealed her white teeth. "There's always room service."

He dropped a few bills on the bar and they left, arm in arm, with several men gazing enviously after them.

Upstairs, he shed his clothes quickly and then took a long time undressing her, kissing and touching like it was the first time they'd ever made love. When she was down to her lacy white bra and tiny satin panties, he knelt in front of her and kissed her belly, pushing his tongue into her belly button. Then he slowly lowered her panties. For some reason, he liked her with her bra still on.

He used his thumbs to open her outer lips and flicked his tongue over her clit. He didn't seem to notice that she hadn't been excited until his tongue began to work its magic. She always found it surprising how aroused she became when most of it was, for her, merely playacting. Maybe that was one of her talents because every man she was with believed that she was truly aroused by his actions. Most of the time she was.

Soon they were on the bed, with Jonas crouched over her, his condom-covered cock delving between her thighs. "This is always so wonderful," he said.

"You make me so hot, Jonas. It's wonderful."

"God yes," he panted. "So good." He plunged into her and she wrapped her legs around his waist.

She felt the heat coil in her belly. Even before she was in the business she'd loved sex in all forms. At first she'd worried that it would become stale and she might eventually learn to dislike it, but that hadn't been a problem. She loved making love and with all her clients it was making love, not just fucking. "Oh God, do it," she said, clamping her vaginal muscles around his thick erection. "Do it, do it, do it." She could feel her heat rising as his thick cock slid in and out of her and he suckled on her nipple through her bra.

He tilted his pelvis so he could reach her clit then squeezed and rubbed until she was, indeed, close to orgasm. "Come for me, baby," he said, his voice hoarse and raspy. "Come for me." A few more strokes and she did come, her muscles clamping on him until, with another few thrusts, he joined her.

She pulled herself back to the present and watched Vicki all but drape herself over Brad.

"Actually, I'm not much of a fan of nonprofessional leagues, Vicki," Brad said, "but I'm sure there are lots of guys here who would enjoy that."

"I was thinking about us going some weekend," Vicki said with a pout, leaning a bit closer to Brad. God, Leslie thought, she's like a spider waiting for a bug to venture too near her web. She smiled inwardly. *Leslie, you're capable of the most deliciously catty thoughts.* She never allowed herself any negativity when she was working because it might creep into the fantasies she created but now she was off duty. Totally and wonderfully off duty.

She turned her attention to Brad. How was he reacting to Vicki? She was very attractive and her overly large breasts almost spilled out of the button-front of the shirt. Men!

Strangely, he wasn't panting, she saw, and she was surprised that she felt relieved. Why? She had no designs on him. Let him hook up with Vicki, obviously what the spider wanted, but Leslie saw from his body language that it wasn't in the cards. Even if Vicki still had hopes, Leslie knew it wasn't going to be. She felt her shoulders relax.

Reluctantly Vicki stood. "Maybe another time, Vicki," Brad said.

"Yes, maybe." She all but stomped off.

"That woman," Brad said when she was out of earshot, "has the subtlety of a load of bricks. Maybe she'll take it out on Gerry."

"Gerry? The guy from the hotel?"

"She and Gerry have an occasional thing going. She thinks it's a deep dark secret but in this little neighborhood everybody knows everything, and tells everyone. I've been filled in by both Suze and Marie on many of her conquests. I guess they were worried that I'll get sucked in too."

"She is quite something."

It was now almost eight o'clock and the gathering was breaking up. The teenaged crowd had already headed off to one of the places on Route 1 and the younger children were being herded off to bed. Many of the grown-ups who didn't have kids to care for had gone off to various Friday-evening activities. Leslie was delighted to have met so many nice people. She'd been asked to meet a few at the beach over the weekend. It was all so simple, so different from New York and her job.

"You know, Leslie," Brad said, "there's a Yankees game on and

I arranged to get the YES network at my place on the hotel's satellite dish. I was thinking of pulling the TV out onto the porch if the wire's long enough. Want to watch with me after we help clean up?"

It was much too tempting. "I don't think so. I'm going to bus a few tables, then pack it in before the bugs come out."

"Sure. If you'd like to go to the gym with me some afternoon, just give me a call or knock on the door. We can have lunch first."

"I might just do that."

"Offer's open whenever," Brad said. "Let's see what we can do to help clean up."

In Marie and Joe's kitchen Brad helped wash bowls and scrub the counters while Leslie folded tables and chairs. He marveled at her ability to get comfortable with people so quickly. He'd watched her during dinner and she had made conquests of most of the men and, surprisingly for someone in her business, most of the women as well. He considered that it might be something she'd learned but decided that this much natural charm had to have been there from the cradle.

His shoulders rose and fell as he sighed. It was sad she was a prostitute, and his business right now. He wondered how it might have been if they'd met under different circumstances, but that was a useless exercise, since these weren't different circumstances.

Chapter

7

Abby turned over in bed and glanced at the red digits on the front of her bedside clock radio. 2:48 A.M. She flipped and pounded her pillow until it was the exact shape she wanted. As she curled on her side, she could hear Damian's soft breathing. She forced her eyes closed and thought about her husband. He was so great with the kids and they adored him. Last weekend it had rained all day Saturday and Damian had suggested that the entire family see a popular movie playing at a theater in Old Saybrook. Then they gorged on pizza and went on to a pinball arcade. Forty dollars' worth of tokens later, the kids had to be all but dragged back to the car.

Sunday he'd spent a good part of the day closeted away in the spare bedroom working, but that was only natural, wasn't it? Abby envied women whose husbands didn't have to work some part of every weekend and could spend time with them. Stop being demanding, she told herself for the thousandth time. He was a wonderful man. He'd told the kids earlier that evening that they could go to the big electronics store sometime that weekend and each pick out a new computer game since he had a lot of work to do. Couldn't he ever spend time with her? "Darling," she'd said that evening as they got ready for bed, "how about we find out when Trish or Eliza can baby-sit and we go out for a nice dinner somewhere? Maybe tomorrow night and then we could see a grown-up movie for a change. There are a lot around I know we'd both like."

"I really wish I could, you know that," Damian had said, "but I've got loads of work and several business calls I have to make."

"What kind of business calls can you have on the week-end?" she'd asked, letting a bit of annoyance creep into her voice.

"Honey, come on," he'd said, patting her shoulder. "Work is my part of this marriage and you're not supposed to worry about it. Supporting you and the kids takes a lot of effort and time. You know I want you and the kids to have everything, like this summer vacation."

Some vacation, she thought and pounded her pillow again. She cooked and took care of the kids all day with no . . . Stop it. *He's right. It's his job to support us and the least I can do is be helpful and not bitch.* She sighed. She didn't worry about the business part of it, but she was beginning to be a little uncomfortable with his secret phone calls all weekend and his often being unavailable in the evening during the week. No, she didn't want to think about that.

He was faithful, she was pretty sure of that, but there was Leslie and the way Damian had behaved. Leslie was such a nice woman but Damian had made a bit of a fool of himself over her and it was embarrassing. She thought back to earlier that evening.

She and Leslie had been sitting with Brad, Marie, and Joe, talking about something innocuous, when Damian finally emerged from the house. He'd arrived about a half hour before and had gone inside to change and visit with the kids. He was really gorgeous, Abby thought as she'd watched him help himself to a burger and some salads, then make his way over to the table. *I love him so much.*

"Hi, Damian," Joe said. "I hope there was enough left. We

got quite a crowd tonight. There must have been more than forty people."

"No problem, Joe. I found just what I wanted." He dragged a chair over from a nearby table and settled himself beside Leslie and across from Abby. "Hi," he said to the newcomer, "I'm Damian."

"Leslie Morgan. You're Abby's husband."

"I am," he said, gazing into Leslie's eyes. "Abby said you were a knockout, and she was right. It's *very* nice to meet you."

"Thanks," Leslie said, seeming a bit uncomfortable. "You probably haven't met Brad either. He just arrived this week."

"He's staying in the Whitson House," Marie chimed in.

"Nice to meet you." The two men shook hands.

For the next several minutes, Damian attempted to monopolize Leslie's attention, regaling her, and the entire table as well, with stories about his activities as an entertainment lawyer, dropping names left and right. Although there wasn't anything overtly out of line, Damian had spent an inordinate amount of time gazing into Leslie's eyes and staring at her mouth and into her cleavage. As Abby turned in bed yet again, she realized that Leslie had seemed to be trying to deflect his attentions.

Was he actually coming on to her? Damian? Husband, father of Abby's children. No, he was just being charming, as he always was. He did touch Leslie's back, however, as he stood to get a drink, and rub her arm when he thought Abby wasn't looking.

Later, in bed, Abby had hinted that she'd like to make love. She'd snuggled against him and stroked his chest. He'd told her he wasn't in the mood. "Anyway," he'd said, "the kids might hear. I think they're still awake."

She listened to his even breathing as he lay beside her. Never mind, she told herself, trying to suppress her frustration. That's just the way he is. It doesn't mean anything. An hour later she fell asleep.

The following morning, she awoke to find the other side of the bed empty. She showered and dressed quickly, then arrived in the living room to find Damian and the children spread on the floor, playing a board game. Tammy's ferret was draped across her shoulder. "Hi, Mommy," Tammy said, brightly. "Daddy made us French toast."

"From a frozen package," her husband said.

"Yeah," Mark chimed in, "but it was really good. He put real maple syrup on it and everything."

"I bought some last weekend when we wandered through that market and I thought they would enjoy it."

"It was great," Tammy said. "Daddy made us feed the animals before we could play."

"That's wonderful. Thanks, Damian. Is there coffee?"

"In the pot," Damian said, turning toward his son. "Okay, Mark, you're goin' down. Those are my pieces there and green's on your other side. Between Tammy and me, you're toast." Her family's delighted laughter filled her heart. She tamped down any negative thoughts, even when she took the kids to the beach to play with the Martinelli children and Damian closed himself in the bedroom with his computer and his cell phone.

The phone woke Vicki later that morning. "You sound deliciously sleepy," the voice said. "Are you still in bed?"

"I'm awake. What time is it?" she asked without opening her eyes.

"I know it's Saturday, Vicki," he said, "but it's after ten and I thought you were going to call me."

"I'm sorry, Marty, I forgot." She tried to sound contrite. He and Cory Bartlett, her financial advisor, had been indispensable.

"I just wanted you to know that, as I'd hoped, I got most of the town and county paperwork in the mail this morning and the lease on the property is waiting for your signature. Did you read the copies I sent you?"

She had waded through about ten pages the previous afternoon, but then had given up on the legalese. She was a shrewd woman, usually able to get what she wanted, but she hated to spend her time on things she had advisors for. "Sure, Marty, I was a good girl. It all seems fine with me."

"Great. You can come into the office on Monday and we can get everything done. Have you made any deals with suppliers yet?"

Actually she had prowled the Internet for wholesalers of lingerie and toys and had found a few places where she could get rentable triple-X-rated videos. She had contacted a few but had quickly become disinterested in the details. This would be Trish's part of the business so she didn't have to bother with it in more than a cursory manner. Trish would quickly learn how to deal with those folks and she'd broker the deals that needed to be made. Marty, however, didn't need to know that she wouldn't be doing it all herself. He thought it was entirely her venture and he was doing it as a reward for her for "good service." "I made a lot of contacts, Marty, but no actual deals. I thought you and I could get together and work out the details."

His voice a little clipped, he said, "Listen, Vicki, I do have other clients and I'm not billing my time when we discuss all this stuff. You need to make some decisions, get some paperwork. Once you've done the legwork, I'll look it over."

Vicki had dealt with this kind of rebellion before. "Oh, sweetie," she purred, turning over in bed and curling her lush body around the phone, "you know how difficult all that language is and numbers have never been my thing. Anyway, isn't your wife out of town next week? We could go over things during dinner one evening then," she lowered her voice still more, "firm things up back at my place."

She heard the catch in his breath. "Do some of your own work," he said, his tone softening his words, "and we'll see what we can do together sometime during the week. But please, don't just hand me a bunch of names. Decide exactly what you want to carry, then call several places, get sample contracts, deal information, percentages, whatever they'll give you, and write it all down. Then we'll organize it. Does that work?"

She hated the idea of doing all that spade work, but she reasoned it had to be done if this thing was going to get off the ground. She needed to discuss it all with her daughter, then Trish could lay the groundwork and, with Marty's help, she could close the deals. She grinned. She was very good at closing deals and with the proper incentives she might even do a little better than Trish could. "Will do, sweetie. You know I hate it when you sound harsh. I like it much better when you're panting, waiting to slide inside of me."

His long sigh told her what she wanted to know. "Just get organized, will you, Vic? Please?"

"Sure, sweetie. I'll make lots of calls on Monday, then I'll call you and we'll set up a time to sign stuff."

"It's only a matter of a few days before the folks in Sound's End find out what you're planning. You'd better be ready for some fireworks."

"They can't stop me, can they?"

"I don't think so. The zoning's right and we have all the business certificates."

"Then that's that."

"Okay, Vic. I'll talk to you on Monday."

As she hung up the phone, Vicki finally opened her eyes. The sun shone brightly around her window shade and the air conditioner hummed in the window. She rubbed her feet on the satin sheets on her king-sized bed, then decided it was time to get up. She slid to the edge of the bed, sat up and finger-fluffed her blond hair. *I've got to make an appointment to have the color done*, she thought. Looking at her hands and feet, she added, *and my fingernails and toes are a wreck*.

As it often did, the bedroom smelled slightly of sex. She recalled Gerry arriving at her back door at about nine-thirty, after Trish and the rest of the barbecue crowd had gone off to their evening's entertainment. Gerry was kind of cute and so young, with stamina enough to make up for a decided lack of talent in bed. This had been their fifth evening together and she'd decided it was time for a little training. She'd seen him talking to Leslie, too, the little slut who was staying in the Rogers' house. She just oozed sex, even in her dumpy clothes. No way was she going to displace Vicki with anyone or anything. She'd show Gerry no one could please him better than she could.

She'd ushered him in and they'd climbed the stairs of the empty house to Vicki's bedroom, Gerry already pulling his shirt off over his head. Eager. That was a good word to describe him. She recalled the scene perfectly.

"Baby," she said as they entered her bedroom, "you're always in such a hurry. How about tonight we slow down a bit?"

"Sure, Vic," he said, grabbing her and pulling her against him.

She put her hand over his mouth. "I mean it. We need to slow down."

"You've never complained before," he said, reaching for her ass, "and you're always wet and ready."

"I know, but that's not all there is to great sex. I can make it even better for both of us."

"How?" He sounded like he was humoring her, but he stepped back.

"I've got a few ideas on how we can play without you getting too grabby."

"I don't get grabby. I just want to fuck your brains out, and you always love it when I do." He stroked the front of his jeans, showing her how hard he was.

God, Vicki thought, *was I ever this young?* "Come here," she said, taking his wrist. "Give me five minutes and you'll see how much better it can be."

She dragged him to the bed and flipped off the quilt to reveal red satin sheets. Then she pushed him down and drew off his sandals. "Now that's the way I like it," he said, assuming she meant to undress him as she'd done several times before.

Nipping at his big toe, she watched him shudder. He was great raw material, she thought as she maneuvered his pants off. Moments later, while she sucked on his thumb, milking it like a small cock, she surreptitiously opened the bedside table drawer and pulled out two pairs of regulation handcuffs. She loved all kinds of bondage equipment and she flashed on the display she'd build at her new store. Mostly demos, of course, since the ordering would be done online, but she could certainly give lots of good advice.

She pulled back and, with a few deft motions, fastened Gerry's right wrist to the headboard. While he was still gasping at her action, she immobilized the other wrist.

"What the hell is this?" he said, rattling the cuffs and quickly discovering he was incapable of freeing himself without breaking furniture.

"Trust me," she whispered, her breath hot in his ear. "You'll love it."

His eyes wide, he stared. "Come on, Vic, let me go. This is too kinky for me."

"I know it isn't, baby," she said, kissing him deeply, "and you do, too. You just don't want to admit it."

"Vicki, I know it's always been good between us but this isn't my thing."

She rubbed the hard ridge of his cock. "Well, little Gerry here says it is. Trust me and go with it." She kissed his eyelids. "Keep your eyes closed and let me do *aaalll* the work," she purred.

He sighed his resignation. "I guess I don't have much of a choice."

"Nope, you don't, so just relax and don't worry," Vicki said, again squeezing his hard shaft through his shorts. "Little Gerry will be very happy before this night is over."

She watched Gerry's next long sigh and the look of resignation that slowly crept over his face. Now she could go at her own speed. "Let's get these off so I can watch your beautiful dick as we play." She pulled his shorts and briefs off, with Gerry lifting his ass to assist in the only way he could. When he was naked, she licked the length of his cock and watched it twitch.

"Open your eyes now and watch what I'm going to do for you." His eyes opened as she untied the knot below her breasts and slowly unbuttoned her shirt. "You like these," she said, cupping her breasts, covered now only by the wisp of lace that was her bra. "Don't you, baby?"

His eyes were fixed on her hands as she fingered her nipples through the thin fabric. "Yes," he said. "I want to suck them."

"I know you do," she said, "but I want to play with them first. See? See how hard the nipples get when I squeeze them? Don't you wish one was in your mouth?"

"Yes."

"Then just ask. Nicely."

"Please," he said. "I want to suck on your tits."

She opened the front clasp of her bra and allowed her large, firm breasts to spill out. Then she leaned over until the nipple hung just out of reach of his lips. "Say please again."

"This is silly, Vic," Gerry said, panting and rattling the handcuffs.

"It's what I want, and what you need to do if you want my tits. Say please."

When he remained silent, she brushed his cheek with her tight nipple. "Hmm?" she purred. "Want it?"

Again his sigh of resignation. "Yes. Please."

"Such a good boy," she said, lowering herself until he could suckle. When he dragged too hard, she pulled back. "Not so hard. Gently. Lick a little, too."

He did as she asked, now licking and sucking gently. "Mmm, that's fine. Now the other one."

He complied. When she'd had enough, she moved so she could rub her now turgid flesh over his heavily furred chest. His groan was loud and long and she chuckled. One of her talents was reading men, and she did it well. She'd known that he'd love slowing down and letting her take control and the handcuffs were allowing that to happen.

Now her body moved lower until she was stroking his twitching cock with her breasts. "Are you going to come, baby?" she asked.

"Soon," he said. "You're making me so hot that I'm going to shoot my load without being inside your wonderful snatch."

"Well, we can't have that, can we?" She climbed on the bed and straddled his chest, stroking her erect clit over his male nipples. She'd learned early on that Gerry loved to have his nipples rubbed and his groans and violent thrashing told her he was about as hot as he could be. She continued to tease until his, "Please, Vicki, please," became almost a chant.

However, Vicki wasn't quite ready. "You'll have to do a little work first, though." She crawled up the bed until her pussy was over his face. "Lick."

In this position, she could control how hard and where his tongue went, so she demonstrated exactly where to stroke her clit with his tongue. "Yes," she gasped, "right there." He learned quickly.

When she was ready, she covered his cock with a condom, then lowered her body onto his straining dick and rode him until they both came, moaning. Later she unfastened his wrists. "You did like that, didn't you?"

Gerry's grin was answer enough. "Yeah, I did. It felt very wrong at first, but later it felt very right."

"Yeah," she growled. "It did, didn't it?"

"Next time maybe I'll cuff you."

Not a chance. She'd never give up control that way. Never. But she said, "Maybe."

Gerry left before dawn. It certainly had been quite a night, she thought as she returned to the present, and smoothed the quilt over the bed. Later she'd have to change the sheets.

After a long, hot shower she walked into the kitchen and poured herself a large mug of coffee. "Trish," she called. "Are you home?"

"I'm in the den, Mom, watching TV."

As Vicki plopped down on the unoccupied lounge chair beside the TV, she again looked at her annoyingly ordinary daughter. "That was quite a party last evening," she said, thinking about Gerry's late-night visit. "I saw you talking to Carl for quite a while."

"We talked a little," Trish said, noncommunicative as always.

"Listen, baby, he's short, and skinny, and really not very attractive. He's also not our kind. I know you can do so much better."

"Butt out, Mom, okay?"

Vicki sat up straighter. "I won't butt out, my dear. It's my job to set you on the right path, and Carl Hernandez isn't it."

"I know how you feel about him, and about KJ, but I want to choose my own friends." There was an annoying whine in her voice.

"This isn't the time in your life for making friends, it's time for making contacts and alliances that will put you on the right road." Had Vicki only done that she wouldn't have to think about getting into business now. Sure, the shop would have its advantages, but if she'd had the kind of guidance from her mother that she was giving her daughter now she wouldn't have gotten pregnant at barely sixteen. She wouldn't have had a one-year-old by the time she was Trish's age. She'd have finished high school and maybe gone to junior college. She'd have met a guy who had more than a nickel to his name. Instead, here she was, mother of an almost-grown daughter, without even a high school diploma, a fact that no one knew.

Vicki had always been a little sorry she hadn't been a bit more careful while having hot, sweaty sex in the backseats of cars and in cheap motel rooms, but because she'd done it with several boys she'd had no idea who Trish's father really was. She'd first accused one of her teenaged lovers, the one she most wanted to marry, but he merely laughed. "You're such a slut, Vicki. There's no way I'm the only guy you've slept with and you'll never prove I'm the father." Sadly, in the days before the popularization of DNA testing, he'd been right. So were the next two guys she told about her pregnancy.

Her parents had been totally unsympathetic, so she'd moved to a new town, had Trish, and worked until her parents' deaths and the subsequent settlement from the bus company. Sadly, that money was slowly slipping away and now she was being forced to start this business.

"Mom, really," Trish said. "Change the subject."

"Okay. Monday, I need you to work with me on finding more suppliers for the store."

"I did all that Internet work for you last Thursday. Now what do you need?" While Vicki watched over her shoulder, Trish had surfed the Net and found a few wholesalers who could help her stock the store. "It's really easy, Mom," she'd said.

Actually Vicki had already become quite proficient with the computer but playing helpless had always worked to get what she wanted. "Well," Vicki said, pouting prettily, "it's still beyond me. Anyway, someone has to call and get prices, percentages, like that. You're the math whiz and you'll understand it all."

"Stop the manipulative voice, Mom," she said, firmly. "I've told you several times I don't want to go into this business with you."

"Don't you talk to me in that tone, young lady," she said, changing from her pout to her motherly voice. "I've done all this so you'll have a job and a business of your own. What I wouldn't have given to—"

"—to have the help and support of my family when I was pregnant and just starting out," Trish said in a sing-song voice. "I know that, Mom. You've told me often enough."

With a deliberate catch in her voice, Vicki said, "Well, I would have given a lot to have help when I got pregnant with you," then dropped her head and stared at her hands, a technique she'd used successfully before.

Trish's voice softened. "I know, Mom, and I'm sorry it was hard for you." With obvious resignation she continued, "Of course I'll help make calls. We can go over the information together. I'll make a spreadsheet and I'll show you how to do all the calculations." She stood and wrapped her arm around her mother's shoulder. "That's the last of it, though." Vicki had always been expert at not doing the things she didn't want to do. "Of course, darling."

"I'm going to the beach for awhile."

As Trish left, Vicki smiled. Things always work out, she thought. Always.

Chapter

8

The walk to the beach was short and soon Trish discarded her flip flops and waded into the cool water. Although it was only late morning, the air was already hot and steamy so the water on her ankles felt wonderful.

Why was her mother so dead set on Trish joining this ridiculous business of hers? Why couldn't she see that there was more to her daughter than she imagined? She had been an A– student and had been accepted in junior college, although her mother would never hear of her wasting her time with more school. She'd also had several job offers with decent salary packages. Why, oh why, couldn't she stand up to her mother?

As she waded, totally self-involved, she almost ran into KJ, walking out to meet her. "Hey, babe, watch out."

"I'm sorry" she said, grabbing his arm to keep from falling. "I guess my mind was miles away."

"Anything you want to share?"

"No. It isn't anything you haven't heard me bitch about before." She looked at him and smiled. He really was her best friend. Nothing even remotely sexual; it was as though they were truly brother and sister. They'd moved into town around the same time and, being new on the school bus, had gravitated toward each other.

"You know you can always unload. By the way, I had a great time last evening."

They'd gone to a club on the Post Road where several of the group, who were underage, could get in without getting proofed. She'd sat with a crowd of guys and girls, many of whom she knew from school. They'd talked about dumb stuff like the latest music and how awful all their high school teachers were, but she'd pretended to have a great time. "I saw you leave with Connie Lesnewski."

With a grin, he said, "I certainly did. She's got a body . . . ."

Trish's eyes narrowed as she interrupted him. "You know, although you think I am, I'm not one of the guys," she snapped. She hated it when he talked about the well-built girls he'd been with while she was still such a stick. She didn't feel sexy about KJ, of course, but she wanted someone to want her.

KJ seemed genuinely surprised at Trish's waspish retort. "Hey, I'm sorry. Don't get so touchy. I thought you and I were best buds." He draped his arm over her shoulder and together they waded slowly down the beach kicking up spray as they walked. Even though he was more than a year younger than she was, he was already several inches taller.

She backed off. "I'm sorry, too. I love you, you know. My mom and I got into it about my future again and I guess I'm just a bit hungover."

"Does this have anything to do with your mother doing something with the old Sherman place?"

Oops, Trish thought. *It seems the word's out. I wonder whether Mom wants the venture to become public knowledge so soon. Suze will have apoplexy.* "I don't know what has to do with what any more. Mom's been doing some scouting around but nothing's definite yet."

"What's she going to do with the place?"

Had Suze sent him out on reconnaissance? "It's a deep dark secret," she said, implying that even she didn't know. She grinned and tried to look innocent. "Very hush-hush. Details to follow, film at eleven."

"I'm really curious. Can't you tell me? I'm your best friend after all."

"Let's let things cook a while. Then everyone will know."

"Sure, Trish. If you need to keep secrets." He looked resentful, then softened.

"Sorry. I don't know what my mom wants to be public yet. Let's just leave it at that." She hated her mother for putting her in this position. Hated her mother? She'd said that a lot when she'd gone through the teenage rebellion thing, but she thought she was past that. Maybe she wasn't.

Did she really hate her mother? She'd arrived home after eleven to hear the sounds of sex coming from her mother's room. She knew what kind of a woman Vicki was, of course, but she hated it when she had her face rubbed in it. Why couldn't she just go to a motel or something? Did she really hate her mother? "Where's your bike? Wanna take me for a ride?"

"Sure," KJ said. "I gotta be back by late afternoon, but it's early yet so let's go."

Leslie spent a good part of Saturday afternoon with Abby and her pair of rambunctious, well brought up children, and Marie and her two youngest, Phillip and Stacy. They talked about everything and nothing, from TV to recipes although she hadn't taken part in a lively debate about whether to put pickle relish in tuna salad.

During their conversation it became clear to Leslie that Abby was a troubled soul with marital problems. Leslie had no idea whether Damian was having an affair or not but Abby had started to doubt his many excuses. Of course Abby didn't say anything directly but Leslie was too good at reading people to miss the signs. If she had to guess, Leslie would wager that Damian was fooling around. His attentions to her had been a little too direct and she was sure that, if she gave him half a chance, he'd quickly arrange some private time together. She had deliberately given him no encouragement.

In the middle of the afternoon Damian walked over to where the women were sitting, told Abby that he was taking Mark and Tammy to pick out their new video game, and asked whether Marie would allow Phillip and Stacy to go along. After admonishments to behave, Marie gratefully let her two children join them.

"I wish he wouldn't encourage their video obsession," Abby said as his car drove off. "They spend too much of their time now with those damned games." Her voice was bitter and Leslie sensed that Abby and Damian had had discussions on the topic before.

She was invited to join Marie, Joe, and their brood for dinner and spent a truly delightful evening with them. It was sad, Leslie thought, that Marie seemed to think so little of herself. Several times during the evening she'd alluded to the fact that she was a housewife and nothing more. She was glad to be able to help her husband with the store but she wasn't really "together enough," as she put it, to work outside the home. Leslie had seldom met a more together woman, but again it was really none of her business.

Although Leslie had sex with her clients, she often found herself in the role of counselor. She advised the married men on how to approach their wives to open up their sex lives so they wouldn't have to come to her for excitement. She counseled men who wanted to date on ways to meet women and on topics of conversation. It was interesting that almost as many of her clients called her for advice as called for phone sex, something she did just as well. If Marie or Abby asked for her advice she'd give it but for now she kept her mouth shut.

Sunday morning Leslie woke up just after eight, the first time she hadn't slept until almost ten. Since she usually worked very late hours, she was seldom up before eleven in the city but here she'd been getting to bed at a reasonable hour and had been sleeping better than she had in months. As she lay in bed she could feel the heat of the summer sun already flooding the room, and hear the gentle, rhythmic sounds of the waves, the scream of the gulls, and the noises of happy children. Occasionally the air was split by the loud barking of a dog.

She wanted to get out into the sunshine and cook her body, and since she'd already come to enjoy some of her fellow Atlantic Beach Road dwellers, she was eager to see who might venture out to join her.

She grabbed a granola bar and chewed as she slathered on sunblock then settled herself on the seawall, gazing at the ocean. The air already had a steamy feel that boded heat and humidity, with no breeze to stir the glass-smooth water. The tide was just beginning to come in so sandbars were visible almost as far out as Short Island and several families wandered the bars looking at the ocean life or digging for clams. A large German shepherd barked loudly and chased gulls from one spot to another, while the gulls hardly bothered to do more than flap several times until the dog splashed off in another direction, two small children laughing at the chaos.

As she finished her "breakfast," she noticed Brad finishing his swim in a section of slightly deeper water. He slowly walked onto the shore a ways down the beach, shaking off like a shaggy dog. He found his towel where he'd left it and wrapped it around his waist. As he approached, she again appreciated his well-developed body. Was he limping slightly? When he saw her he straightened and the limp disappeared. Interesting.

"Hi there," he said, pulling himself onto the seawall beside her. "It's really going to be hot today."

"Don't people spend summers at the shore to be cooler? This air feels like Manhattan."

"It certainly smells better."

Laughing, she admitted, "No asphalt, hot dogs, or dog poop."

"You forgot car exhaust," he sighed. "I find I miss the city, though."

"What do you miss most?" Leslie asked. "I have been enjoying this so much that I haven't allowed myself to think about the city."

"I've been here a few days longer than you have and I still find it difficult to sleep at night. It's too quiet. I miss garbage trucks, sirens, and horns." He sighed again. "It's going to take me a few more nights to get used to it."

She'd listened to crickets the first evening and had also noted the absence of normal city noise, but it hadn't kept her from sleeping. "How long are you here for?"

"I've actually got the place for another week with an option for two more."

"I didn't think cops got that kind of time off."

"I'm a bit of a computer geek so I have quite a bit to do on my laptop, and I've got so much vacation time that I thought getting away might do me good."

Her radar antenna told her there was more to his simple statement. Curious about him, she continued, "What do you need to get away from?"

She could see him close in on himself. "Being a cop is difficult, both physically and mentally, so when I had the opportunity to get away, I took it." He quickly added, "What about you? How long are you here for?"

"I'm here until Labor Day weekend."

"A whole month? Lucky you. How did you get to take so much time off, if I'm not prying?"

"It's okay. August is really slow in my business and I haven't really taken a vacation in several years, so I'm treating myself."

"Like it so far?"

"Mostly," she said, being strangely honest. "It's so much slower than Manhattan and that takes a bit of getting used to.

Without my work it's difficult to find things to do. I really like the people, but during the day they have other things to do. I'll get used to it and I really need some downtime."

"That pretty much sums up my problem, too. Part of me isn't sure this was such a good idea, but I paid for the place and I'm determined to make the most of it."

"We're on the same wavelength. What do you do with your time? You don't strike me as the lie-on-the-beach-and-soak-up-the-sun type."

"I swim every day. I think I mentioned that I found a gym and I spend quite a bit of time there, keeping in shape. I spend several hours a day online, doing research on some cold cases, and I watch baseball on TV."

"Do you read? I've brought several books I've wanted to get into, and I figure Amazon.com can supply more when I'm ready."

"Actually, there's a huge Barnes & Noble superstore in the mall just down from my gym. If you're interested, I can drive you over this afternoon. You can either go to the bookstore or work out with me on a day pass, then shop."

The sun was pounding on her head and already making her a little too hot for total comfort. She couldn't spend the whole day in the water, and spending an afternoon with an attractive man, without the pressure to be what he wanted, was intriguing. She merely had to remember that he was a cop, but she was used to being closed-mouthed so that shouldn't be a problem "I think I'd like that, both the gym and the bookstore. I'm used to working out almost every day and even though it's only been a few days I'm starting to feel flabby."

As she realized she'd intended, he looked her over. "Right. Flabby. I should be so flabby."

She looked him over. His skin was almost dry and his abs rippled beneath smooth, lightly furred skin. "Back at you." She laughed. "Okay, enough of this silly mutual admiration thing."

"Early dinner afterward?"

"You mean like a date?"

"I mean like dinner. There's a great seafood place on a little inlet a little farther out than the gym. It's very casual, with wooden tables and plastic glasses, but they have the best fish and seafood around. You a fish person?"

This was sounding like a date, and she realized that it was fine with her. A casual relationship with a nice-looking man with no strings, no need to satisfy, sounded wonderful. And there was that little frisson of sexual attraction that felt really good. "Actually I am, and that sounds lovely."

"Wonderful. I gather it gets very crowded so I'll call and make sure they'll have a place for us at, say five-thirty? That too early for you?"

"No, that sounds great." She frequently ate early before a long evening of entertaining.

"How about I knock on your door about two?"

"I might still be out here, but I'm sure the detective in you can find me."

"I'm sure I can." Towel still around his hips, he trotted across the street to his cottage.

At two o'clock Leslie was sitting waist deep in the lapping waves, with Marie, Abby, and Suze. She'd been so deep in conversation that she'd lost track of the time until Brad called to her.

"Ladies," she said, "I've got to go." She stood up and ran a hand down her wet legs, then across her forehead and the back of her neck to cool herself off.

"Got a date with the hunk?" Suze asked.

"Not a date. Brad is going to take me over to his gym so I can work out. It's been almost a week and I feel like I really need it."

"Need?" Suze said, looking Leslie over. "That sounds like something exercise people say. Not me. I prefer to stay sitting down. How about having dinner with Kevin and me when you get back?"

"Well . . ."

"Ah," Marie said. "So you're also having dinner with the gorgeous Brad."

"Snagged," Leslie said, a bit embarrassed. Why shouldn't she have dinner with anyone she wanted? "It's not a date, though. We're just friends and that's all."

"Good for you," Abby said.

"That should keep him out of Vicki's clutches," Suze added. "Oh, before you go, anyone have any idea what's up with Vicki and the old Sherman Gallery property? I've heard that she's interested in leasing it."

"If that's the place across from Joe's market, then I think I saw her little silver car over there on Friday. It's hard to miss. Why?"

"Vicki doesn't seem the kind to open a T-shirt shop, that's all," Suze said. "I'm very curious and as mayor . . ."

"I've no idea," Marie said, "but Joe's seen her there, too."

Brad walked up, looking really hot in a pair of tight, knee-length black bicycle pants and a red T-shirt. "Hi there, ladies. Mind if I steal Leslie for a few hours?"

"Not at all," Marie said, "and enjoy your dinner together."

Brad feigned exasperation. "Is nothing secret around here? Ask a lovely woman to dinner and almost immediately everyone knows about it."

"The curse of a small town within a small town," Marie said. "Have fun."

"You all keep cool," Brad said.

Leslie quickly changed into a pair of loose shorts and a polo shirt and put a change of clothes for afterward, along with a few toiletries, in a small tote bag.

The Fitness Club was impressive, with large rooms filled with light, music, and an array of exercise machines that rivaled her gym in the city. She bought a day pass, glad that Brad hadn't made any noise about treating, and was directed to the ladies' locker room. She put her things in a locker, then spent the next hour using the equipment. Since they were in different areas of the room she didn't talk to Brad, but couldn't help being aware of him. There were several good-looking men with beautiful bodies but her eyes kept straying to him. She caught his eye occasionally and, if her hands were free, she gave him a wave.

The treadmills faced a wall of windows that looked out on Route 1 and later, as she trotted along, she watched cars and people. Sweating, she realized that she was relaxed and felt wonderful. At about three-thirty, Brad stepped onto the treadmill beside her and quickly revved the speed up to about five miles an hour. He ran silently, but as she ran Leslie couldn't deny the heat of his presence. Well, not actual heat, but there was a flush that felt really nice. *Don't get too involved*, she told herself. *He's a cop and you're a prostitute.*

Running on the treadmill, Brad felt the heat as well. He had been unable to concentrate on his workout, his eyes straying to her more frequently than he'd liked. Although her body was hidden beneath loose-fitting clothing, he was aware of her large breasts and great legs. *Stop it*, he told himself when his mind strayed to thoughts of large beds with satin sheets. *She's a hooker and you're a cop.*

Chapter
9

After a quick shower and a change of clothes, Leslie met Brad at the front door of the gym. He was wearing a pair of knee-length khaki cargo pants with a black knit polo shirt that had a small tiger on the left chest. His hair was still wet and he looked sexy as hell and very desirable.

Brad obviously appreciated the way she looked as well. She'd decided to dress a bit more attractively and hadn't taken time to examine her motives for it. She'd chosen a small yellow tank top with a swishy white summer skirt and white sandals. "Nice," he said. "You dress up nice. Why do you always play down your looks?"

"I don't know. I matured early and first girls then women always seemed afraid of me. Maybe that I'd steal their man or something. So I've always dressed conservatively."

"I wouldn't call it conservative. I'd say you were hiding your gorgeous figure. I like the way you look now much better."

She laughed. "Thank you kind sir." He should know how she dressed when she was working.

After about a half an hour in the bookstore Leslie walked toward Brad's rental car with a large shopping bag filled with books she wanted to read or reread. Brad had a small plastic bag that obviously held only one or two small volumes. "What did you buy at the bookstore?" she asked.

"It's silly. There's a fad, puzzles called Sudoku. My partner is pretty good at them and I tried a few last week. I thought they might be fun so I bought a book of them." He pulled a small paperback book from the bag. "I bought one for you, just in case." He handed the book to her.

"Thanks." She flipped through a few pages. "I know about these. It's the number thing with the grid. I've done a few," Leslie said, "but I get frustrated easily."

"I told you I was a bit of a computer geek and I've always loved logic puzzles. I could show you a few tricks for solving them if you'd be interested."

"Yeah. They would be perfect for doing while sitting on the beach. Thanks." It wasn't like taking a gift from him. He was just being nice, not expecting anything in return.

Brad drove Leslie to Soundings, a seafood restaurant on a small inlet near the sound. Since they had reservations and it was an odd hour, they were shown to a wooden table at the edge of the outdoor patio overlooking the little river. Below was a small dock for diners who arrived on motorboats and surrounding it were several dozen ducks and gulls being fed french fries by two small children in a motorboat. The birds' noises were deafening.

"Is it too hot to eat outdoors?" Brad asked, although the patio was shaded by a large, striped awning.

"Not at all. It's delightful." They settled opposite each other near the railing. A family sat at the table behind Brad, their brood of children also feeding bits of crackers to the birds below. The quacking of the begging ducks and the squawking of the gulls forced Brad and Leslie to raise their voices. "Nice place, if a bit loud," she said, laughing.

"Want to find another table?" Brad asked, seeing that there were a number of empty ones both inside and out.

"Let's give it a minute." As Leslie looked over the large menu, the families both left and the waterfowl quieted. "This is quite a menu," she said, unable to decide among all the choices on the four-page, plastic-covered tome.

"I know," Brad said. "It seems that restaurants around here specialize in making it difficult to decide. When I came here last Wednesday evening I was totally overwhelmed. I saw a guy at the next table eating something that looked good so I told the waitress to bring me whatever he was having. It turned out to be a good choice."

She was surprised that he would have gone to a restaurant on his first night in town rather than have fast food. "Do you eat out a lot back in the city?"

"I must admit that I like good food. That's part of the reason I work out. It lets me eat what I want and still not gain any weight."

Leslie was surprised to hear a man talk about weight. "I eat out a lot, too," she said. "I do quite a bit of entertaining with clients and all." She let him think she was talking about clients of her decorating business.

"Have you found anything on that menu that tickles your fancy?"

"What did you have that you enjoyed so much?"

"They make a dynamite bouillabaisse."

Leslie snapped her menu closed. "Done."

"I think I'll try their fisherman's platter. Do you share? When I'm with friends, we often get two different entrees and go halvsies. Interested?"

"Sounds like a deal to me. I do that on occasion, too."

"What kind of food do you particularly like?" Brad asked and they slipped into desultory conversation. When the waiter arrived, Brad asked her whether she'd like some wine. When she nodded, he said, "Since you do a lot of entertaining and I don't drink when I'm by myself, you probably know more about picking wine than I do." He handed her the card with the limited list of choices and, surprised and pleased, she ordered a Pinot Grigio.

"I'm not used to people letting me choose the wine. It's usually such a macho guy thing."

"I know when I'm outclassed. I'm just a poor civil servant. When I entertain, it's usually a snitch and they don't have a particularly educated palate. Burgers and beer are the extent of it."

He was so charming it was difficult to keep him at arm's length. It would be easy to treat this like a real date and slip into another, and another. *Stop it, Leslie.* He's a cop and he'd go ballistic if he ever found out she was a pro so she remained determined to keep it light. She already knew that he'd grown up on Long Island, so, when their salads arrived, to keep the conversation moving she asked, "Do you have a family?"

"Two older brothers and a younger sister. Tom works for a construction company in Deer Park, married with a pair of four-year-old twin boys, and my brother Matt works for an electronics firm, wife, no kids. My sister Sheila's married, with a new baby. Both she and her husband are grammar school teachers out in Merrick. You?"

"I'm an only and I really envy you your large family. My folks just moved to Florida and I miss them. I get down there a few times a year, particularly in the middle of the winter."

"Is your dad retired?"

"Yeah. I was born late in their marriage so they're already collecting social security."

Throughout the salad course, they told stories about growing up. They quickly discovered that she had graduated from high school in the same year as his younger brother. Brad and his brothers were very close in age so they had an active childhood, getting into all kinds of mischief. "We had one of those cops-in-schools programs in middle school and I got really close to the one who came in to counsel us about not using drugs and not drinking and driving. He was really a sane guy and answered lots of my questions about girls, the ones I couldn't admit to my brothers that I didn't know the answers to. He's the one who got me interested in the police force."

"You've wanted to be a cop ever since?"

"I guess. I went to John Jay College of Criminal Justice in the city, thinking that I would become a lawyer, but when I graduated I took the NYPD entrance exam and passed with flying colors. And, as they say, the rest is history. How about you? Have you always wanted to be an interior decorator? How does one become one of those?"

"I'm a Manhattan girl, born and bred, so I just sort of slid into going to City College. I majored in English literature. Being an only child, I spent a lot of time by myself as a kid and I've always liked to read so it seemed a natural thing to get into. Little did I know that with that kind of degree the chances for a career were limited. Teaching didn't appeal to me." She thought about how much to tell him about her past. "I modeled for awhile, then a friend got me into what I do now." That was pretty much the truth, and the "what I'm doing now" part left Brad to fill in the rest.

It had begun pretty much as she said. She'd been convinced by several friends that, with her height and good looks, she should try modeling. Almost immediately she knew that high-class, fashion modeling jobs were not going to be offered to anyone only five-foot-seven, with a 36C bustline and generous hips. She'd been approached by a lingerie company, housed in the garment district, however, and had gone to work several months after her college graduation. Her lush figure and innate sensuality quickly had her earning enough to rent a small apartment in Brooklyn Heights, a subway ride from Midtown. Finances were tight, but doable. She made friends with a few of the other models and one evening went to a small local bar with Kayla Peters, a tall, absolutely gorgeous black woman with dark, smooth skin, short black hair, a tiny waist, and large breasts that spilled out of most of the gowns and bras she showed customers. The two women had gotten close in the past few months and been out several times before.

After a few beers Kayla confided, "I haven't told too many people but I'm moving to the West Coast in a few weeks. I met a guy from a talent agency and he said I had a great look for TV."

Leslie's bullshit radar vibrated violently and it must have shown in her face, so Kayla continued, "I know, I know, but I checked him out seven ways from Sunday and he seems legit. The agency he says he works for exists and when I called and asked for him, they said he was out of the office, so he does work there." She sighed. "I've really got nothing to lose. I've always wanted to live on the West Coast and I've got enough money in the bank to tell him to go to hell if this is just a scam. If he wants sex in exchange for getting me interviews it won't be the first time."

Not wanting to pry, she said, "That might turn out to be a lucky break for you and I wish you all the luck in the world. Having kiss-off money in the bank must be so great."

"You've got to be raking it in, Les," she said.

"I make ends meet but let's just say that my savings account isn't bulging."

Kayla leaned closer and said sotto voce, "You haven't gotten any work on the side yet?"

Leslie knew a few of the models "entertained" outside of work, but she hadn't imagined Kayla, who was bright, lively, and seemed so conservative, would be one of them. "No," she said, curious.

"You know what goes on, don't you?"

"I'm not blind, but no one's actually told me anything."

"Have you ever considered doing more than modeling? You know, being with guys for money? It's such an easy way to earn a bundle."

She could feel her face tighten. "I don't think so, but if you say so it must be okay for you."

"Don't get all moralistic on me, Les. Oh I know you didn't say anything, but I can see your judgment on your face." She put her hand on Leslie's arm. "It's really nothing. I've been on dates with guys and had sex afterward just for kicks, right? You're not a virgin, are you?"

"Of course not. I've been with quite a few guys." She almost felt defensive.

"No one special?"

"Not at the moment."

"Okay, let's say you go out with a guy and he wants sex. He's not repulsive and you haven't had any in a while, so you agree. What's wrong with that?"

Leslie huffed out a breath. Kayla wasn't going to try to convince her that it was okay to be a prostitute. "Nothing, but it's a long way from being paid for it."

"Not that far, actually. What if someone had set you up with a date and there was cash in the deal? You go to dinner and, if the guy's not repulsive, you have sex. What's so different?"

Leslie was about to bark an answer when she allowed herself to think for a moment. When she hesitated, Kayla jumped in, "It's not. I used to give it away, now I get paid. This isn't 'stand on a street corner wearing a sign on my forehead saying For a Good Time Call . . .' kind of stuff. The guys I go out with are businessmen, stockbrokers, insurance executives, like that, all set up and checked out beforehand. Most of them are out of town guys who just want a little fun while they're in New York City."

"Married, I assume."

"There you go being judgmental again. If it weren't me, it would be someone else. I'm not luring them out of a good marriage, and frequently it is a good marriage. I'm entertaining lonely guys who want things that their wives aren't interested in. It's not up to me to make their moral judgments for them."

Leslie had never given any thought to the kind of thing Kayla was talking about. "I guess," Leslie said, noncommittally. "Who sets these things up?"

"It started with Lenny at work, but he's a bit of a sleeze. After a while I met a woman named Marnie who worked at a place called Courtesans, Inc. How I met her is a long story and not worth going into. Anyway, she introduced me to the folks there and that was that. Now I go to parties and dinners and I even got to go on a cruise to Bermuda, with fascinating men, and occasionally with women, too."

Slightly shocked, she blurted out, "You're a lesbian?"

Kayla's smile showed a mouthful of white, even teeth. "I swing both ways from time to time, but I'm mostly into men. I've been with a few women, too, just to see what it was like."

Leslie sipped her drink, trying to take in all that Kayla was saying. Oh, she wasn't totally naive. She knew that the sort of thing her friend was talking about went on, but this was the first time it had been talked about so matter-of-factly. "It's a bit much to take in," she said.

Kayla took a large swallow of her beer. "I guess it is, but to me it's just the way things are. That's the one part of moving that upsets me. I'll be leaving my clients, and several of them have become friends."

"Friends? You mean you see guys more than once?"

"Sure," Kayla said. "I see lots of the guys every time they come into town. On the books, of course."

Leslie sat back in her chair. "Okay, my mind is blown."

"Would you be interested in meeting Erika? She runs Courtesans, Inc., and I know she'd like you. You're intelligent, knowledgeable, interesting, and a good conversationalist."

"That's really funny. You listed things that I would have thought only peripheral. Isn't she looking for knockouts, perfect 10s?"

"Oh, of course looks are important and you're more than beautiful enough, so stop fishing for compliments. In her business, however, good-looking women are pretty common. The men I go with want something much more than just a pretty face and big boobs. They want to go out to dinner with a charming companion, talk about the news or sports or tell the latest joke. I think you'd be good at it. I'll be leaving a few really great guys, ones I'd like to introduce you to."

"Phew. That's quite a load you just dumped on my head. I'll need to do a bit of thinking about it."

"No hurry. There's somewhere around five hundred dollars a night if you're good at this."

Leslie almost choked on her rum and Coke. "Five hundred dollars for being with how many men?"

Kayla's grin was priceless. "One. I charge eight hundred, of which I get to keep five. Of course I have to pay a bundle to Uncle Sam, but my bank account is in very good shape."

"You pay taxes on your income as a . . . ."

"Prostitute, although I tell Uncle Sam I'm an entertainer and escort. You can say prostitute. I don't mind. I use *my* body to make money, I give pleasure to men who want it, and I enjoy it. What's to be ashamed of? I'm totally healthy, not on drugs, and all the men I'm with use condoms and are carefully vetted by Erika and her folks. What's wrong with that?"

Leslie's eyebrow lifted. "It's . . . it's . . . I don't know, it's illegal." Many of the things Kayla had said made sense, but prostitution?

"Yes, it is, but why? Who gets hurt? If I rob a bank, the savers or the insurance people get hurt, if I kill or maim, that's obvious. Who gets hurt if I take something I own, my body, and rent it out to someone who wants to use it? Stop the knee-jerk stuff and think seriously." Kayla lifted her beer and took a long swallow.

"You're blowing my mind, Kayla."

"I know and I wasn't sure you'd still be my friend if I told you but my moving changes things. Erika will need a good-looking, charming woman to take over for me and you fill the bill. I'd love for you to think about what I've told you. I don't feel like a bad person and I'd hate for you to have bad feelings about me either. Let's have a drink after work one afternoon next week, after you've decompressed."

During the following week, Leslie thought about little else. Everything Kayla said made sense and yet it was wrong. Very wrong. Wasn't it? Five hundred dollars? No, not for any price. But Kayla was such a lovely, cultured woman and didn't seem to be worried about it. She was totally comfortable with the idea. Leslie's brain was boggled. Kayla's words kept echoing through her head. "I'll introduce you to Erika if you want. What have you got to lose?"

Chapter
10

A week later Kayla met her at a trendy Indian restaurant in Midtown. "I've invited Erika," she'd told Leslie, "but you're not committed to anything." Leslie had changed her mind several times, both about the encounter and about what to wear. Finally she decided that she had nothing to lose by meeting Erika so she dressed in a becoming pale green linen dress with a light crocheted shawl over her shoulders. "Tell me about this woman," Leslie asked over glasses of white wine.

"What can I tell you that you don't already know? She's nice, used to be married, and I gather she has a teenaged daughter in school somewhere in Europe."

"How in the world . . . ?"

"Here she is," Kayla said. Leslie turned and saw a tall, slender, perfectly dressed woman in her early thirties, she guessed, wending her way between tables.

"You're Leslie, of course," Erika said, settling herself opposite the other two. Her voice was low and cultured. "Kayla has told me so much about you and she certainly didn't exaggerate about your looks."

"Thank you," Leslie said as Erika put her leather purse on the floor beneath her chair. She started to mouth the usual modest reply but stopped. She didn't think Erika would be impressed by false modesty. She knew she was good-looking and her dress set off her ash blond hair and hazel eyes.

"Have you two ordered?"

"Just drinks," Kayla said. "I didn't know whether you'd have time for a meal."

"I'll make time," she said, picking up the menu, "and I'm ravenous."

Erika ordered a glass of red wine and then the three of them collaborated on a dinner order, deciding quickly to share whatever they selected. When the waiter arrived, they listed two appetizers and two main courses that they'd agreed on. "And I'd like raita and mango chutney." Erika looked at the other two. "Nan?"

"Definitely," Kayla said. "I'm a bread person but I usually don't eat it—weight and all—but tonight, what the hell."

To Leslie, Erika said, "In case you're not an Indian food devotee, raita is that wonderful yogurt and cucumber side dish that cools your mouth in case one of the dishes is too hot."

Leslie wasn't usually too experimental with food but she didn't want to show any hesitation in front of Erika. She'd eat what was put in front of her.

When the waiter was gone, Erika said, "Tell me about yourself, Leslie."

They chatted like old friends through appetizers, bread, and their main courses. When spicy tea had been served, Erika got to the point of the dinner. "Kayla has told you what I do, correct?"

"Yes. You provide escorts for out of town businessmen who want to have beautiful, cultured women on their arm for an evening."

"Afterward, too," Erika said. "I don't want you to misunderstand."

"I don't," Leslie said.

"Are you interested in pursuing Kayla's line of work once she's gone?"

"I don't really know. It's a bit scary."

Erika's warm smile took away a lot of Leslie's misgivings. "I can understand that and if you decided to say good-bye after dinner and we never see each other again I'll be disappointed, but I'll get over it."

"Disappointed? I thought I was doing a sort of job interview. You make this sound quite personal."

"We are interviewing each other, and I think you'd be perfect for us at Courtesans, Inc. You're well spoken, interested and interesting, with that wonderful, sexy voice. You're a good listener and, of course, you're gorgeous. However, this line of work isn't for everyone." Her laugh was warm and her expression slightly self-deprecating. "Actually it isn't for almost anyone. You have to have a well-developed sense of who you are because you'll be playing many roles. You'll be burying your real self beneath layers of other women, the teases, the debutantes, the dominant, and the submissive. You'll spend a great deal of time being what some man wants you to be not what you really are. I think that you're certainly strong enough to be all of that."

"I'm flattered."

"Don't be. You didn't have much to do with that part of who you are. You picked your parents correctly, that's all. But you are responsible for how you behave now, too. You've done a lot with what your parents gave you. All that would make you an asset to my business. That is, if you're interested."

Leslie's smile was warm. "The way you talk about it, it sounds interesting."

"What about the sex part?"

"That doesn't really bother me much. I'm a pretty liberal woman and I'm certainly not new to the date 'em and do 'em scene. I enjoy a good evening in bed with a nice guy. All the guys you entertain are nice guys, aren't they?"

"They're men, just like other men. They're carefully checked out from many angles and my service is so exclusive that the men are very well behaved, afraid of being blacklisted. I have a few rules that everyone adheres to, men and women. No drugs. Period. Condoms always, no exceptions. I don't care how many times you've been with a guy and how much you trust him, even if he begs, no bareback riding. The rest is common sense."

"Like?" Leslie asked, respecting this woman more and more as the evening progressed.

"Like taking care of your looks, manners, and personal hygiene if you're on a job. Like 'the customer's almost always right.' If he asks for something you're not willing to give, however, you are encouraged to say no. We refund his money or find him another lady."

"Does that happen often?"

"No, because I usually know what a man wants beforehand and only connect him with women who enjoy the same things. I keep a detailed record of what each one of my women like so I can match men with the appropriate woman."

"I see," Leslie said.

"It's my business and my reputation on the line so I want to keep both my women and my customers happy." Erika glanced up as the waiter brought the check on a small silver plate. She dropped a gold credit card on the bill without looking at the amount. "Why don't you take some time and think about what I've said? Talk to Kayla and, if you like, I can introduce you to other employees in case you want more feedback. I'm sure I can trust your discretion, so here's my card. I think you'd be a great addition to my company but only if it's what you want to do." She handed Leslie an engraved business card with only Erika's name and phone number on it.

"I'll think about it and call you in a few days."

"That will be fine."

Leslie did think about it, often. She was surprised at her lack of shock and revulsion. Weeks ago, before Kayla's revelation, Leslie's immediate reaction to a discussion of prostitution would have been negative. Her mental picture would have been of scantily dressed women hanging out on street corners, leaning into passing cars pedaling their wares. She'd certainly seen enough of that on cop shows on TV.

This sounded nothing like that—intelligent women entertaining well-heeled men for mucho bucks. Why should selling her talents in bed be any different from selling her talents as a lingerie model, or a plumber, or a movie actor? The more she thought about it the more she thought she might do it. Her only worry was whether she was good enough in bed to warrant the amount of money men would be paying her.

She decided to talk to Kayla about it. Over drinks a few evenings after their dinner with Erika, Leslie sat with her friend over beers in a small bar near work. "I've thought a lot about what you and Erika told me," she said without preamble. "I have one worry."

Kayla giggled. "Only one?"

"Yeah, it surprised me, too. I want to do it but I'm concerned that I'm not too knowledgeable in bed." She raised her hand to preclude Kayla's immediate retort. "Oh sure, I've been with lots of guys and had my share of fun in the sack, but most of the men who use Erika's service want more. You know, kinky stuff. I don't think I want to be tied up or peed on."

Kayla giggled. "Ugh, not peed on at all. Never. No. No. No. The bondage thing, however, well don't knock it until you've tried it. Quite a few of the men I've been with don't want anything terribly off base. Oral sex both giving and getting, and being told that they've got the biggest cock I've ever seen and that they're the best I've ever had. That's what I've found gets guys off.

"Sure, some of the guys want more, but as Erika said, she keeps meticulous records of who wants what, and who's willing to do what. She matches men with us and, when and if we're ready to move on to, let's say bigger and better things, she accommodates. I've expanded my horizons since I've been working for her, but it's not a necessity. She's got more than a dozen girls working for her and she can arrange for most things men desire."

"Do you know any of the other women?"

"Only a few," Kayla said, sipping her beer. "They're nice women. One of the ones I did a double with has two kids." When Leslie looked shocked, Kayla continued, "I was surprised, too, so I talked to Erika about it. Several of the women are married, two are getting graduate degrees and using the money to pay for classes. Most are heterosexual, but a few women are bisexual and service both male and female clients."

"Female clients?" In all her thinking she'd never considered that women might indulge with either sex.

"Hell yes," Kayla said. "It's a small part of her business, but Erika employs several men who entertain women in the same ways we entertain men. I would guess there's more public, social stuff when a woman hires a man. You know, divorcees who want to look like they're involved with a good-looking stud. Like that."

"I'm afraid I'm still really naive about stuff like this."

Kayla winked. "I was, too, but you will learn very quickly."

"You're pretty convinced that I'll do it."

"Yup," she said, raising her glass. "To new things."

Leslie raised her glass and touched the rim to her friend's. "To new things."

The following Monday evening, Leslie had another dinner with Erika. "I'm so glad you've decided to join our little group," Erika said. "I knew when Kayla told me about you that you'd be perfect."

"I'm not sure about that. Perfect? I'm scared to death. What if I don't satisfy someone?"

"I'll give him a refund, but that won't happen too often, I'm sure. I've got a few guys who love the thrill of being with someone new to the business. They love to play teacher. How about I set you up with one of them for one evening soon. Regular fee, of course."

"Now that I've said yes, I think I have cold feet."

Erika's laugh was calming. "Of course you do, and that's what Cameron will love about you. Will you trust me on this?"

"Erika, if I didn't trust you I wouldn't be here."

Erika patted her hand across the white tablecloth. "Good girl. I'll call you."

She met Cameron Wallace the following Saturday evening at the same Indian restaurant in which she'd first met Erika. He was of average height, with a full but neatly shaped beard, jutting nose, and heavy, bushy eyebrows. She was surprised by the wide streaks of silver in his hair and beard and the deep lines in his face. Leslie guessed that he was in his late fifties or early sixties. She had envisioned her dates being young, virile men, men in their thirties and forties, men in their sexual prime, in need of more outlets for their excess sexual energy. She was being well paid, however, so she'd take what came her way. He stood as she approached his table. "Good evening, Leslie," he said, his smile warm and open. "I can't tell you what a pleasure this is."

"Thank you, and it's nice to meet you, too." What the hell did one say to a man who's paying to have your company? She felt that it was incumbent upon her to keep the conversation lively. Start with small talk. Think of something clever to say, maybe about the weather.

"It was quite a hot one today," he said, breaking her train of thought.

"Yes, it certainly was." What now? What did she know about him?

"This is really awkward, isn't it?" he said. "Erika told me quite a bit about you. I know that you're really new to this whole thing so I feel it's my responsibility to keep the conversation going; to keep you from feeling too awkward and bolting."

With a smile, she said, "I'm not going to run, and I was just thinking that it was on me to keep things light and interesting."

She could almost feel his deep chuckle. "So here we are, both trying to make small talk." He leaned forward and placed his hands over hers on the tablecloth. "Let's get a bottle of wine to grease the wheels and then you can tell me about yourself."

Over glasses of exceptionally good Cabernet, she told him about college and her interest in English literature and he told her a little about his background. His father had founded a small electronics firm in the early fifties. It had originally made radios but had quickly graduated to more sophisticated products. Eventually the firm got into computers and small devices that controlled other devices. The multi-million-dollar company was now his, but he no longer took part in the day-to-day operations.

It turned out that he was a voracious reader and they had many favorite books and authors in common. They both enjoyed movies and had seen many of the same recent films. Dinner sped by.

"Brandy?" Cameron asked.

"Sure."

"Important point here," Cameron said. "You're not to do things because you think I want you to or that it's the 'done thing.' Be yourself. That's why I'm paying to be with you. You will have to judge how to behave with other men, but most will be happy if you're comfortable and friendly. Now, once again, brandy?"

"I've never really had any so I'd love to try."

"That's the attitude I want for this evening, all of it."

Over glasses of what she assumed was superior brandy, Cameron said, "This has been a delightful dinner. You'll go far in Erika's business. You're charming, and certainly good to look at."

She was glad he thought so. She'd pulled dress after dress

from her closet, and rejected them all. Finally she'd settled on a pair of white linen slacks and a black sleeveless sweater that showed off her ample bosom and long neck. "Thanks. And you're such good company I almost forgot why we're here."

"Does this evening make you nervous?"

She took a deep breath. She had heard his admonishments earlier and didn't pretend to be something she wasn't. "Very."

His grin showed his white teeth. "Good. That's what I like." He signed the credit card receipt and stood. "Let's make you even more nervous." He guided her out of the restaurant and into a taxi. He gave the driver a Park Avenue address, then draped his arm around her shoulders.

"Lesson one," he said, stroking her collarbone with the pad of his index finger. "Never wear slacks on a date. No access." He slid his hand up the inside of her thigh and lightly fingered her crotch. "Men will like to know what they're getting."

"I never thought of that," she said, with a slight catch in her voice. His fingers were doing devilish things to her clit.

"I hope that little hesitation is because I'm making you a little crazy."

In addition to turned on, Leslie felt panicky. "You certainly are. I'm not sure what you want me to be doing in return, however."

"You're not expected to do anything except be who and what you are."

She leaned back against the seat and he leaned over and kissed her long and very well. His hands rested quietly against her thighs while his lips played with hers. His tongue teased the joining of her lips until she opened for him and let his tongue stroke hers.

When he sat back, he whispered, "How do you feel about the cab driver watching what we do?"

She glanced at the driver's eyes in the rearview mirror, clear through the transparent plastic shield between front and back seats. "Honestly?"

"I never want you to be anything but honest."

"I sort of like it. It's exciting to be watched."

"Great," he said, slipping his hand inside her blouse. "Let him watch."

She reveled in the feeling of Cameron's fingers playing with her nipple and through slitted eyelids she watched the driver's eyes. When the taxi stopped at a red light, she reached down and lightly squeezed Cameron's rigid erection as the driver adjusted his rearview mirror so he could watch the proceedings. The light changed but the cab moved only when the driver behind honked. Leslie almost giggled. "Watching him?"

"He didn't see the light change," she whispered. "He was so busy watching us."

Cameron covered her hand in his crotch with his. "Watching this, I'm sure."

"Yeah. Let him watch."

Too quickly for all concerned, they arrived at Cameron's building, a very exclusive high-rise in a very exclusive neighborhood. He paid the fare and, she saw, included a big tip. "For entertaining us while we entertained him," Cameron said as they entered the marble and crushed velvet lobby. Leslie loved her little apartment in Brooklyn Heights, but this was spectacular. A uniformed concierge said, "Good evening, Mr. Wallace," then walked over and pressed the button to summon the elevator. When it arrived he reached inside and pushed the penthouse button, then backed out. "Have a good night, Mr. Wallace."

"Doesn't that bother you?" When he looked puzzled she said, "He has probably guessed what we're up to."

Leslie loved Cameron's rich laugh. "I hope to hell he's envious."

They rode up in what was really a room, with a small teak table topped by a vase of dried flowers and two small side chairs. The carpeting was deep gold pile and the walls were upholstered in embossed satin up to the chair rail, then mirrored, not a fingerprint allowed, she was sure. It was all she could do to keep her cool. This was money displayed in a way she'd never dreamed of. Not that she wanted to live with it, but it was beautiful to visit.

The doors opened onto a small vestibule with two doors opening from it. Cameron took his key and opened one of the doors, letting her into his sumptuous apartment. Although Leslie would have loved to look around, Cameron took her in his arms. His lips were soft, yet insistent, and she parted her lips to allow his tongue access. "You're so desirable, Leslie," he purred, "and you turn me on."

The bedroom was as lavishly decorated as the other living areas, but he gave her no time to appreciate the decor. "I want to see you," he said. "Would you undress while I watch?"

Here was her first challenge. Could she do this? She looked into his eyes as he seated himself on the edge of the bed. He was so nice that she wanted to please him so she slowly removed her blouse, glad she'd chosen the pale satin and lace bra and panty set from her company's collection. She'd been modeling for over a year and suddenly understood the desire for luxurious lingerie.

As her slacks fell to the floor Cameron said, "You're as lovely as I thought you'd be. Erika's other customers will love you. Will you use your own name?"

Babbling to cover her nervousness, she said, "I've considered it and I think I'll use Carolynne. It was my best friend's name in elementary school. She spelled it with an 'e' at the end."

"Come here Carolynne spelled with an 'e' at the end," he said, "and undress me. I like to watch your hands." Her panic slowly lifting, she pulled off his tie and dragged his white shirt from the waist of his slacks. He wore no undershirt so once she'd removed his shirt she could touch his skin. His body looked its age, but when she'd removed his briefs his need was obvious.

"I want to be inside you," he said, opening the bedside table drawer and unrolling a condom over himself.

She stretched out on her back and he climbed over her. She could feel the tip of his turgid erection prodding her to open her legs further. When she did, he pushed into her. She splayed her hands on his back, then slid her palms down to his buttocks. "You feel so good inside of me," she purred, totally honestly. He did feel wonderful. "Do more, just like that."

He did as she'd asked, then, with a few more thrusts he came with a bellow. She didn't climax, and she didn't fake it.

"That was wonderful," he said when he'd regained his breath. "Thank you for everything." He padded to a small refrigerator in the corner of the room and returned with two bottles of ice cold water. He twisted the cap off one and handed it to her then took a long pull from the other. "Exercise always makes me thirsty," he said with waggling eyebrows and she couldn't help but laugh. Then he continued, "I have a little problem you could help me with from time to time." He took a small chocolate truffle from his nightstand, unwrapped it, and when Leslie opened her mouth, popped it in. "As you can probably tell I'm a very wealthy man and, sadly, my wife died about ten years ago. Therefore, I'm considered quite a catch. I date occasionally, but I find that the women I spend time with are as interested in my bank account as my company."

Leslie savored the taste in her mouth, then took a sip of her water. "So that's why I'm here. No strings, no future."

"Actually I'd like to have a future of sorts. If you're willing, I'd like to see you several times a month, for a few reasons. First, you're dynamite in bed."

Leslie wondered at that. She hadn't really done anything, no oral sex, no hand job. He must have sensed her confusion.

"It's not your technique I value, it's your honesty. You asked for what you wanted, and you didn't fake orgasm. Next time I'd like to give that to you, by the way. Second, you're good company. You're knowledgeable and willing to express an opinion, yet also eager to learn about things you don't know about." With a sudden chuckle he continued, "You have no idea how insipid most of my companions are."

He reached for the quilt at the foot of the bed and spread it over both of them. "Third, you'll be my defense against the hoards. When I'm with you they'll keep their distance and, if we're seen together more than two or three times, everyone will think that this old fart has a new love."

"Stop the old part, Cameron," Leslie said quickly.

He patted her hand. "Leslie, I'm sixty-eight and some of the women I've dated are sure I've got one foot in the grave. A quick marriage and they'll inherit some of my fortune."

Leslie was surprised at his age. "You're quite a guy for sixty-eight."

"Exercise, vitamins, and healthy doses of Cialis. I don't know whether you've decided how often to let Erika book your time, but I'd like to be part of that. I'll pay Erika's fee, of course. The money means little to me, but your company does. May I talk to Erika?"

"I'd love to see you again, Cameron."

"In exchange, in addition to the money, I'd love to introduce you to my world. Plays, concerts, fine restaurants, the works. I'm sure you'd be a quick learner and it would make you all the more valuable as an escort. How does that strike you?"

"I think we'll have some great times together. One caveat. I've been to a few concerts and I tend to fall asleep."

Cameron roared with laughter. "There's that honesty again. That's what I like most about you."

Over the next year she saw Cameron several dozen times, enjoyed his company and learned, both about the world of the very rich and the many areas of sexuality he enjoyed. At first he was her only client, but she eventually began to see other men. About six months after joining Courtesans, Inc., she quit her modeling job and concentrated on entertaining.

About eighteen months after her first dinner with Cameron, she was both delighted and saddened when he told her over dinner that he had found a companion much closer to his own age, a woman he'd asked to marry him. "She knows all about you and is glad you've given me the joy you have. However . . ."

"Say no more. I completely understand. I wouldn't want to share you either." She leaned across the table and kissed him. "I will miss you like crazy," she said, her eyes filling, "but I am so happy for you."

For the first time they parted without making love.

Chapter

11

That had been the beginning. Carolynne with an "e" had been born.

Now, looking at Brad over the wooden table, she knew that Kayla had been right. There was nothing inherently wrong with what she did. There was nothing wrong with what Leslie did now. Actually, aside from being burned out, as people were no matter what they did, she was happy being what she was.

"Do you like being a cop?" Leslie asked.

"I do. Most of the time I get to put away the bad guys. Unfortunately it's not always easy to tell which ones the bad guys are, but I do my best." For the next several minutes Brad regaled Leslie with stories of being a cop in the big, bad city, as he called it.

They finished dinner before seven and Brad drove back to Atlantic Beach Road. "How about a walk on the beach to work off all that great food?" he suggested.

Leslie looked around, glad to see that no one from their little neighborhood was around. She didn't want to have to deal with the questions that Marie, Suze, or Abby might ask. This wasn't a romantic walk in the light of the setting sun. It was merely two friends getting some exercise. *Liar*, she told herself. Something is going on here. That little tingle doesn't lie.

They left their shoes on the seawall and, barefoot, wandered along the beach, talking about nothing and everything, and when Brad took her hand, it felt natural. The water felt cool on their bare feet, in contrast to the heat still remaining in the sand above the tide line. He turned to her as the sun set in swirls of fuchsia and gold and kissed her gently. Her knees melted and the tender area between her thighs moistened. How long had it been since she'd been kissed just for the pleasure of it?

He was a wonderfully gentle kisser, soft, easy, with no pressure. She could back away at any time, but she didn't. His hand spread lightly on her back and she could feel his heat through her blouse as he held her close. Smiling down at her, he said, "This is like a cliché scene in a movie. I hate it that you might relegate me to the cliché trash pile."

"Some scenes become clichés because they work well." She draped her arms over his shoulders and pressed her lips against his. They played, tongues dueling, hands stroking, bodies barely touching. She touched the tiny uneven spot on his front tooth with her tongue, then tunneled her fingers in his hair, dislodging several curling strands from the wave across the top. With a sigh, she said, "And this one works really well." When they finally turned to walk back toward their respective cottages he again took her hand.

It was almost dark when they reached the seawall. Anticipating his question, she said, "It's much too soon."

"Take out the word *much* and I'll agree, but there's something going on here and I'd like to explore it some more."

With a sigh of acceptance she nodded. "Me, too." She found her shoes, hooked them over her index finger, kissed him lightly, and entered her house. *Leslie*, she berated herself, *what the hell are you doing? Heading for disaster, that's what.*

*   *   *

Brad, you're an idiot, he told himself as he watched her door close behind her. You're getting involved. *Wake up you jerk*. It's hormones and lust. He realized that he'd been fighting a hard-on all day and that was ridiculous. She was a hooker, plain and simple. Well, maybe not plain and certainly not simple. He'd been wonderfully surprised by her all day. He reasoned that to command the prices she got for her time, and it wasn't just in-bed time, she had to be intelligent and charming in addition to hot, but she was so much more than any of that. Damn. He was very attracted to her and that was a gigantic mistake. It would get in the way of everything. And, aside from her being a pro, what would happen if and when she found out he was in Sound's End to get information from her. Too tangled. But he was finding her almost irresistible.

In his bedroom he undressed, turned out all the lights, and stretched out on the bed. What was it about Leslie that intrigued him so? She was good to look at, sexy in an unobvious sort of way, but he'd met and even dated prettier women. She had that erotic voice, but that was just a gift of nature. She was intelligent, but that wasn't something he often thought about looking for in a woman. She was charming but again, he'd been with lots of charming women, actually lived with one a few years before. So what was it?

It had to be some kind of chemistry. He'd read about pheromones, chemical signals that animals sent out to attract members of the opposite sex. Maybe that was what it was. She sent out just the right chemicals, deliberately or not, and he was being reeled in like a fish. Whatever it was, however, he was having a difficult time keeping her in perspective.

Several years before, a friend of his on the force had been having trouble clearing his head after his live-in girlfriend decamped with another guy. He'd taken the advice of a TV shrink and imagined his ex in the most unflattering way possible and he'd laughed with his friends over beers. Now Brad tried the technique. He pictured Leslie with a terrible head cold, nose red, coughing, sneezing. It didn't help. He saw her in his mind with a john, straddling his waist, rising and falling on his hard cock. He reversed the positions, the guy on top, pumping. That was a worse picture. Erotic. Hot. He felt his cock hardening. He wanted her and it wasn't doing any good denying it. He might as well go with it, fuck her brains out and get her out of his system.

During his teenage years he'd masturbated while looking at Victoria's Secret ads, ladies in revealing lingerie with just enough showing to be tantalizing. He pictured Leslie in a long gown of deep blue satin, with lace over the breasts, a matching long robe over it, tied just beneath the bosom. He'd gotten an idea of her lush body over dinner so now he was able to build his fantasy properly.

She was in the bedroom of his apartment at home, standing near the window that looked out over lower Park Avenue. She had her back to him when he walked in and she turned as she heard the door close behind him. "I've been waiting for you."

"I'm sorry I'm late," he said softly. "You are very beautiful."

"I thought about you when I bought this. Want to touch?"

Of course he did. He loved the feel of the satiny fabric as he slid his large, rough hands over her hips. He could feel the heat of her flesh through the material and he slid his hands to her rear and squeezed her buttocks and pressed it against his groin. She stood still as his hands roamed, touching all of her except her breasts.

Finally he slipped the robe off her shoulders and, as it fell softly to the floor, he leaned down and pressed his lips to the side of her neck. Her skin was almost as soft as the satin and she smelled faintly of perfume and soap. There was also the faint odor of her arousal. His cock was so hard that he wriggled his hips to adjust his slacks. "Let's get rid of those," she whispered, and slowly unbuckled his belt and unfastened his pants.

He felt exposed with his erection pushing at his cotton briefs but she smiled at the sight. "Now?"

"No," he said, his voice quavering, "not yet."

He kissed her, their mouths fusing, changing position often to taste every angle, every facet of her, his hands still drifting idly over her flesh. He was so hungry and it was delicious torture to wait, but he wanted to savor every nuance. He kissed his way down her neck as her hands pulled his shirt up and her nails firmly scored his back, not enough to break the skin but enough to make his flesh tingle.

His mouth found hers again and, as they kissed, he backed away and removed his shirt. The feel of his naked chest against the cool, slippery satin of her gown was erotic, sending shafts of heat directly to his penis. She undulated against him like a cat in heat, her thigh between his, rubbing. She made purring noises, her breathing thick and raspy.

He could barely control his panting and he felt his pulse pound in his ears as he lowered the straps of the gown to bare her beautiful breasts. They were white and full, with erect strawberry nipples that begged for his mouth. He crouched, holding her satin-covered mound against his chest as he feasted, licking, suckling her perfect tits.

She let her head fall backward and cupped her breasts, offering them to him, moaning as he sucked. His hands pushed the gown down further so he could bury his face between them and inhale her personal fragrance, now combining with the heat of her excitement.

He started to lower his body, to lick her pubis, but she guided him backward until he was lying on the bed. She pulled off her gown and his briefs, then her mouth took over, ever so slowly licking the length of his straining cock, her blond hair flipped to one side, stroking his belly. The feel of her blowing on the wetness made him catch what breath he had left. She rubbed her tight nipples over his cock, then licked and blew again. When he didn't think he could stand it any more, she made an O with her lips and surrounded his cock, not quite touching it, bathing it in the wet heat of her breath.

Slowly, so very slowly, she took his cock in her mouth, only occasionally lightly caressing his skin with her tongue or teeth. When she'd captured all of him, she gradually closed her mouth over him, his cock filling the hot, wet cavern. She created a vacuum and pulled back, drawing his cock from her, then lowered herself again.

It was the best blow job he'd ever gotten and he wanted it to go on forever, yet he also wanted to bury himself in her sweet, wet pussy. She obliged, eventually, straddling him and lowering her sopping cavern onto his erection.

In his bedroom he groaned. God, that vision had caused his cock to swell almost painfully and he put one hand on it, the other cupping his balls. It only took a moment for him to come all over his belly and hands, ejaculating for what seemed like hours.

As he lay, his breathing slowing, he realized that he hadn't come like that in months, maybe years, and certainly not from masturbating to an old fantasy. But the face and body had been Leslie's. Rather than getting over this ridiculous obsession, he found he was more fixated on her than ever. Shit. Shit, shit, shit.

"She's doing what?" Suze said into the phone the following morning.

"Vicki Farrar is going to open a store in the old Sherman Gallery space." Her friend Frank Lovejoy worked in the town clerk's office and he knew everything about everything. Although it was only nine-thirty, he'd called her as soon as he'd found out one more juicy bit of information.

"Vicki? I don't believe it. I saw the plans at the zoning board meeting but it was all in the name of some corporation. I didn't think she had it in her. Good for her. It will keep her busy and out of my hair."

"Don't be so happy so fast, Suze. I'm afraid you don't know one little detail."

Suze was sure he was dragging this out just to make her suffer. "What 'little detail?' "

"I got a call from someone first thing this morning, asking for information on Vicki's Erotic Emporium. He gave me the address of the old Sherman place."

"Vicki's Erotic Emporium? No, no, no. She can't be serious. I can't, I won't let something like that into my town, whatever she's selling."

"She's done all the right paperwork from my end, and I assume she's up to date with the county and the state as well. I'm not sure you can do anything about it."

"Don't bet on that," Suze snarled.

An hour and five phone calls later, Suze was no closer to putting an end to Vicki's Erotic Emporium than she had been when Frank called. She'd discovered that Vicki and her attorney had all the permits she needed and she'd signed a one-year lease on the property. Suze knew the building and realized that it would need little renovation to become a store. *Won't happen*, Suze said to herself for the twentieth time. *Never. Not in my town! Not in my lifetime!* She stormed out of her house and along Atlantic Beach Road.

"What is this I hear about you opening some kind of erotic store in the old Sherman place?" Suze asked Vicki without preamble when she answered the mayor's knock at her door.

"I guess the cat's out of the bag," Vicki said with her characteristic pouty lower lip. "I think it's a great idea." She didn't step back to allow her to enter so Suze had to stand on the top step.

"I don't think so at all, and you won't be able to make this happen so don't put a lot of money into it."

"Listen, Suze," Vicki said, her voice stronger. "I've got all the permits I need and I've already started to talk to the contractor who's going to do over the interior. It's a done deal and it won't be long until it's open."

"Over my dead body," Suze spat. "This is my town and you won't get away with this."

Vicki's laugh tinkled, sounding to Suze like clinking ice cubes. "You sound like the sheriff in an old western movie." She lowered her voice and put on a thick Texas drawl. "This town isn't big enough for both of us."

She hated to be taken so lightly, so Suze switched her tack. "What about your daughter? Is that any way to bring up a teenager?"

"Trish is going to work there with me. Come on and stop being so mid-Victorian. You see more stuff on daytime TV than will be available in my store. Anyway, you should talk about raising teenagers. Have you looked at your kids recently? Do you even know where they are?"

"Don't change the subject," Suze snapped, putting Vicki's comment about her children out of her mind. "This won't happen."

Vicki put her hands on her hips. "My lawyer says it will, so cut the crap, Suze. You can't bully me." She stepped back and closed the door in the mayor's face.

Flabbergasted, Suze started back down Atlantic Beach Road. Seeing Marie and Leslie sitting on the seawall, she stalked over. "You'll never believe what that slut is doing." She took a deep breath and tried to calm her racing pulse. The nerve of that woman. She'd just called Vicki a slut, and she never used that kind of language.

"I assume you mean Vicki," Marie asked, her voice infuriatingly calm. "What is she doing?"

Suze crouched and told the two women about Vicki's Erotic Emporium. She'd grabbed a picture of the old Sherman

Gallery from one of her albums and showed it to the women. "In this building right across the street from Joe's market."

"Can she do that?" Marie asked.

"I won't permit it."

"Why not?" Leslie said. "It's a legitimate business and from the number of empty storefronts I've seen around, the town could use some new ideas."

"A triple-X-rated store? You've got to be kidding. How will it affect the children?"

"First of all, from what you tell me, you don't know that it will be triple X rated, and I'm sure that kids will be barred from the store in any event. Set an age limit and have the cops patrol if you think it's being violated." Leslie looked Suze straight in the eye. "I know you're the mayor and all but it seems to me that you'd be happy to have some additional tax revenues. If the local folks object, she'll get no business and will have to close."

"Not a chance. That store isn't going to happen. Marie, you've been here a long time. How do you feel about a lingerie and toy store opening right across from Joe's place?"

"You know, maybe Leslie's right," Marie said. "After all, there's a Victoria's Secret store in the mall in Old Saybrook. If you can't beat 'em, join 'em. It might bring some new blood into town and new patrons to Joe's place."

Leslie's right? Since when did Marie disagree with her? She was almost as annoyed at Leslie for butting in as she was at Marie for agreeing with her. Everything was falling apart. She stood and stalked off, then the two women heard her front door slam.

Chapter

12

"Privately," Marie said, grinning as Suze's door banged shut, "I'm not too keen on the idea of X-rated stuff being sold right on Main Street across from Joe's store, but I do like to see Suze fume."

Leslie's heartbeat was just returning to normal. Suze's reference to "what that slut is doing" had really frightened her. Was her secret out? She'd only relaxed when she realized that it was Vicki who bore the brunt of Suze's fury. "Victoria's Secret doesn't sell anything X-rated. Some toys are even being sold right out in plain sight in novelty shops. Why do you think Vicki's store will be so different?"

"I know Vicki and I can sense the way her mind works. There will probably be books and videos at least."

"One would think that Suze can control that if she tries. Wouldn't the zoning board have something to say about it? Aren't there laws about how far that kind of store can be from a school or church? Or people's houses for that matter." She should talk, Leslie thought, about X-rated businesses.

"Actually, Vicki's picked a great spot. There's nothing around that would cause a problem. If Suze is already pissed, she probably knows that Vicki's got all the permits in order." Marie's smile relaxed her face and took ten years off.

"It will be interesting to see how this all plays out," Leslie said. "I just hope some of the fireworks happen before I leave. It should be fun, but I don't have to live here."

"Changing the subject and being nosy, how was your dinner with Brad last evening?" Marie asked.

"Very nice. We went to Soundings."

"Good choice. Joe and I go there on special occasions. Did you get to feed the ducks?"

"Half my bread went over the side of the deck," Leslie said with a laugh.

"Those ducks are famous in the area. Some get so fat it seems they shouldn't be able to fly, just waddle around on the far side of the inlet."

They chatted for awhile, then were joined by Abby and her two children. "I didn't see Damian yesterday," Marie commented. "Did he have lots of work?" To Leslie, she added, "That man works all the time."

Abby looked sad. "He had to leave around noon. Some meeting or other."

Before she could control her mouth, Leslie said, "On a Sunday?"

"Oh, it happens from time to time. He's in entertainment law and often those folks can only meet on the weekends." Abby's sigh of resignation was genuine, but everything was all too obvious to Leslie. "We're really lucky that he sends us here for the summer so we're not stuck in the city while he works."

Leslie bit her tongue as Abby sent the children off to play in the sand. Once they were out of earshot, Marie told her about Vicki's plans and, for the next hour they debated the advisability of an erotic business in Sound's End.

In the middle of the afternoon Brad finally emerged and joined the three women. Dressed in his knee-length cargo pants and no shirt, he looked sexy as hell and the look he gave her smouldered so much that she looked away. Fortunately neither of the other women noticed.

"You're skin is still so white. If you don't get out in the sun more," Marie told him as he settled on a towel on the warm sand, "you're going to go back to New York City just as pale as you were when you arrived."

"I burned very badly as a kid at the beach so I use lots of sunblock and stay out of the midday sun. Anyway, I had a project I had to get into," he said, "and I was on the Internet most of the day. Using a dial-up connection is really slow. I'm used to having instant access the way I do at the precinct."

"Leslie said you went to Soundings last evening."

"I think you recommended it the first evening I was here, Marie. Great choice."

"Joe and I really love the place." She turned to Abby. "Have you and Damian been there yet?"

"I've heard a lot about it but we haven't been there. We don't go out much. Damian loves my cooking so when he's here I make his favorites." She put a grin on her face. "That makes me sound like some kind of kitchen drudge, but I really love cooking for him. The kids love to be with him, too." She pondered. "I guess we could take the kids there."

"They'd love the ducks," Brad said. "They're such a riot, and a real danger to your hearing."

"You and your husband should take some time for yourselves," Leslie said. "I'd be happy to baby-sit if that's the problem."

"Oh, I couldn't let you do that and there are plenty of kids around who'd be old enough. We seldom use sitters. Damian says I should be with the kids in case they need me during the night."

Drop it, Leslie, she told herself. *It's none of your business.*

Later, as the sun began to lower, Brad said, "Want to grab a bite in town, Leslie? I'm done on that little laptop for the day, and I do mean done. I'm not sure my squinty eyes will ever recover."

"I thought I'd make something here," she said, trying to discourage him.

"Ah, come on. Take pity on a poor working stiff."

After some hesitation, during which she recited all the reasons that Brad was entirely wrong for her, Leslie said, "Sure. Okay. Let me throw some better clothes on."

They ate at a small Italian restaurant and took another late walk on the beach. At her door, their kiss was long and passionate. Brad made no demands on her and, although she'd thought a lot about sex with him, Leslie made no moves either. The situation was impossible and she said that to herself over and over until it became like a mantra. It didn't seem to help.

Friends. That was what they were becoming, making great conversation and enjoying each other's company. Most evenings they'd walked on the beach holding hands but going no further than a good night kiss. By Friday, Leslie's frustration was rising. She knew he found her attractive so what was holding him up? He was single, not seeing anyone that he'd ever mentioned, so . . .

She knew what was keeping her from making a move. Her sane mind knew it would only bring pain. She wanted him and the combination of a friend and a lover might be difficult to keep in proportion. She recited her mantra: *He's a cop.*

It was late Thursday evening when KJ arrived home on his bike. He was used to slipping into the house after everyone was asleep and he was surprised when he found his mother still up. He'd barely seen her all week. Tonight he'd spent the evening with a group of friends enjoying a bonfire on Middle Beach, with food, girls, and lots of beer. He wasn't drunk, but he wasn't totally sober either. He'd probably been over the legal limit driving home but in Sound's End he knew he could get away with anything. There were a few advantages to having a mayor for a mother.

"Did you know about it?" Suze snapped when KJ tried to pass through the kitchen. She waved the local paper at him.

"Know about what?" God save him from obtuse conversations when his mind was fogged.

"Vicki's Erotic Emporium. Trish must have told you. Why the hell didn't you tell me?"

Erotic Emporium? No wonder Trish hadn't let him in on the secret, and no wonder his mother was in a snit. "Please. Do you think I knew something you didn't? You, who knows everything?"

"Don't get snippy with me. You knew, and you didn't tell me. What kind of a son are you?"

"Why should you care?" he muttered.

"What did you say?"

"Nothing, and I did know," he said, lying through his teeth, "but I was sure you did, too."

"In the future, if you find out something that affects this town, you tell me." She paused, then continued, emphasizing each word, "Do you hear me?"

"Yes, Mother," he said with a sneer.

"Where's your sister?"

"Isn't she in bed or on the computer?" KJ said, knowing all too well that she was still at the beach.

"No, she isn't," Suze said. "Have you seen her tonight?"

"She was at the beach earlier," he said, not lying. "It's not my turn to watch her. She has her life, and I have mine."

"You're older so it's your job to keep an eye on her. After all, she's only fifteen."

"Right, Suze," KJ said, heading for the stairs. Slightly off balance, he tripped on the first step but his mother didn't notice.

Later he heard Eliza climb the stairs, lock the door to her room, and then the Windows jingle. She was on her computer again.

By Friday, Suze was in full cry. During the week Vicki had had construction firms measuring the building and Suze had begun what was turning out to be a more difficult task than she'd imagined, organizing the local residents into a grassroots campaign to keep Vicki's Erotic Emporium from getting off the ground. A lead article in the local paper stated the facts about the construction while letters to the editor campaigned for one side or the other.

Vicki basked under the attention. Everywhere she went people talked to her, either supporting her efforts or berating her for her audacity. "Trish," she told her daughter late Friday afternoon, "this is growing bigger than even I expected. The publicity is enormous."

"I still want no part of it." Trish and Vicki had hardly seen each other all week. Trish had gone off each morning and returned late in the evening. "I spent the day with a few friends in New Haven on Thursday," she said, "and when they made the connection to you, they bombarded me with questions. They wanted to know whether they'd be able to get porno tapes and whips and handcuffs. Most of it was in fun, but it was embarrassing, too. I don't want to be connected to this."

Vicki's face turned stormy. "I've allowed you to go your own way this week because I didn't really need you. I've developed relationships with several of the guys from the construction company and they're helping me make the critical decisions about the layout of the inside. Once the building's organized, however, I'll need you to begin setting up where things will go, ordering and all."

"Mother, you don't seem to be hearing me. I don't want to get involved. I've got other plans for myself."

The creases between Vicki's eyebrows deepened. "You listen to me, young lady, I've broken my back for you for eighteen years. It wasn't easy. . . ."

"Stop. You've banged me on the head with that for as long as I can remember, and I'm done feeling guilty for your mistakes. Leave me out of this. Two of my girlfriends are getting an apartment in New Haven and they showed it to me this afternoon. They've invited me to move in with them."

Vicki panicked and decided she'd taken the wrong tack. "I'm sorry, baby," she said, wrapping her arm around her daughter's shoulders. "I know I get carried away sometimes, but I do need you." She lowered her voice and spoke conspiratorially, "I really need you. They're all against me. Suze is whipping the town into a frenzy and I can't go through this alone. Stay with me, at least until the Emporium gets off the ground. Then, if you insist on going off on your own, I guess it will be all right. It will only be a few months."

"Mom," Trish said, frustration obvious in every line of her body, "please."

Vicki heaved a deep, theatrical sigh. "Okay. I guess you should go, if you must. I can try to get along without you." She wondered whether she was spreading it on too thick, until she felt Trish's shoulders slump. Vicki hid her small smile. "I know this is difficult for you," she continued, "but I want you here, by me, supporting me in this. There's nothing wrong with what I'm doing."

"I know that, Mom." Her sigh was long and deep. "Oh, I guess I can hold out another few months since you really need me."

Vicki squeezed her daughter's shoulders. "Thank you, baby. It will be great. You'll see."

Although it wasn't a Friday cookout evening, the neighborhood got together and combined cooking skills for an outdoor dinner. Since it was low tide, everyone decided to move dinner down onto the sand. Abby and her two children made a macaroni and cheese casserole, while Marie contributed home-cooked Philly cheese steak sandwiches. Suze brought a large bowl of potato salad and Leslie put together a large green salad, with tomatoes, peppers, and olives, and brought it out with several bottles of dressing. Brad had kept her company into town and while she shopped for salad makings, he went to the local Carvel and bought an ice cream cake and a supply of mosquito coils and citronella candles. "I've gotten chewed to pieces several times," he lamented, "and I'm not going to let that happen again."

"Bug spray seems to work for me," Leslie countered.

"Maybe for you, but on me the bugs see it as A.1. Sauce."

Suze's husband, Kevin, along with Joe Martinelli, joined them as the group gathered on lawn chairs with paper plates on their laps, cans of soda and beer on the beach at their feet. Their plates loaded, the two Croft children had returned to their house to eat in front of the TV. All the other young people were off doing whatever young people did on a Friday evening.

The major topic of conversation, as it had been all week, was the Emporium. Once they finished eating and most of the paper items had been thrown into the garbage, Leslie said, "You know this is all pointless. There's really nothing we can do. The town will decide what it wants."

"I represent the town and I don't want it," Suze snapped.

Fed up with Suze's attitude, Leslie said, "You may represent the town, but the people in it will make the decisions. You've checked all the permits, board approvals, and everything else you can think of, and you're done. Let it go and see what happens."

"I can't do that. I just can't."

During the discussion, Damian arrived, ascertained that the children were in the house, and disappeared after them. When Suze and her husband gathered up the last of their dishes and went back to their house, Leslie could tell that Abby was upset. While Brad was talking to Marie and Joe, she skootched her chair closer to the sad-looking woman. "Want to talk about it?" she asked.

"No. Yes. I don't know."

"I'm a good listener," Leslie said, "but that's an offer not a demand."

"I know and although you've only been here a week I feel like we're friends. It's Damian. I hardly see him anymore." Her eyes grew large as tears glistened. "When he's here he spends most of his time with Mark and Tammy and almost none with me. I mentioned going out to dinner just the two of us and he immediately put the idea down. He doesn't like me to leave the children with a baby-sitter."

"They're certainly old enough."

"I know, but he . . ." The tears she'd been trying to control trickled down her cheek. "I'm so scared."

Leslie reached over and grasped Abby's hand. "Of what? Or do you not want to talk about it?"

"I don't want to talk about it because that will make it more real. I'm pretty sure that he doesn't love me anymore and I think there's someone else. I think he's parked me and the kids here so he can be with someone else all week. I think he resents spending time with us, especially with me."

"Do you have any basis for your suspicions? Anything more than a wife's feelings?"

"No, not really, but my feelings are pretty strong." She leaned back and pulled a tissue from the pocket of her shorts. Mopping her eyes, she said, "We were so in love when we were married and I thought it would be perfect forever. We were both quite young, though. He had just graduated from college and I had been working as a receptionist in a doctor's office for a year after high school. The early years were great. He did well in law school and I worked and supported us. He got hired at his current firm and moved up quickly. I continued to work until Mark was born. Then Tammy came along and I became just a housewife.

"Don't get me wrong," Abby continued, "there's nothing wrong with staying home with the kids, but when they both started school I wanted to get a part-time job, just while they were gone."

As she talked the words came faster and faster. "Damian

objected strenuously. He makes more than enough for all of us and, well, I guess he's a bit old-fashioned. Now the children are gone all day and I'm bored to death. Oh, I keep the house, cook, do the laundry but that's not enough for me anymore." She dabbed at her eyes. "I think he's bored, too, with me, with our marriage, with everything."

"Being bored doesn't mean he's seeing someone else."

"I know, but he is. I just know it."

"So what are you going to do about it?" Leslie asked.

"I've no idea. I've never talked about it out loud before so I haven't allowed myself to think about it. I don't have many choices anyway. I can either stay or go and leaving isn't an option."

"Of course not, at least not yet. I would never encourage anyone to leave a marriage without exploring every avenue possible. Have you considered marriage counseling?"

"I mentioned it once over the winter and Damian went crazy. He isn't interested in telling anyone about our life. He told me I was overreacting and, for a short while, he was a model husband. Not for long, however."

"Let's consider the gigantic elephant sitting right here." Leslie's voice softened. "Have you given much thought to getting out?"

"That's out of the question. He's a great father and I couldn't deprive the kids of that. Ever."

"What about you? What are you depriving yourself of?"

"Nothing I can't do without." She turned and tuned in to Brad, Marie, and Joe's conversation, effectively putting an end to Leslie's discussion with her. It was sad that she was merely a visitor in Abby's life, Leslie told herself. *Abby has to make whatever decisions she needs to make. First she has to think about herself as a real person, not as Tammy and Mark's mommy and Damian's wife.*

Chapter

13

After the others went back to their houses, Brad and Leslie sat on the edge of the seawall. They'd spent a good part of the previous week together and it was becoming more and more difficult to keep the relationship at arm's length. The sun slipped below the horizon, leaving streamers of rose and raw gold. Gulls and terns wheeled and screamed, backlit by the setting sun. "How about a swim?" Brad asked.

It had been a brutally hot, humid day with a slight offshore breeze that did nothing to cool anything off. "Love to," Leslie said. "Let me change into a suit."

In her bedroom, Leslie considered. She had several one-piece bathing suits, demure and comfortable, that she'd been wearing all week and a black bikini that she hadn't put on yet. She had no desire to attract the attention of any of the men to her body. Well, maybe one of the men. She might as well admit that she wanted to attract Brad. It was a mistake and she knew it; there was no future and very little present. She knew that he'd had great success with his computer projects and that he was staying one more week, but that would be that. There was no way that they could remain friends, lovers, or whatever once he found out what she was. There was little chance that she could keep her occupation private once they were back in Manhattan.

There was now, however, so she pulled the bikini out of the drawer and put it on. She pulled on a thigh-length beige cotton coverup, grabbed a towel, and found Brad still sitting on the seawall in his cargo pants. "No bathing suit?" she asked, then winked. "Skinny-dipping?"

With a long, serious sigh, he dropped off the wall and pulled off his shorts to reveal a pair of brief black trunks. "I guess it's time for me to come clean about one of the reasons I'm here."

In the fading light, Leslie saw a deep, angry, red scar that began a few inches above his knee and continued across his upper left thigh. Not only was it ugly, but it was deeply sunken, so there was obviously a large amount of muscle missing. Seeing the scar she realized that in the past week he had always worn long pants or shorts that were long enough to cover his leg. Even when they worked out, he wore knee-length bicycle pants. She reached out to touch the wound, then pulled her hand back. "Want to tell me about it?"

He hoisted himself back onto the edge of the seawall. "It's so cliché. Brooding cop trying to recover from a bad shooting. I'm almost embarrassed."

"You don't have to tell me," she said softly, climbing back onto the wall and settling beside him. How bad was it? Where was his head?

Brad still had nightly screaming nightmares about the evening it all happened three months before: the domestic dispute with a man holding his toddler hostage, the sudden appearance of a gun, the kid screaming as he fell then silence as he hit the sidewalk below, Pete going down then the searing pain in his thigh, then nothing. Nothing for several hours while the doctors struggled to save his life. A severed femoral artery, they told him, his life pumping out of the hole, all over the grimy linoleum of the third-floor tenement apartment. Considerable damage to the muscles, tendons, and ligaments. Mike Mitcham's face when he awoke. "It's okay buddy. You are going to be okay and you got the bastard."

"He's dead?" He heard himself as if from a distance.

"As a doornail."

Brad's voice was flat as he said, "I couldn't save the boy."

"I know. No one could have done more than you did."

"Is Pete okay?" What had they done wrong? Domestics were always a bitch but who could have known the bastard had a gun hidden beneath his shirt. He still saw the scene in flashes: the man pulling the nine-millimeter from his belt and holding it to his toddler's head while he dangled the shrieking little boy out the window, then letting the kid drop, whirling and turning the nine millimeter first on Pete then on him, firing, firing, firing. Then, as if in slow motion, he was twisting as Brad pulled his gun and fired at him. Brad's gun continued to fire as if by itself as he fell, pulling the trigger until he passed out.

"He took several in his vest, one in the neck, and, like you, one in the leg," Mike said, "but your call got us there in time."

"My call?"

"You screamed into the radio, 'Officer down!!' over and over. When the first guys got there you had a death grip on your gun with one hand and the radio with the other even though you were in bad shape."

"The boy?"

Mike's chin dropped. "I'm sorry, he didn't make it."

Brad hesitated, then asked, "What about Pete? Is he going to be okay?" he said, trying to process. One in the neck. That sounded bad.

"I won't lie to you. He's going to live, but we don't know how much long-term damage was done. The bullet in his neck nicked his spine. The docs think there won't be any permanent damage, but no one's willing to bet money either way."

He remembered being hit in the chest, but his vest, like Pete's, must have saved his sorry ass. Brad had reached down to feel the thick bandage on his thigh.

Seeing Brad's motion, Mike continued, "You're going to be good as new eventually. The docs say it was touch and go there for awhile, but you're in one piece. You'll need lots of rest and physical therapy and you'll be on a desk for awhile. You lost a lot of blood, buddy. Most of the precinct donated."

The surgeon and later the department doc had assured him that, with time, he'd recover full use of his leg. There had been a departmental investigation and the shoot was declared to be a good one and the child's death to be the result of his father's actions, but Brad still suffered from what the department shrink labeled posttraumatic stress. He relived the scene over and over, both awake and asleep, trying to figure a way to keep the toddler alive and defuse the situation without any bloodshed.

Leslie was such a good listener, he realized, that although he told her a slightly abbreviated version of the story, it was more than he'd told anyone except his shrink. Even his family didn't know the entire chain of events and the horror of that night.

"I think I read about it," she said, turning to him and breaking her silence. "Several months ago? The wife pitched a fit at the department?"

"That's the one." Early in his story she had seemed to sense how difficult it was to talk about it so she had turned and gazed at the ocean. Now her voice was soft and sympathetic, but not cloyingly reassuring. "It got quite a play in the press," he continued, "because the woman wanted to sue the city for her baby's death. The powers that be put the squash on that quickly enough. It's difficult to feel any sympathy for a guy who dangled his two-year-old by one arm, with a gun in his ear, laughing at us while the kid screamed, then dropped him onto the concrete."

"It must have been terrible."

With a rueful smile, Brad said, "It would have to improve a lot to be terrible, but it's in the past now. Actually that's why my boss urged me to take a few weeks here. I still need to get my head together."

"It must be tough on you," Leslie said, finally turning back to him. "There must be quite a bit of guilt, even though you weren't responsible for either the death of the child or the injury to your partner."

Strange that she was the first one who talked openly about it without tiptoeing around the subject. She seemed to understand exactly what he was dealing with and what to say, to neither accuse nor minimize. "Yeah, but it did have its good points," he said, redirecting the conversation. "I've always been a computer nerd and since I've been on a desk I've been learning more and more about forensic computer work. It's really been fun."

"What about your partner? Is he okay?"

"Pete foolishly credits me with saving his life, for killing the bastard who was doing the shooting. In truth, we were both lucky to have great vests and a shooter who didn't go for a head shot. Anyway, Pete's well on the road to recovery. I talk to him several times a week and he's doing fine. There's no paralysis or permanent damage of any kind. Like me, he's on modified duty and happy to be off the street."

Leslie wanted to say the right things for Brad's sake and for the future of their relationship. Was the scar the reason he hadn't wanted to go further than kissing?

"Is the scar on your leg the reason for the longer pants all the time?"

"Sure."

"Why?"

"Why? That scar's about as ugly as it comes." He paused. "It's also visual proof of what happened, of what I did."

"It certainly is a nasty scar, but what did you do exactly? I didn't hear anything in what you told me that had anything directly to do with you."

"If I hadn't been there the guy and his kid might still be alive."

"And if your parents hadn't met when they did, you and your brothers and sister might not be here. That kind of 'what ifs' are totally counterproductive."

"So you say."

Leslie placed a hand on Brad's knee at the base of the scar. "You brought those tiny trunks with you and wore them tonight so somewhere in your brain you were considering letting some of this out. I think it's more than time."

"You sound like the department shrink."

Leslie allowed her face to relax for the first time since the beginning of the conversation. "Maybe we're both right."

His grin was boyish and revealed the chipped tooth. "Did your tooth break then?"

"When I fell. The dentist has sealed it temporarily but I have to go in to have a cap made. I've been putting it off. I hate the dentist."

Leslie laughed out loud. "You go into a dangerous situation and get shot, but you're afraid of the dentist?" Brad's self-deprecating laugh joined hers. Eventually, she asked, "Will you go back on the street when the powers that be say you're fit?"

She'd hit on one of the problems Brad was facing. It would be several weeks before he was physically able, and the shrink had to declare him fit for duty as well. He smiled ruefully and decided to give her a real answer, not the macho stuff he gave to his friends on the force. He unconsciously rubbed the scar and his tongue found the uneven spot on his front tooth. The break had happened during The Incident but he still didn't know exactly how. Maybe when he fell . . . "I don't really know. I've really become fond of this forensic computer stuff and it puts my geeky talents to good use. That's why I can work from here. The idea of getting into another situation like that one scares the hell out of me." Would he have the nerve to go back to the street if he was needed? He couldn't face that question yet.

"I'll bet. Does it hurt much?" Leslie asked, her hand gently touching his, then lightly stroking the ugly scar.

"It's not too bad anymore. I'm still taking the occasional pain pill but, for the most part, I can deal with it."

She withdrew her hand from the unintentionally sensual gesture. "You work out without too much discomfort, at least that I've seen."

"I used to work out occasionally before the shooting, but now its part of my program of physical therapy. I lost a considerable amount of muscle and I have exercises to do each morning and evening to get full use back. I've got at least another month on limited duty and by the end of that time I hope to be pretty much back to my old form." His head might be another matter. "Enough about this," he said, slapping his other thigh. "Let's go for a swim."

He jumped down from the seawall and watched Leslie remove her opaque coverup. "Oh shit," he hissed between his teeth, suddenly aroused. "Why do you hide that gorgeous body beneath all the baggy clothes you usually wear?" he asked. "And those sports bras." He made an ugly face. "Yuck."

She laughed as she dropped the coverup and her towel on the sand. "I know what I look like and it's often more of a problem than a joy. Men come on to me and I have to fend them off in the nicest way possible so I don't make enemies. Most men want what I'm not willing to give and women worry that I've got designs on their husbands. It becomes difficult to make friends with anyone and this month I wanted to be friendly, not sexy. It's much simpler this way."

"But much less decorative," Brad said, his gaze wandering appreciatively over her body, revealed to its best by her bikini. He had known what she looked like, of course. There were several pictures of her in her file, but in the flesh, well, there was all that flesh, a slim waist and flat belly, full, sexy breasts, and shapely thighs. He let out a long, low wolf whistle. "So why tonight?"

She took his hand and urged him toward the water's edge. "Because you're not just any guy."

The mid-August water was warm and the bottom sandy. Leslie had done little swimming since she'd arrived but when she did she found that her buoyancy was enhanced by the high salt content of the water so she floated easily. They swam for awhile, then stood in chest-high water, salt water streaming off their faces. Brad reached over and smoothed her sopping hair from her face, then licked drops of salty liquid from her lips. Leslie had already made the decision. If the situation arose, she'd let him make love to her.

How long had it been since she'd made love with a man just for fun? She draped her arms around his neck and rubbed her nose against his. When their lips met it was as natural as breathing. Mouths warm, lips pressing, their heads adjusting to find the perfect angle. When she parted her lips, his tongue found hers and the kiss deepened. Her hands stroked his shoulders and his pressed into the small of her back, kneading her flesh and pressing her mound gently against his erection. He held her buoyant body easily as she wrapped her legs around his waist and linked her ankles.

They kissed for a long time, then his hands unfastened the back of her bikini top, leaving the neck strap still fastened, and his hands found her breasts. She bent her head back, exposing her throat. He licked the pounding pulse he found there while his fingers played with her erect nipples.

Eventually, she whispered, "I want you, but not here."

He grinned at her, his white teeth with the small, endearing chip in the front the only things visible in the deepening twilight. "Your place or mine," he said.

"Mine's closer." She fastened the back of her bikini and, hand in hand, they dragged themselves through the gently undulating water onto the deserted beach.

They found their towels, but as Leslie started to head for her cottage, Brad took her towel and began to slowly rub her dry. "Suddenly I'm in no hurry," he said, then bent, moved her bra aside, and licked salty water from her breasts. "It's dark enough that no one will see."

"Two can play at that game," she said, flicking her tongue over his flat, male nipples.

They played, teased, licked, kissed, until they were both hot and almost insatiably hungry. Leslie reached down and found the length of him hard and pulsing. "You show a lot of patience," she said, squeezing gently, "but patience can be overrated."

He slipped his hand down the front of her bikini bottom and found her erect clit. "It certainly can, but a little delayed gratification can be wonderful."

She arched her back as his clever fingers rubbed all the perfect places. She wanted to duplicate his motions and rub his cock, but she couldn't quite make her brain work. Suddenly she felt the small spasms start deep in her belly. "Oh God," she moaned. "Don't stop."

He braced her back with his free arm and continued to play with her clit. "Do it for me, baby," he whispered. "Come right here in my arms."

She did, smothering her screams against his shoulder. "I want to be inside of you," he growled as he picked her up and carried her toward her cottage.

It was only moments until they were in her bedroom, pulling off their wet clothing and quickly toweling their hair. "Shit," he hissed. "I'm not prepared."

"I am," she said. "A twenty-first-century woman with any brains is always prepared." She opened the lid of her suitcase, pulled out several foil packets and tossed them at him.

"So many?" he said with a laugh. "You're certainly an optimist."

"Always."

He opened a packet and quickly covered his cock. Then, as she lay back, he covered her body with his own. The tip of his erection found her opening and plunged inside. "I'm usually pretty good at delaying stuff," he said, lifting his hips, then burying himself in her again, "but you make that impossible." Seemingly unable or unwilling to stop, he pounded into her until he came with a roar. As he calmed, he rubbed her clit until she came again.

It was quite a while until, finally catching their breath, they were able to talk. "Holy shit," he said. "That was wonderful."

She giggled. "It was, wasn't it. I've thought a lot about making love with you but I never imagined it would be this good."

"You say making love *with*, not making love to."

"That's the way it should be, at least according to the women I work with." She caught herself. That phrase, the women I work with, could mean in her interior decorating business but she had to be more careful in the future. "We talk a lot about sex, as I guess lots of women do."

"I like that way of putting it, Leslie," he said sleepily, pulling the bedspread over them both, then pulling her close. "Making love *with*."

They dozed, then made love again an hour later, then about 2 A.M., after making love yet a third time, he rose and dressed. "I guess you weren't overly optimistic about those condoms," he said as he scooped up wrappers scattered around the room and tossed them in the trash.

"I guess not." She hadn't felt so well fucked in a very long time. "The hotel staff will probably be scandalized by my garbage."

He grabbed the wrappers from the pail and stuffed them in his pants pocket. "Can't have that." He dropped a light kiss on the tip of her nose.

"I guess not," she said sleepily, curling beneath a blanket. "Are you sure you have to go?"

"I don't want to start more gossip than necessary. At least not yet." He pulled on his now-dry trunks and shorts. "How about brunch? I need to get some sleep first, so why don't I pick you up around eleven?"

"Done. I definitely need a nap, too," she said, curling on her side. "I didn't get too much sleep last night."

"Funny thing," he said with a chuckle, "neither did I."

Leslie lay in bed and listened to her front door close behind Brad. Somewhere between waking and sleeping she thought about how her friends back at Club Fantasy would react if they ever learned that she was sleeping with a cop, and by choice. How could this possibly have a good ending?

For now, however, she was too happy with the present to worry about it. Wasn't that what led most people into trouble?

As Brad crossed the dark, empty road he thought about the mistake he had just made. She was a prostitute. A hooker. Of course she had pleased him in bed and of course she'd let him believe that he'd pleased her. What if it was all phoney? What if his current state of bliss was just a product of a professional temptress and her ability to make fantasies come true? And what about his job? Someone higher up had a bug up his ass to find out details of Club Fantasy's client list. She was his assignment. Okay, maybe Mike had used it to get him some much needed rest, too, but still. . . .

He really should back off, he thought as he climbed the stairs and dropped onto his bed, but not just yet. For the next few days he would just enjoy what was happening and let the devil take the hindmost. Dumb? he thought as he drifted off to sleep. Probably, but he was too happy to worry about it.

Despite his exhausted and sated body, the nightmare still came, and now she was woven into it. Now she was holding the gun that had shot Pete and was now aimed at him.

Chapter

14

Saturday was blazingly hot and the neighbors hid in their air-conditioned houses as the sun baked the Connecticut shore. Brad and Leslie worked out at the gym, then grabbed a quick bite of dinner at the Wayfarer. When they arrived back at Atlantic Beach, three couples sat on lawn chairs behind the seawall, watching the setting sun. There was no breeze and the still, humid air brought out clouds of mosquitoes. Skin slick with insect repellant, huddled close to several citronella candles, Suze and Abby waved them over.

"Back from the gym?" Marie said as Leslie walked over, picked up a bottle of bug spray, and covered every exposed surface.

"Yeah. It was blessedly cool there. Mind if we join you? Brad's getting chairs and more bug juice."

"Of course," Abby said, holding Damian's hand. "You and Brad are becoming quite an item."

You've no idea, she thought, but said, "We enjoy working out together."

"Right," Marie said. "Two healthy people should be enjoying each other's company. Why not?" Her husband, Joe, nodded his agreement.

Everyone but Damian and Suze raised a glass and said, "Hear, hear."

"Suze," Kevin said, seeing his wife's slightly disapproving expression, "stop being such a prude. They are unattached and healthy. What's wrong with that?"

Suze put on her professionally charming smile. "Nothing at all," she said, raising her beer bottle.

Brad arrived with two folded lawn chairs in one hand, a pair of beer bottles in the other, and a can of bug spray under his arm. When they were sprayed and settled, Damian stood. "I'll just take a listen to the kids, make sure they're getting ready for bed." He walked toward their house, leaving Abby alone.

"That's a good idea," Abby said to his back.

"Where are KJ and Eliza this evening?" Joe asked.

"KJ's out with his friends and I think Eliza is in her room on that damned computer. She spends more time on that these days than she does out of the house."

"What's she into in cyberspace?" Abby asked. "I've been worried about my kids on the Net so I have the computer restricted. They can only be on the Internet when I'm around to supervise."

"That's silly. You're making a big fuss over nothing," Suze said. "Most kids, Eliza included, are smart enough to know about giving out personal information. What can they see there that their friends haven't showed them or told them about? It's a big issue over very little."

"I think you're right most of the time," Leslie said, "but there are predators out there, so I think parents have a duty to know what's going on with their kids."

"You know this from your vast experience with having children, I guess?" Suze spat.

"Anyone for a dip in the ocean?" Kevin asked, redirecting the conversation. "It's almost high tide and the water's like a bathtub."

"That sounds like a great idea," Leslie said, remembering the previous evening. Water was so sensual.

"How about some skinny-dipping," Kevin continued, "just for fun?"

"Don't be ridiculous," Suze snapped, slapping his arm hard enough to make him wince. "Maybe you're one of the degenerates we're trying to get rid of." Kevin looked away.

Everyone stood, all anxious to end this suddenly unpleasant gathering. "I'm too lazy to go back to the house," Marie said, "but I can swim in my clothes." Like Leslie, Suze, and Abby, Marie was wearing a T-shirt and lightweight cotton shorts.

"Yeah, me too," Leslie said quickly.

"Sounds good to me," Abby said.

"I wish I were a guy," Marie said as the guys pulled off their shirts. "Then I could just strip to my shorts and forget the rest."

Damian returned and with lots of more-relaxed giggling, the couples trooped to the water's edge and into the gentle waves. "Just stay together," Brad said. "It's a little dangerous to swim in the dark."

"I know just how dangerous," Leslie whispered into Brad's ear.

For several minutes they paddled around, forming and re-forming into pairs and threesomes. As she stood in the warm, chest-high water, Leslie felt someone behind her. Arms reached around her beneath her shirt and hands cupped her breasts, covered only by a lacy bra. Fingers found her nipples and squeezed.

As she closed her eyes to savor the sensations she saw Brad talking with Marie and Joe. Brad? She swivelled her head and saw Damian behind her. "What the hell?" she hissed.

"I saw you and Brad out here last night so stop fussing and admit that I got you hot." He flicked his thumbs over her erect nipples.

"What do you think you're doing?" she hissed. Had he discovered who she was or what she did at Club Fantasy? And, if he did know, did he think that gave him the right? The feel of his hands revolted her and she pulled away and turned to face him. She'd made love with hundreds of men, but it had always been by mutual agreement. This was an assault. She kept her voice low, not wanting to alert any of the others to what was happening. "Keep your hands off me."

"I couldn't resist those tits you keep pushing in my face. What's Brad got that I haven't?"

She tried to keep her voice even. Okay, he obviously didn't know what she did for a living. He was just a macho shit. "Damian," she hissed, "Abby's my friend and you're her husband. Cut it out right now." Her words came out with a vehemence she hadn't known she possessed.

He reached for her, cupped her buttocks, and pushed his erection against her mound. "See what you do to me?"

She reached down and grabbed his erect cock and squeezed. Hard. Then she slid her hand between his legs and grabbed his balls. "I think I've had more than enough of this and if you don't take your hands off me, you'll be very sorry. Very, very sorry." She squeezed more firmly.

He backed away. "All right, slut, take your hands off. I thought you'd want something to liven up the long weeks here, but I can see I was wrong. Maybe Brad's cock is keeping you happy and I guess that's your choice. And your loss."

As he swam away, Leslie dunked her head under the water to try to clear her mind. Good God, what a shit! she thought. Poor Abby—she was obviously right about him. How long before it all blew up? It was none of her business but she would be there if things blew up. Beneath the water, her entire body trembling, she rubbed her breasts through her shirt and bra to scrub off the feel of Damian's hands. How dare he?

She shuddered and tried to calm herself when she saw a shape approaching in the darkness. Had Damian decided to try again? She slumped when she heard Brad's voice. "You're here all alone," he said. "Want company?"

With a sigh of relief she said, "Sure." She took his hands and used them to cup her breasts. The feel of his hands erased the lingering impression of Damian's. "That's what I really want."

As if sensing something, Brad said, "Is everything all right? I saw you talking to Damian."

She wanted to tell him about her encounter but it was a tiny community and telling him might make being in the same place as Damian awkward. She didn't need to make Brad uncomfortable, or worse. She smiled softly as the picture of Brad driving a fist into Damian's nose flashed through her mind. Satisfying as that might be, she wouldn't tell him. After all, Abby was her friend. "Everything's fine. I just missed you."

"We can take care of that later."

The eight of them spent another hour playing in the ocean. The moon rose and there was enough light to sort of see each other so she managed to stay clear of Damian. There were several water fights and, as the full moon rose, lots of romantic floating and kissing. She managed not to stare at Abby and Damian, behaving as if they were lovers. She hoped Abby was happy. Eventually everyone but Brad and Leslie went back to their houses. "Ready to go in?" she asked.

"Not just yet. Take off your shorts and panties and throw them up on the sand." There was a deep sensuality in his voice and she did as he asked. "How well can you float?" He lifted her hips and she lay back on the surface of the ocean. Bracing his feet, Brad held her buttocks and moved between her thighs. Then his mouth found her, sucking at her mound. He rubbed his brushy moustache over her engorged clit until her head went under. He slid his hand up her back to keep her afloat and began to suck.

Between the cool of the water and the heat of his mouth, she was in ecstasy. As he sucked, the hand at her back kept her floating while the other found her opening. He slid his thumb inside her, his mouth never leaving her clit. Heat bubbled in her belly and suddenly exploded, spasms filling her. His tongue didn't stop until he'd rung every ounce of orgasm from her.

He guided her to a standing position, then said, "Drowning isn't part of this. How about we go inside?"

"I'm for that, but I'm not sure I can walk."

He swept her into his arms and carried her to her cottage, and to her bedroom.

Sunday afternoon was heavily overcast so Leslie sat on the sand with her book of Sudoku puzzles. At Brad's suggestion she'd bought a soft lead pencil and a large, pink eraser. Now, after several sessions, she'd moved from easy to moderate and found she was able to solve them without too much difficulty. Occasionally she got to one of the last squares and discovered that she'd reached an impasse so she'd erase and begin again but she was enjoying the mental exercises tremendously.

Most of the other residents were off about their own business and Brad was engaged with his computer so midafternoon Leslie was happy to see Abby arrive at the beach with her two children, who ran off to scamper around the rocks near a jetty. After a bit of small talk, Abby said, "Listen, Leslie, forget what I whined about a few days ago. Damian's fine and we had the best sex ever last evening."

Sure. Right after he grabbed me in the water. She put on a big smile on her face for Abby's sake. "That's fabulous. I'm delighted that he's eased your mind."

"Leslie, it was so wonderful. I just wish he didn't have to leave at noon most Sundays. It's less than an hour's drive back home but I guess he's got business to tend to."

"If I'm getting too nosy please feel free not to answer, but is he good to you?"

"In bed, you mean?"

"Not specifically. You don't have to go into details about your sex life. I just meant anyplace."

"Sure he's good to me. He's the best. In bed he's loving and he's always happy with our lovemaking, and out of bed he makes a good living, is great with the kids, and well, he's great. He brings me presents sometimes and takes me out to meet his show business friends from time to time. He's a terrific husband."

"I'm glad," Leslie said, wishing that Abby sounded a little more convinced. They chatted for about half an hour, then Abby headed off to walk to Middle Beach with her children.

As Abby walked along the beach with Tammy and Mark, she answered their questions and kept a running conversation, but she had time to consider Leslie's question. Was Damian good to her? He certainly had been eager in bed the previous night. They'd come back from the beach, checked on the sleeping kids, then showered off the ocean's salt slick. In bed he'd reached for her and stroked her body over her nightgown. "Take that off," he'd growled, and she had, delighted that they were going to make love. How long had it been?

He was already erect and he quickly covered her body with his. He'd rubbed her inner lips until she was lubricated, then slid his penis into her. He'd come quickly and she'd been so happy that she'd pleased him. Soon he was asleep beside her, snoring gently. It was wonderful—wasn't it?

"Hey, Mom, can we go collect a few more shells?" Mark asked, breaking her reverie.

"Sure."

"Great. Dad says we've got the start of a real good collection." He turned to his sister. "Come on. There are usually some great ones over by the jetty." The two ran ahead and, with a sigh, Abby followed.

* * *

Monday morning, as they sat on the beach, Brad told Leslie that he had to go into the city the following day. "I've got to see the NYPD docs to check on the condition of my leg and the shrink about the condition of my head. Between the two of them they'll decide when I'm fit to go back to the street." He was dreading the visit. He'd have to tell the shrink that the night-mares hadn't abated. Somehow he'd hoped that his relation-ship with Leslie, whatever that was, would chase the demons, but it hadn't.

"Do you want to go back to the street?"

Brad hesitated for several seconds. "I don't know. As much as I love working out there, foiling the bad guys, I'm getting to enjoy my computer work. I'm helping to build cases against bad guys there, too."

"Does the shooting play into that reluctance to go back? You wouldn't be the first or, I suspect, the thousandth, cop to decide that they'd missed getting killed once, and maybe that's enough."

How was she able to understand his thoughts so easily? "I don't know." He shook his head. "Want to drive back to New York with me for the day? Got any shopping to do?"

"Let me think for a moment. If I did, could we stay long enough to have dinner at one of several places I could recom-mend?"

"Sure, and I'd really love the company. It's such a boring drive."

"Oh, so you want me for entertainment."

"Of all kinds, my love." He kissed her lightly on the nose.

Leslie took a moment to consider. Club Fantasy was usu-ally closed on Mondays and Tuesdays so maybe she could have lunch with Rock and Chloe and whatever other folks were around. Marcy would probably be home with the baby but she might be able to get out as well. She looked at her hands. She badly needed a manicure and pedicure, and she might be able to slip in a quick trip to the hairdresser, too.

Somewhere along the line, Leslie had to make a decision not unlike Brad's. Would she go back to entertaining clients? Was her burnout problem solved? Maybe now, with some distance and maybe a little perspective, she could talk to her friends about it. "Sure," she said to Brad, "I'd love to keep you company. I have some friends I might have lunch with, too. What time are your appointments?"

"The doctor's at one, the shrink at two-thirty, then I have to see my boss. Would that work for you?"

"Love it." She started toward her house. "Let me make a few calls and see who's around. August is so undependable."

Within an hour she'd made noon lunch plans with Marcy McGee, one of the owners of Club Fantasy. "I'm really sorry Rock's out of town," Leslie said to Marcy on the phone.

"Me, too. He'll be sorry he missed you. We're really pretty empty and when we have customers, Zack goes over. Rock's back in California with his folks and most of the girls are away, too," Marcy told her.

"Not Rock's dad's heart again, I hope?"

"No, everyone out there's completely healthy. Zack's got the day off tomorrow so he can stay with the twins. How about we have a girl's day out?" Marcy's babies were now toddlers. "I'll give Chloe a call and see whether she can join us."

"That would be great. Need hair or nails? I'm a wreck. Sand and salt are hell on the beauty regimen."

"Always, and since Daddy will be baby-sitting, I'll set things up for both of us," Marcy said. They set up time parameters and Leslie found she was looking forward to seeing her old friends.

While Brad headed downtown to deal with his issues, Leslie joined Marcy for lunch. "I'm really sorry that Chloe couldn't make it," Marcy said. Of medium height, Marcy had always been overweight but dressed stylishly to play down her extra pounds. "She got a last-minute call so she's out on business." Today she was wearing a loose-fitting navy summer dress with big white jewelry. She sported a large brimmed white straw hat that carried the eye away from her size.

"I'm sorry, too. Not that you aren't wonderful company, you understand, but I want all the gossip and since you're not around the building much you're not privy to the good stuff." Since she wasn't one of the entertainers, and never had been, Marcy ran the club, which her sister Jenna and Jenna's friend Chloe had founded, primarily from her apartment via computer. She vetted prospective clients, booked most of the jobs, and took care of the billing, employee compensation, medical insurance, and taxes, everything a thriving business needed. It was a full-time job, one that allowed her to stay home with her eighteen-month-old twins.

"Actually, I do have a bit of gossip," Marcy said with a conspiratorial wink. "I'm pregnant again."

"That's fabulous!" Leslie jumped up and hugged her friend. And that was what she was. When Erika had turned her business over to Jenna and retired to Long Island with her husband, Leslie had been only too happy to join Club Fantasy. It was such a delicious concept, fulfilling fantasies with realistic settings, costumes, whatever was needed to bring life to dreams that men had been masturbating to for many years. "When are you due?"

"Around Christmas. Zack's in shock. With the twins now toddling always in opposite directions, my place is a madhouse, and he's had a bit of trouble adjusting. But he loves it, too."

Leslie reached across and patted Marcy's still flat belly. "This baby's in there by himself? No more twins?"

"No, thank God, and I'm feeling great. And just to balance it all, Jenna's pregnant as well. We seem to do everything in tandem." Jenna, Marcy's twin, was now retired from the Club and living upstate with her lawyer husband. "She's due just after the first of the year. . . ."

"And?"

Marcy giggled. "She's having twins."

"No."

"Yup."

"You two—there must be something in the water. How does Glen feel about that?" Jenna's husband was also a friend.

"Zack's teasing the hell out of him of course, but it's all good-natured. Glen's thrilled."

They chatted for a long time. It turned out that Marcy was tuned in on most of the news. "How about you?" Marcy asked. "How's the vacation going?"

"It's really good. I'm getting lots of rest."

"You're still so pale. I expected you to have one of those sexy tans."

"Not a chance. Number 45 sunblock every day keeps skin cancer away."

With a laugh, Marcy said, "You're right, of course. Have you managed to keep your occupation a secret?"

"You're looking at a designer of professional space." She grinned. "I do design the rooms at the club from time to time."

"Right," Marcy said with a hearty laugh. "That's as good a story as any."

"I considered what to tell folks about what I did and that just sort of came out. They accepted it and I didn't disabuse them of the idea."

"What about guys? Is this strictly a couples area or are there men worth flirting with?"

Leslie briefly debated what to tell Marcy, then blurted out, "There's a guy. His name is Brad and he's sexy and nice and I'm a little too involved for my comfort."

"Why? Geographically undesirable?"

"That's not the problem. He's a Manhattanite all right, but he's a cop."

Marcy's voice rose. "Are you out of your mind?" Several nearby diners turned so she leaned forward and lowered her voice. "A cop?"

"I know, I know. It happened gradually. He found a health club and we went together. We had a few meals. Shit, Marcy, he's really special."

"He's still a cop. Have you . . . ?"

"Yes, and he's great in bed, too." She held up her hand to forestall further comments. "I understand all the problems and I'm going to have to deal with them as they appear."

"I assume he doesn't know about the Club or what you do there?"

"He doesn't know anything and I intend to keep it that way as long as I can."

"Just your luck. You finally meet a great guy and he's occupationally undesirable."

"I love that phrase," Leslie said with a snort. "Occupationally undesirable. Exactly right."

Their lunch lasted several hours: good linguini and a high-calorie dessert, then they sat at adjoining tables at the nail salon and occupied side-by-side sinks at the hairdresser. Leslie caught up with all the news about Club Fantasy and a few of her clients. "Several have asked whether you might make an exception and come back from vacation for an evening. I tried to convince them that you're truly unavailable, but a few are quite persistent."

"Actually, that's gratifying," Leslie said with a chuckle as Marcello combed her out. The color was a bit lighter, but it looked like she'd merely spent time in the sun, as she had. "They can't live without me."

Laughing, Marcy said, "It must be tough being so indispensable."

Her face serious, Leslie said, "That's the real problem. I feel like I'm tied to all these guys somehow. I feel trapped."

"You're never trapped here," Marcy said. "You are your own person. I've got an inkling of what you've been feeling and I sympathize. You've got enough money in the bank, why not take the rest of the year off, not just a month. Find other things that interest you. There must be something you've been itching to do."

"There's really nothing. I've been such a part of this business for so many years that the thought of not entertaining makes me feel empty. But the thought of doing it also makes me crazy." She watched Marcello fluff her hair and untie her apron. "I'm so confused."

"Have you considered working only part-time? Maybe two evenings a week."

"I've thought about a lot of different scenarios, but nothing seems to fit with the way I feel right now. I'm damned if I do and damned if I don't."

"Take your time. We'll field all the calls. You do need to decide about next month, however. It's almost the middle of August and your customers want to set up dates for September. I need to know for scheduling."

"Can I handle it on a case-by-case basis for the moment?"

"Sure. I can see what your guys want and call you from time to time. I assume you've got your laptop with your calendar."

"Sure. Let's just do things week by week. At least that won't make me feel so closed in."

"What about new clients? Shall I consider you off the books?"

"For the moment, yes."

"I'm really sorry about that. You're a great employee and a good friend. I don't know what Jenna would have done without your services when Club Fantasy began."

Leslie took Marcy's hand. "I've loved you both and I'm so happy to see you so happy. Jenna and Glen, you and Zack. It makes me hungry for that kind of life for me, too."

"Might Brad be the one?"

To her surprise, Leslie began to cry. "It's just a summer romance, I'm sure, but it makes me want things I probably can never have. The really sad part is that he's got no idea what I do for a living and I know he'll run when he finds out."

Chapter

15

"The funny thing is that I know exactly what she does for a living, and it doesn't seem to matter. I'm crazy about her." Brad stretched his long legs in front of him and gazed at Dr. Vinour, the department's shrink. "It's really screwing with my brain."

Brad had a lot of respect for the doc, or the head-man, as members of the force had dubbed him. He was in his late forties and because, in addition to being a psychiatrist, he had two brothers who were cops, he seemed to have a unique understanding of the problems that confronted police officers. "Why should it?" the doc said, leaning back in his chair and chewing on the end of his pencil. "It's summer, and she's no doubt attractive. Why shouldn't you have a little fun?"

Brad particularly liked the fact that the doc wasn't into dogma or condemnation. Rather, he was practical and very down to earth. Therefore Brad was more forthright, and he listened and carefully considered what the doc had to say. "It's moving beyond just a 'little fun.' "

"And the problem with that is?"

"It's unprofessional and I feel like I'm sliding down a very slippery slope."

"Has this relationship helped with the dreams?"

Brad dropped his head. "No. I still have them just about every night."

"As bad?"

He hesitated. Every night he dreamed the same ugly encounters with the same ugly people. "I'm afraid so."

"Even when this new woman's in bed with you?"

"We haven't spent the night together yet so I don't know." He shifted his hips and crossed his legs at the ankles. "When Mike asked me to do a little investigative work on this Club Fantasy thing I never thought about the people, the women who work there. I went into it with lots of preconceived notions, which have proven to be nonsense. You know, hookers as drugged-out sleaze, money grubbers, you get the idea. Leslie's such a nice person." He uncrossed his ankles, then propped one calf on his other thigh. "She's warm, and charming, not professionally charming, just, well nice."

"Go on."

"I was a little daunted by the thought of going to bed with a professional, but when it happened I knew it had been inevitable. And wonderful. She's just like any other woman. In bed, I mean." He dropped his feet to the ground. "That's not what I mean. She's special, and great in bed." He shifted in the chair. "I don't know why I'm rambling on like this. It's really nothing."

"It's not nothing, Brad," the doc said. "It's something you have to straighten out in your mind. However, it's not really germaine to getting you back on the job. It's the nightmares that still worry me. It's been more than three months. I'm not saying that the shooting will ever really leave you, but you should be moving past it."

"Do the other cops in my position *move past it* easily?"

"Many do, but some take more time than others, and a small percentage aren't able to get beyond the trauma. I think you'll eventually be able to move on."

Angry, mostly with himself, Brad said, "I'll move on when I'm ready to move on."

"Of course you will, and posttraumatic stress resolves itself in lots of different ways at lots of different speeds. My job here is both to help you, and to make a recommendation to Mike and the folks upstairs about when you're ready to go back into the street. That moment hasn't come yet, in my opinion." He leaned back in his chair. "You haven't had that tooth fixed yet."

"I know."

"It's a constant reminder of everything that happened that night. You feel it when you speak or chew, you see it in the mirror when you shave."

"I know. You keep telling me that. I'm not big on dentists."

"Are you sure that's the only reason? Are you punishing yourself for not being able to save that little boy?"

"Don't be silly," he snapped. "I'll do it when I'm ready." Maybe he was punishing himself but it would all take care of itself in due time. Then he'd make an appointment to have the tooth capped. Brad sighed and crossed his legs at the ankles again.

"You need to figure out when it's time to move on. For everything."

"Actually, Doc, I know I'm supposed to be gung ho to get back on the street, but I'm not sure whether I'll ever be ready."

"Some guys in your situation never go back. You can take disability for awhile and get away from the job entirely for some time. I can recommend it if that's what you want. Or you can stay with the desk job. Either way, you need more time to heal, and decide what you want. You only get one shot at a life, and you need to be sure how you want to spend your three-score and ten."

"Yeah. I guess."

"And let your relationship with your lady go wherever it wants to go."

"I don't know how to do that without letting the fact that she's a hooker get in the way."

"Do you have problems when you're with her or when you think about it afterward?"

"Afterward, mostly. When we're together it all feels right."

"Maybe that fact deserves some serious thought."

Brad recrossed his legs, but said nothing. He'd think about what Dr. Vinour said later.

"Give yourself some time," the doc continued, "and let's see where you are in, say, another month." The shrink checked his appointment book. "We need to see each other in a few weeks. I'm going away the week after Labor Day so let's make it the Thursday of the following week." They agreed on a time and the doctor gave him an appointment card. "Take your time and see what happens with your lady friend. Maybe she'll be of some help to you."

Brad groaned. "How can I deal with her finding out what I know?"

"I've no idea."

Later that afternoon he met with Mike Mitcham in his office at the precinct. "How's it going, Brad? Any intel on Club Fantasy or Carolynne with an 'e'?"

"It's not going too well, I'm afraid," Brad answered. "Carolynne with an 'e' is going by her real name, Leslie, and she hasn't told anyone that she's an escort so it's been impossible for me to pump her for information. I've been getting great results with my computer, though."

"I know. Perry and McLean have been delighted with what you've done on the East Coast Recycling deal and the Volkov matter. Giving you uninterrupted time to follow the money trails has really paid off." He sighed and his shoulders slumped. "However, I can't free up any more money for more time there."

"I've thought about it. I'm paid up there through the end of this week and I thought I'd fund another two weeks myself.

The head-man won't certify me for at least another month so I might just as well be there as here, that is, if you can get the off-site authorization. I'll continue with the searches I've got going and you can add anything else that needs to be done."

"I don't think the time should be a problem if you fund the house yourself. We still want whatever you can come up with on Club Fantasy, too. What did the lady doc say about your leg?"

"I've been working it pretty hard and she says I'm in pretty good shape. The shrink's not so sure. It's my head that's the real problem and that's why he wants me to wait another month."

"Works for me." Mike leaned forward and rested his elbows on his desk. "Brad, that was an ugly time and I really want you to be one hundred percent before you think about going back on the street." He paused. "I've asked around. You seem to have such a talent for the computer stuff that I might be able to get you a transfer if that's something you want. I said *might*, not can, but it's something to think about."

"Yeah, it is," Brad said.

The following Saturday evening the four couples were again together. Since the tide was low, they sat on legless beach chairs on the sand, watching the sun set and eating ice cream sandwiches from the ice cream man. Kevin, Joe, and a bunch of the kids had gathered driftwood earlier in the day and now the bonfire blazed. Mark, Tammy, and Marie and Joe's two youngest had roasted marshmallows after dinner and then had gone home to bed. Leslie had asked a while ago how the two women could be so comfortable leaving their kids home alone.

"It's not too far away," Abby had explained, "and they're in bed before I come back out." She patted her pocket. "Great invention. Both Marie and I have baby monitors and can listen to what's going on in the house, and the kids know it."

"We'll know if anything goes wrong," Marie said, "and it's only a short sprint back home."

The past few days had been idyllic for Brad and Leslie. Brad had told her that he'd been authorized to take two more weeks away, and she was thrilled. They spent the middle of each day apart, Brad working on his computer, Leslie sitting on the beach with some combination of Marie, Suze, and Abby and whichever of their children happened to be around. The evenings and nights were just for the two of them. Their deepening relationship didn't go unnoticed. Damian was the first to mention it. "It seems that there's a summer romance blossoming right before our eyes."

Summer romance. *Keep reminding yourself that this is just that*, Leslie told herself. No real connection with the real world of cop and prostitute. It had been only two weeks since they first met. Two very intense weeks. "We can all feel the heat of those smoldering glances," Damian continued, a nasty edge to his voice. "Isn't once a night enough for you two?"

"That's enough, Damian," Joe said angrily. "It's really none of your concern."

"Oh," Damian said lightly, "I was just commenting on what we've all been aware of."

"It's still none of your business," Kevin said.

"Mark and Tammy don't need to be exposed to all the goings-on."

"Exactly what goings-on would those be?" Brad hissed. "What terrible things have your kids been talking about?"

"We see you out here every night, necking on the beach and naked in the water," Damian said.

"Stop it," Abby said angrily. "The kids haven't said anything, except maybe that they miss you during the week. I miss you even when you're here."

Too bad, Leslie thought. Abby was so sure last weekend that everything would work out. I guess things have changed again. It was difficult for her not to take sides but having experienced Damian's aggression the previous weekend, her already low opinion of him kept getting lower.

"Children, children," Marie said, obviously trying to defuse the situation. "That's quite enough."

Damian looked contrite. "I'm so sorry. I get a bit carried away where my kids are concerned."

Abby merely turned away.

"Let's all let it go," Marie continued. "We've only got two weeks until Labor Day so let's all make the most of them."

"We've had a great time, especially these last two weeks," Joe said, looking at Leslie and Brad. "You two have been a great addition to our little enclave."

"To our little enclave." Kevin raised his beer and they all toasted. "Any chance either of you might come back next summer?"

"I'd like to, but taking time off isn't easy," Leslie said.

"We won't be here next summer anyway," Damian said.

"Why not?" Abby said, totally nonplussed. "I love it here." Leslie knew that Abby didn't enjoy her weeks alone, but she was obviously so angry with her husband whatever he said, she'd argue.

"I heard about the new sex store opening in town and with sex on the beach and all, I don't think this is the right atmosphere for my family."

"Nothing's been going on on the beach that's bothered anyone," Kevin said. "Except you, Damian."

"What about Vicki's store?" Abby said. "I don't know why everyone's getting so upset about it. It's just a store. Maybe, if I'm here when it opens, I'll go in and buy something silly and sexy."

"It's not the kind of place I want to see you patronize," Damian snarled at his wife, "and that's that."

"I think we'd better change the subject and talk about this later," Abby said, standing up and snatching up her things. "I think I'll go back home and lie down. I'm getting a headache."

"I'll come with you," Damian said.

"You don't have to." She stalked off with Damian following.

After they'd left, Brad said, "He's really a shitty guy. I don't know how or why Abby puts up with him."

Leslie thought, *You've got no idea how shitty the bastard is.* "She's most interested in keeping her family comfortable and together, I think."

"People can overlook quite a bit if they want to. Many of us see what we want to see and don't see what we don't," Marie said. Changing the subject, there was a chuckle in her voice as she said, "It's nice to see you two getting along so well. It warms the heart."

Leslie took Brad's hand. "We do get along well." She winked at him and the conversation moved on to other topics.

Later that evening, they were sitting in Leslie's living room. They'd discovered their shared interest in 1940s big band music and the room was filled with the strains of Glenn Miller's *String of Pearls* from a CD she'd bought, with Brad's effusive agreement. "I can remember my folks dancing around the living room to this song," Brad said, his eyes distant, a small smile on his lips.

"They sound like nice people."

"They were and I was really lucky to have had them. I had a great childhood, full of laughter and fun. We spent summers on the Jersey shore, in places not unlike this one. My mom was a schoolteacher and she helped us with our homework, all five of us. She managed to treat each of us as an individual. Sometimes, when I listen to my cohorts at work talk about their ugly memories I worry that my family was too nice to harden me enough."

"I'm sure you can be tough when you need to be."

"What about you? Good parents?"

"Yeah. They were the best. As an only child I guess I longed for a brother or sister, but my mom and I were, and still are, best friends. My dad was great, but Mom was something special. I could talk to her about anything. She answered all my questions about sex. My school friends would ask me stuff so I'd ask her, then relay the answers. She was amazingly enlightened and unflappable—for a mother."

"She sounds wonderful. I hope I can meet her some day." Leslie felt her stomach clench. Thinking about the future was a minefield. Therefore she was glad when Brad stood and held out his hand. "Dance with me."

Leslie did quite a bit of slow dancing with her clients. In addition to being sensual, it lightened the atmosphere and often helped smooth over the rough spots at the beginning of a session. This, however, was different, delightfully so. Brad was a great dancer, smooth, flowing, leading her with gentle pressure in the small of her back. He made it all feel comfortable and natural. "Where did you learn to dance?"

"From my folks," he said, his mouth close to her ear, his warm breath heating her blood. "My mom felt that, although this kind of dancing had gone out of style long ago, it was a skill that would stand me in good stead eventually." He held her more tightly and whirled her around the room. "She was certainly right."

They felt so good together that Leslie felt as if she could go on this way forever. That was dangerous. Whenever Brad made reference to things they'd do when they got back to the city after Labor Day, she aimed the conversation in another direction. There was no way that anything could come of their relationship after Labor Day. He'd go back to being a cop and she'd go back to being a prostitute. Suddenly the fact that their idyll was half over leaped into the front of Leslie's mind. In two weeks they'd go back to the real world and probably never see each other again.

She snuggled close and draped her arms around Brad's neck as they danced. She wanted him fiercely, to hold her, to make love with her, to help her enjoy their remaining weeks and stop thinking about what might have been. She tipped her face up, and he lightly touched his lips to hers. Throughout the next cut on the CD they danced, mouths together, tasting, questing. Finally their feet stopped moving and the kiss deepened. Purrs and low growls filled their ears, so mingled that it was impossible to sort out who made which sound.

"God, you feel and taste so good," he said, his palms making slow circles on her back.

She tangled her fingers in his hair, longer now than it had been when she arrived. "Back at you," she said, her voice hoarse.

She was wearing a white tank top so it was easy for his hands to slither beneath the back of her shirt and touch her skin. "Before this goes any further," she said, "I feel all sticky. Too much bug spray and sunscreen. I need a shower." She pulled away and winked. "Wanna join me?"

"I get the soap first," Brad said with a grin.

They stripped in the bathroom, each taking time to appreciate the other's body. When he reached for her, Leslie slipped away and turned on the water. When it was adjusted to the right temperature she climbed into the stall shower with Brad behind her. "Hey. You have one of those handheld shower things." He unhooked it and sprayed water on her back, then she took it and wet him down. She poured body wash on her scrubber and began to wash the scum from her body.

"That's girly stuff," Brad said, reaching for the bar soap. As they washed they kept bumping into each other in the small enclosure. When his back was turned, she rubbed the scrubber over his back. "Girly stuff indeed."

"It smells like a girl," he said, "but it feels nice when you rub it over my skin." She rubbed, continuing down to his cheeks.

"Turn around." She scrubbed his chest, whirling the scrubber over his swirls of hair. Then she moved lower, stroking his cock, watching it swell.

"You're wasting soap," he said with mock seriousness, "making me larger. More area to wash."

She giggled, cupping his balls in her slippery fingers. When his breathing thickened, he grabbed the scrubber from her hand and poured more body wash on it. "My turn." He moved behind her and slowly washed her back. The scrape of the rough fabric made her skin tingle delightfully.

Then, rather than turning her to wash her front, he pressed her back against his chest and picked up the bar of soap. "I like it better this way." He wiggled his body so it rubbed against her back as his soapy hands roamed over her breasts and belly. She rested her head against his shoulder, closed her eyes and reveled in the feelings, his slippery hands, the hot water pouring over her body, all conspired to increase the sensuality.

"Let's see what this can do," Brad said, lifting the shower head from its hook. He sprayed her chest, then moved the spray down so it shot water onto her mound.

"Umm," she purred, then took the shower from him. She turned a knob on the side until the water pulsed from the head, then turned it on him, spraying jets of water onto his rising cock.

"Damn, that's dynamite. I want you right here, right now, but I'm afraid of doing bodily injury in here." He took the shower from her and replaced it on the hook. He dropped his voice. "You know that most household accidents happen in the bathroom."

"I'm not sure this is what they mean," she said, grabbing a towel, "but last one to the bedroom is a rotten egg."

They dried each other, then he stretched out on the bed and she straddled his legs. She rubbed her erect nipples over his chest and licked her way down his body. Her tongue delved into his belly button, then lower still until she could flick her tongue over the tip of his cock, already hard and reaching for her mouth.

She'd never been able to "deep throat" but she licked the length of him, then sucked the head of his erection into the hot depths of her mouth. Her head bobbed, sucking and releasing until he grabbed the back of her hair. "You'd better cut that out before I do something I don't want to do."

"Why not?" she said with a grin, then sucked a bit harder, making his hips twitch.

"It's really okay?" he asked, sounding surprised and using her hair to force her to look at him.

"Most definitely okay." She returned her mouth to his cock and brought him to the brink, then over it. He groaned loudly, thick semen filling her mouth. Although she swallowed most, small amounts dribbled onto his belly.

"Oh God," he groaned as she crawled up beside him. As she stretched out next to him she realized that, although she was quite skilled at oral sex, nothing she'd done had been the least artificial. She'd done everything because she knew he was enjoying it, not because, as she did with customers, it was the next step in a plan to give ultimate pleasure.

"Two can play at that," he said, crouching between her thighs.

"You don't have to do that."

"I know, but I love doing sexy things with you." His mouth covered her mound and he sucked at her clit while his finger found her vaginal opening. One, then two fingers filled her as he sucked and nibbled. He wet her thoroughly, then blew on her wet flesh, while his fingers slid in and out. She felt herself climb and orgasmic tension build low in her belly.

She looked down at the top of his head, then closed her eyes and let her climax take her. The rhythm of her spasms matched the rhythm of his mouth while his fingers held still.

Later he said, "I felt you come. I could feel your orgasm clenching my fingers. It was the most erotic thing I think I've ever experienced."

"Umm," she purred and curled against him. He pulled the light blanket over their damp bodies and they slept.

Until she awoke to his moans. "Don't. Please." His limbs twitched and his head thrashed back and forth.

"It's okay," she said, shaking his shoulders. "I'm right here. You're in bed. It's okay." She watched him slowly surface, the nightmare fading as he lay beside her catching his breath.

After a quick trip to the bathroom he returned to the bed and cuddled beneath the blanket beside her. "I'm so sorry I woke you."

"It's okay. That must have been quite a nightmare."

"I have them a lot. I'm really sorry I woke you. That's why I prefer to sleep at my own place."

She smoothed her palm over the deep scar on his thigh. "The shooting?"

His sigh was long and deep. "Yeah. I can leave it for hours at a time during the day but at night it's much more difficult."

"I can imagine." She stroked his leg. "It's really okay if I wake up. Do you think you can rest now or should we watch some TV?"

"Usually I can't but with you here," he said, pulling her close, "I think I might be able to fall back to sleep. If this happens again, I'll go back to my place."

"Don't. I want to be here for you. Sleep is highly overrated."

He quickly fell back to sleep but it was a long time before she did. She wanted to help, but didn't know how. She pulled him close, hoping that her presence would drive out some of the evil spirits. Eventually, they both slept, and slept soundly until morning.

Chapter

16

Around ten o'clock Monday morning Suze knocked on Leslie's door eager to have a talk with her about this erotic emporium business. Leslie had become one of Vicki's staunchest supporters and Suze knew that a few well-chosen words would turn her around. If Leslie finally saw what was right, many of the rest of her friends would follow along.

Suze couldn't fathom how Leslie and her friends on Atlantic Beach had managed to get so many of the locals convinced that this business was a good idea. Why couldn't they see that it would cheapen their perfect little town? Suze had gotten very little sleep the previous night and had finally come to the conclusion that Leslie was the key, the one she had to convince. "It's Suze," she called loudly through the screen door, "and I've brought donuts."

Donuts. She'd driven all the way to the Dunkin' Donuts on Route 1 to get this offering and she was sure it would work.

"I'm in the bedroom on the phone, Suze," Leslie called from the upstairs bedroom. "Come on in and just give me a few minutes."

"Sure, Leslie," Suze said, setting the donut bag on the table in the dining area. "How about I make coffee?"

"Great. I'll just be a few minutes." Leslie closed the bedroom door.

In the kitchen Suze found the coffeemaker the hotel had put there with a can of coffee beside it. As she counted the scoops, she wondered at the secretiveness of her neighbor. This call was probably just Brad, but even when they were together on the beach, when her cell phone rang, and it had rung several times over the past week, she answered it then made sure to hold the conversation in complete privacy. What could be that private that often? Was she dating a married man? She was evasive about the exact nature of her business, too. What was that all about?

Suze heard the musical chime of Leslie's cell phone and, since it was out on the counter in the charger and in plain sight, she looked at the screen. The Club and a phone number was all it said. The Club? What kind of club? Was she doing the decorating for some kind of nightclub? The chiming stopped and Suze assumed that Leslie's voice mail had picked up. The Club? Curious, she made a mental note of the phone number. The Club?

When Leslie emerged from the bedroom Suze told her that there had been a phone call on her cell and that the caller had probably left a message. "I thought it might be important," she said.

Leslie took her cell phone into the bedroom and reappeared a few minutes later. "Suze, I'm so sorry. Things have been really hectic this morning. Business stuff."

Suze considered asking what The Club was, but thought better of it. Maybe she'd do a little sleuthing later.

The two women sat at the small dining room table rehashing the now well-worn arguments about the shop over coffee and donuts. Little was being accomplished, Suze realized, and she was so curious about the phone call that she didn't even make her strongest case. There's something going on here, she thought, and maybe it will cut Leslie down to size. Miss

Perfect. Even Eliza had been hanging around her recently. Something was nagging at her and Suze couldn't let it go.

"Suze, I'm sorry, but I really think you're wrong about this. I guess it isn't the type of thing a mayor wants, but it's free enterprise and from what I understand there's nothing against it in the zoning laws or anything else for that matter."

Suze finished the last of her coffee and stood. "I'm sorry, too, but I guess we might as well agree to disagree. Vicki's not going to get this done if I have anything to say about it, and that's that."

Leslie shook her head. "I don't think there's much you can do about it but you're the mayor."

"That I am and Vicki better not forget that." She picked up her mug and plate and put them into the dishwasher. "Okay, well, I'm off."

Suze couldn't wait to get back to her house. Although it was probably something totally innocuous, she had the bug in her brain and she couldn't shake it loose. She flopped on the sofa and, after giving the matter a bit of thought, she dialed the New York City number. "Good morning, this is Rock," a man's voice said. The voice was soft, soothing, and rather sexy. "Can I help you?"

She was fishing in the dark, but she'd done this kind of thing on occasion. She needed to say very little and let the person at the other end of the phone do all the talking. She realized that her phone number would come up on the other person's caller ID so she had devised a story. "Leslie told me about you and I thought I'd call." That was open ended enough.

"What did she tell you about us?"

That was a question she didn't know how to answer. Us? Well let's give him a bit more rope. "She told me about The Club." Whatever that was.

"And?"

God, he was such a pain in the ass. Hmm. What now? "Well . . ."

She heard a huff of breath. "Okay, I'm sure this is a bit awkward for you. I assume you're in Connecticut, where Leslie is. I don't know how much she told you, but I'm sure you know that we cater to women as well as men. Leslie usually gets a better idea of what fantasy you want but maybe it's easier to talk to a man. How much did you discuss with her? Do you want to set up a date now?"

Suze's mind was whirling. What the hell was The Club? They cater to women as well as men? It didn't sound like a nightclub. What kind of fantasy? "Date?"

"Listen, maybe you better talk to Leslie a little more," he said, suddenly sounding suspicious. "She can set things up."

"Okay," Suze said, "I'll do that." She quickly hung up, her breathing rapid and her hands sweaty. What the hell was going on? Whatever it was, she knew how to begin to find out. She'd call local police headquarters and start with the desk sergeant. When a familiar voice answered, she said, "Hi, Owen, this is Suze. Can you do me a favor and use your reverse directory and find out the address for this phone number? And see whether anyone around knows anything about it." She gave him the number she'd just called.

"What kind of things are you looking for?"

"I haven't the faintest idea but I smell something fishy. Just do it for me."

"Sure thing, Madam Mayor."

An hour later, the phone rang. "Mayor Murdock, this is Owen Childress over at police headquarters. Where did you get that number?"

"That's neither here nor there. What did you find out?"

"I got the address then phoned a friend in that precinct. I asked about it and got quite an earful."

"Earful about what?"

"The address is a brownstone in the east fifties. It's listed as a residence of a man named Martin Rockford but in reality it's a place called Club Fantasy. He lives there but he's really the bouncer for a sex club. The cops have had it on their radar for a long time but they've never been able to pin anything specific on him or anyone there. Of course, those high-priced places usually have the dirt on lots of guys in high places so the bigwigs usually don't want any waves."

"Huh? What exactly are we talking about?"

"I'm sorry, Mayor. I guess you wouldn't know anything about places like that. It's a brothel, catering to a very high-class clientele. You know, two-thousand-dollar-a-night stuff. Oh, the cops can't get any real evidence on them. It supposedly entertains without any sex, but everyone over there knows what really goes on. I hear it files taxes and everything." His laugh was rich. "I wonder whether they have a health plan."

Suze's mind was whirling, fixated on one word. "It's a brothel?"

"That's what my friend tells me. It's owned by a pair of twins named Jenna and Marcy Bryant—they're both married now, he says—and a single gal named Chloe Whitman. I need to ask you again. Where did you get that number?"

"Never mind. Thanks." She hung up. Leslie had something to do with a brothel. She smiled. Of course. It all suddenly made perfect sense. She was a hooker. A high-priced call girl, like the kind who worked for Heidi Fleiss. She'd read all about that woman. Her grin widened. No wonder she could afford to take a month off and rent a house and car. No wonder she was so vehemently in favor of Vicki's sex shop. No wonder!

What a dynamite piece of information, but what to do with it? How could she handle this to make the most mileage? How to best discredit her and her damned support of Vicki's Erotic Emporium? That was a question worth pondering for awhile. She had two weeks before Labor Day.

In the end, the secret didn't even keep past that day. Late that afternoon, Suze, Marie, Leslie, and Abby were watching both of Abby's children and two of Marie's play in the sand.

Brad was closeted with his computer, Joe was at work, and Kevin was playing tennis. "If anyone wants to try some, Joe called before and told me he was bringing something new home. Carl's created a sort of jelly roll with veal rolled around mozzarella cheese and spinach. He's going to bake it at the store and you're all invited to sample some."

The agreement was immediate and unanimous. "He also said that Vicki's place looks to be almost ready. He's got no idea how she's gotten it done so fast, but some guys are putting up an 'Opening Soon' sign just below one that has the name Vicki's Erotic Emporium in deep pink script."

"She told me she was hoping to have it ready just after Labor Day," Leslie said.

"You still don't see anything wrong with that?" Suze glared at Leslie until it made her truly uneasy.

"I really don't," Leslie said. "The way she explained it to me it sounds like it won't even be offensive to the most delicate sensibilities. The back will have locked doors so no one can wander in without permission."

"It figures you'd think so," Suze snapped, "being what you are."

"Excuse me?" Marie said. "What the heck are you talking about?"

Suze just shook her head and glared at Leslie, her fingers twisting at the hem of her shorts. "It just figures."

"Come on, Suze, what's up?"

Leslie was pretty sure she knew what was up. Somehow Suze had found out about her real occupation. It was written all over her face. "It's okay, Suze," she said. "You might as well spit it out."

"She thinks everything about sex is okay. Do you know why?" When everyone stared at her, she continued, "Because she's a whore. A professional hooker. She has relations with men for money."

There was a long period of absolute silence during which Leslie couldn't control the urge to glance at Brad's cottage. No sign of him. "Leslie?" Marie finally said.

"Suze is right. I'm not an interior designer, I'm a very highly paid escort."

Abby stared at her. "You mean you're with men for money?"

"That's what it means," she said, miserable that Suze's revelation would mean the end of her relationship with everyone at Atlantic Beach, especially Brad. "I'm sorry I lied to you all, but I was hoping that I could make some friends without the judgmental stuff I'm seeing now." She squared her shoulders. "I'm not ashamed of what I do but I know people's knee-jerk reactions and I was hoping to avoid that."

"Not ashamed?" Suze snarled. "You're a call girl. You should be ashamed."

"I'm not going to apologize for what I do, but I will explain. I make love with men for money. Actually, I think most of you did that too at one time or another."

"I've never . . ." Suze sputtered.

"Did you make love with Kevin before you were married?"

"That's none of your business!"

"Okay, you're right. Let's just say that a woman has a nice dinner with a guy, then they go to a movie. He pays for everything, hoping he'll get lucky. She knows they'll make love afterward because she sort of likes him. At the end of the evening they do. How is that so different from what I do, except that I take the money up front? And, by the way, it's a lot more than just the cost of dinner and a movie but my clients feel it's worth it."

"Oh, please. It's not the same at all," Suze said, her voice rising. "It's illegal and immoral."

"It is illegal but it wasn't always. A hundred years ago, before Queen Victoria got all huffy about it, having a mistress was perfectly acceptable. I assume you've all seen movies like *Gigi*. The guy has had a series of mistresses and offers the job to our heroine. She wants marriage and that's her choice, but it wasn't an evil, behind-closed-doors offer. It was perfectly acceptable."

"That's not the point. We're living now, not then."

"True. It's a crime, but who's the victim? Not the guy; he gets what he wants. Not me, I'm very well paid for something that's mine—my body—that I have a right to sell."

"How about family values?"

"That's a cliché of the worst kind. Do men cheat on their wives? You bet, but is what I do so much worse than standing around a bar and letting some married guy pick me up? Or doing it with my boss on lunch hour?"

Suze was obviously outraged. "I can't believe you're defending prostitution."

"Actually some of the things she's saying make sense," Marie said. "I guess I never thought about it that way."

Suze whirled on Marie. "You can't mean you agree with her?"

"All I said was that I understand where she's coming from. It's worth thinking about." She reached out and took Leslie's hand. "How in the world did you get into"—she stumbled over the words—"what you do?"

Leslie told the three women a little about Kayla and Erika, and eventually Marcy and Jenna and Club Fantasy, using only first names and calling the brownstone The Club.

"You mean they fulfill men's fantasies with costumes, props, and stuff?" Marie asked.

"That's quite an idea," Abby said, speaking for the first time since Suze's revelation. "I can understand a guy wanting something like that."

"Abby! You of all people should understand how dangerous this is for all marriages."

"If Damian were going to do something outside our marriage I'd certainly want him to do it with someone he's not going to fall in love with or get some disease from. It is safe, isn't it?"

"It most certainly is. Condoms, no drugs. Little risk of any kind."

"What about cops? Don't you worry?" Marie asked.

"Not really. My bosses are very careful, and I think they have quite a client list, people who wouldn't want their names revealed."

"What about Brad? Does he know?"

Leslie's face fell. She'd been so involved in defending what she did that for a moment she'd forgotten about him. "He doesn't know. Yet."

"He will now," Suze said, her face contorted with anger. "You can be sure of that."

"I'll tell him. You don't have to," Leslie said. Suze stalked off and a moment later the three remaining women heard her front door slam.

"Where is Brad today?"

She again glanced at his house. "He's working on his computer." Now he would find out about her and that would be the end of their summer fling. She already missed him. Her gaze flicked between the two women. "I'm sorry I was dishonest with you both. I guess I was hoping that I could spend my month here without any of you ever finding out."

"I'm sorry you didn't trust us enough to be honest," Marie said, "but seeing Suze's reaction I can understand why you did it."

"I just wanted to have normal friends with normal jobs and normal lives. I have wonderful friends at work." She told them about her deep friendship with Jenna, Marcy, and Chloe. "There's Rock, too. He lives on the premises and is a bouncer of sorts. We've never had to use him as such but he's built like a brick wall and when guys meet him, if they had any hanky-panky on their minds, it disappears."

"Ever had anything bad happen?" Abby asked, her eyes wide.

"I've had the occasional dissatisfied customer who demanded money back, but other than that, no."

"Did he get his money back?"

"Sure. It's not worth hassling a guy but the penalty is that he's not welcomed back. A guy who's looked long and hard to find someplace like ours doesn't usually make a fuss. He makes his dissatisfaction clear and we fix the problem the next time."

"I have to say that I'm dying of curiosity," Marie said, leaning closer. "Have you ever been with someone famous? Someone I might have heard of?"

"Absolutely, but that information is strictly confidential." She grinned. "We don't kiss and tell at my place. If we did, we'd be out of business in a New York minute."

"Of course. That makes sense. I'm sorry I asked."

"Don't be. It's a natural question and, frankly, I wish I could tell you about some of the people I've been with. Actors, musicians, politicians, all kinds of celebrities."

"Leslie," Abby said, and Leslie could see that she was blushing. "What's it like, doing what you do?"

Chapter
17

Leslie kept it light, not mentioning the negative, burned-out feelings that had led her to Sound's End. "I have to say that I love my job. I get paid to be with wonderful men, go to interesting places, and have great sex. What's not to like?" Okay, occasionally one of the guys was a jerk, with bad breath and body odor, but that wasn't worth mentioning. On the whole she loved her job.

"That's a wimpy answer and not what I wanted to know," Marie continued. "Come on, fess up. What's the sex really like? Lots of kinky stuff?"

Leslie thought about downplaying the things that went on at Club Fantasy but decided to be honest. "Kinky has different meanings for different people." She put her hand up to forestall their comments. "In the beginning I would have thought lots of the things I do now as a matter of course were kinky but I've grown in the years I've been doing this and now there are only a few things I won't do and actually few things I don't enjoy." She remembered Cameron. He had been wonderful, teaching her about wine, foods of varied countries, music, sports. He was interested in almost everything and thoroughly enjoyed teaching her. Delightfully, he was as eclectic about his sexuality as he was about everything else and he taught her about the more off-center areas of sex.

She recalled one particular evening several months into their relationship. After a rather boring concert they had ended up at his apartment.

"I want to play tonight," Cameron said as they walked into his bedroom.

"I'm always eager to play with you," Leslie said, aroused by the gleam in his eye. "What kind of game?"

"My kind." He leered at her playfully. "Will you trust me?"

"Of course, Cameron. What do you want me to do?"

His grin revealed his white teeth. "Oh, Carolynne," he winked, "with an 'e,' you're fabulous. I predict that the name Carolynne with an 'e' will become famous in some circles. By the way, is that a new dress?"

Puzzled by his abrupt change of subject, she shook her head. "I've worn it a few times. Why?"

"It's not very becoming. The color's wrong and I don't really like it. I want to destroy it. I'll pay you to replace it, of course."

Her gaze dropped. The dress was a pale, mossy green with a tight bodice and deeply scooped neckline. Since Cameron's comments in the taxi months ago, she always wore skirts on dates and this one was full and calf length. His dislike of her dress reminded her that she hadn't been sure about the color when she'd purchased it but the saleslady had insisted that it brought out the blond in her hair. She'd have to learn to trust herself more. "No need to replace it, Cam. You have impeccable taste and if it doesn't do it for you, then let's get rid of it."

"That's my girl." He pulled a length of soft rope from a dresser drawer. "Stretch out on the bed and extend your arms straight out from the shoulders."

She guessed immediately what he wanted and gladly did as he asked. He quickly tied the cord to one wrist then to the side of the bed frame then did the same to the other wrist. She tested their tightness and discovered that the movement of her torso was totally restricted.

He'd tied her a few times before, and they'd agreed on a safe word, but each time her arms had been secured above her head, giving her a little freedom of motion. At first she'd been a bit skeptical about bondage, but she'd quickly enjoyed the helpless feelings the bindings created. While she was tied he had teased and played with her and, since she couldn't do anything to bring on her orgasm, she'd gotten more excited than she'd been previously. She'd also learned how to perform oral sex to his exacting standards since, if she didn't get him sufficiently erect he'd refuse to let her climax. She wondered exactly what he was planning this time, but she trusted him completely and was sure he had something erotic in mind.

While she watched intently, trying to guess exactly what he was up to, he rummaged in the drawer again and withdrew a length of padded wood about eighteen inches long. "We haven't gotten too adventurous as yet, but tonight I'm in the mood."

He put the spreader between her ankles and tied one ankle to each end, preventing her from drawing her knees together. With a few deft movements he fastened the bar to the foot of the bed then he slowly removed his jacket, shirt, and slacks. "Time for some fun. You know that all you have to do is *holler uncle* and I'll stop, right?"

"I remember." "Holler uncle" was their stop signal.

"I want you to have no distractions so you can concentrate on your pleasure." He showed her two cotton balls, then placed them over her eyes and held them in place with a long silk scarf tied over one temple. "I wouldn't want you to have to lie on the knot," he purred. She was unable to see anything. "They say that being deprived of one sense enhances the others," he purred, then kissed her deeply. "You'll have to let me know."

She focused on her other senses. She inhaled and smelled a

trace of his cologne then licked her lips and tasted him. She heard him move around the room, then felt him settle on the edge of the bed.

"Listen. What do you hear?"

She listened. "Scissors," she said, easily identifying the snick.

"Right you are, so you get a present." His kiss was warm, and his hand on her breast kneaded her still well-covered flesh. She moaned, already aroused.

"Now I get a present," he said. She heard the scissors rend fabric and realized that he was cutting her dress up from the bottom. The shears were cold against her skin as he worked his way up the center of the bodice, splitting the center of her lacy bra, then sliced up one sleeve to the neckline, parting her bra straps too. "They make this look easier in dirty movies," he said, yanking the pieces of her dress and bra out from under her. "There," he said with a deep breath. "Much better." The cold of the scissors against her hips as he cut her panties made her try to bring her thighs together, but the restraint between her ankles made that impossible.

"Okay, here's the next sound for you to try to identify." She heard a sort of whooshing sound but had no idea what it was. "Stumped?"

"Yes," she admitted.

"I'll give you a minute to think about it." She heard him walk into the bathroom, then return. "Lift your hips." She did and he slipped what felt like a sheet of plastic beneath her. "Okay, let's try this sound."

"That's water. In some kind of bowl or pitcher."

"Right you are again." When she felt the warm cloth on her pubic area she started to put the pieces together. She said she trusted him, but was this outside her comfort zone?

He washed her carefully, then she heard the shears working on her pubic hair. "You've figured it out, I assume," he said, scissors snicking. He stopped. "Is it okay with you?"

She hesitated. She knew he'd stop if she hollered uncle, but did she want to? What about afterward when it started to grow out? Would it be uncomfortable? This was his evening and she cared for him a lot, wanted him to enjoy her. "Does this excite you?" she asked.

"Very much."

"Then go for it."

"I'm egotistical enough to think that you'd do almost anything for me, but I don't want that to be the only reason."

Leslie thought. "It's not. Everything we've done together has been an adventure and I've learned so much, sexual and not. I want to try."

He kissed her again. "Good. And thank you for trusting me."

She heard the whooshing sound again and felt his fingers rub shaving foam over her skin. Slowly and gently he stroked her with a razor until her pubic area was smooth and hairless. She felt him settle back and wash her completely. Then he untied one wrist and placed her hand on her crotch. "How does it feel?"

She slid her fingers over her newly shaved skin. The feel of her fingertips on her naked flesh was exciting in an entirely new way.

"You look so sexy. I can see your lips clearly and I can now watch them swell as you get more and more excited. It's a singular pleasure."

She lay her hand at her side. "I'm glad I please you."

More rustling then something cool was being spread on her newly shaved skin with deft fingers. "This is supposed to take care of any razor burn."

His fingers burrowed in all her folds, rubbing the lotion into her skin. "You need to see this," he said when he'd finished. He removed her blindfold and wheeled a free-standing mahogany mirror next to the bed, then adjusted it so she could see her completely shaved crotch. It was the most erotic thing she'd ever seen. She could see her hairless outer lips and the inner lips peeking out from between. "Now watch," Cameron said.

From the dresser drawer he pulled a thick, plastic dildo. "Watch as this disappears." He pressed it against her already-wet opening and, her eyes never leaving the mirror, she saw it slowly sink into her. She could feel it filling her and see him pull it out, then push it in again. Watching and feeling, she was starring in her own erotic spectacle.

"I can see how hot you are," he said, his cheek against her upper thigh, near enough so she could feel his hot breath on her clit, "so come for me now." He thrust the dildo in and out, then flicked her engorged clit with the tip of his tongue. She could see herself in the mirror clearly, see the back of his head, then as he leaned back, his hand on her flesh. It was amazingly erotic and she soared.

"Oh, God," she yelled. "Yes." His tongue flicked out again and she came. "Yes, yes. Do it, do it."

Later, untied, she asked him why he'd given her such pleasure with none for himself.

"I don't understand why you don't get it by now," he said. "I love giving you pleasure, seeing you writhe with it. I thought watching yourself in the mirror would convince you that watching is totally erotic." He patted his crotch. "It makes me hot. Look in the mirror and touch yourself."

"What?"

"I'm going to get undressed while you play with yourself as we both watch. I know you well enough to know you can come again, and I want to be inside you when you do. So play with yourself." He moved the mirror to the foot of the bed so the image of her pubis filled the glass. "I think the vagina is the most beautiful part of a woman's body. Now do it."

Tentatively she touched herself and she saw her fingers move. "I've never seen myself before," she said, stroking her long fingers over her smooth, denuded flesh. "It's making me really hot."

"I knew it would," he said, now naked. "I want to watch you while I stroke my cock." He sat on the edge of the bed and stared at her fingers while he rubbed his hands over his cock and balls.

"It feels almost like I'm touching someone else and other fingers are stroking me."

"Show me. Touch all the best places. It's making me hotter."

Her vaginal tissues were soaked with the juices from her earlier orgasm and she spread the juice over her skin, rubbing all the special spots that Cameron had taught her about. Soon her hips were moving in rhythm with her fingers. As she stroked herself she also watched Cameron's hands on his swollen erection. "Want to make love to me now?" she asked, her voice throaty.

"Make love 'with' you."

She grinned. "Yes, with me."

"I do," he said, "but I'm delaying my gratification." He handed her the dildo. "Use this."

She closed her eyes and slowly inserted the dildo as she touched her clit. "I like to think it's your cock inside me," she said.

"It will be," he said, unrolling a condom over his penis, then pulling the dildo from her fingers and inserting his rigid cock deep inside her. It took him only a moment to come and, as he did, she felt the bubble of her second orgasm grow in her belly. "Don't stop," she begged. "Oh, God, don't stop." His fingers found her clit and, with a few strokes, she came again.

She snapped back to the present and as she looked over at Brad's cottage she thought she saw the second-floor curtains move. "Yeah," she said, turning away and deliberately letting out the breath she'd been holding, "lots of kinky stuff. I do whatever gives my client pleasure."

"Do you always—you know—have an orgasm?" Marie asked, her entire body radiating her curiosity.

"No, not always," Leslie answered honestly. "On occasion I'm not in the mood, but giving a guy pleasure is usually enough to give it back to me."

"Do you pretend? I've seen the occasional erotic movie and the girl always pants, screams, 'Yes, yes,' and explodes. That can't be real."

"It's not, and I do have to fake it from time to time, but whether I come or not, I always give my clients a good time and that's what they pay me for."

"What about your family? Do they know?"

"When I started it was difficult telling my folks but after we talked for awhile and they stopped their knee-jerk, negative reaction, they went along. 'It's your life,' my mom said, 'and you have to live it your own way.' Now that I'm happy and safe, they're fine with it."

"Do they live in the city?"

"They used to but now they're down in Florida, living in one of those retirement places. My mom plays bridge almost every day and my dad's taken up woodworking." She grinned. "For my last birthday he carved me a totem that looks like a giant dildo. When I mentioned it to him, he laughed and winked at me."

"He sounds like quite a guy."

"My folks are really understanding, and mentally very young for retirees."

"Do you use your own name?"

"Sometimes. At others I'm Carolynne. With an 'e.' "

"What's the downside to—you know—being what you are? There must be a lot."

"I'm a prostitute and you can say it that way. I know there's a stigma about it, but it's what I am and it's really all right to say it."

"Okay," Marie said. "What's the downside of being a prostitute?"

Leslie let another long sigh slip out. "I diet all the time and can't allow myself to gain so much as a pound. My clients want me a certain way and I've got to be what they fantasize about. I've eaten and enjoyed things during these two weeks that I haven't had in years. I've eaten onions and garlic, and beans without worrying about the gas."

The women laughed, then Abby asked, "That can't be all of it?"

"I know it will sound trivial but I have to read all the time to stay informed and be good company over dinner. I read *Newsweek* and *Time* every week, along with *People* and *Sports Illustrated* and occasionally the *Inquirer* or the *Star* if there's something men might be interested in. Sometimes I study something for a specific guy. Earlier this year I spent considerable time trying to learn about the futures market for a stockbroker who felt that everyone should know how the commodity exchanges work. When I told him I knew very little, he gave me two books to read so I could discuss the subject with his business friends. I had to plow through them even though they were deadly dull. His business associates were really impressed, however, and that pleased him and increased my tips." She looked wistful, then giggled. "I've actually put some of his ideas into practice and my investments are doing really well."

"From what you say," Marie said, "it seems you have guys who see you lots of times. I would have thought it would be a one-time thing. Well, the fulfilling a fantasy part, at least. Wouldn't it be enough to live it out once?"

"I thought so, too, when I joined The Club, but that hasn't been true. Men hone their particular fantasy and then want to relive it over and over. Having returning regulars means it gets easier and easier to give them exactly what they want, and makes filling my calendar easy. If it's the first Tuesday of the month, it must be Bob." Actually Bob *was* the first Tuesday of every month and the sheer predictability was what led her here in the first place. "But I'm well paid so I can't complain too loudly."

"How well-paid?" Abby slapped her hand over her mouth. "Sorry. That just slipped out, and I know it's none of my business, but I'm so curious."

Leslie smiled. When she'd first talked with Kayla, she'd been most interested in the pay scale too. "I make enough to keep me going." When Marie tilted her head to one side questioningly, Leslie continued, "Okay. I'm so used to hiding the details that it's difficult for me to be honest. I make anywhere from five to as much as twelve thousand dollars a week, before taxes."

"Five to . . . ?" Abby sputtered. "A week? Oh, my. That's more than Damian makes. It doesn't show." Abby turned her wedding ring on her finger.

Leslie remembered the large diamond solitaire and two-carat ear studs she wore on weekends. Damian probably likes showing off his money on his wife. At least, she thought, he has good taste. Leslie looked down at her bare fingers. Jewelry had never been her thing. "I guess I don't show it off." She got thoughtful. "Where do I spend my money? I live in an expensive condo in Manhattan, a building with a doorman and concierge, and I suppose the exorbitant rent is my major vice. I have a wardrobe that would choke a horse, but I need it since I go out a lot with my clients. They like to show me off so many of the men entertain us both with dinners and the occasional Broadway show or concert. I have some nice jewelry, too, if that's what you mean, but most of it was given to me my grateful clients."

"How about travel? Damian says when the kids are older

we'll spend an entire summer in Europe, seeing all the famous places."

"I don't travel, except when a client takes me on a cruise or something. This is my first real vacation in several years and I'm not a thing person so I don't buy stuff. Most of what I make I bank."

"Damian likes nice things around him. We have three cars and a big house in the suburbs. He also keeps an apartment in the city for when he can't get home because he's working late."

Leslie gazed at Abby wondering whether she was quite as naive as she appeared. Apartments in the city were usually for only one purpose. "My mother always used to say that there's nothing as individual as the way people spend their money."

"Will you tell Brad what you do?"

Brad!! She'd been so involved in telling Marie and Abby about Club Fantasy that she'd actually pushed Brad to the back of her mind. She thought about the curtains she'd seen move earlier. "I'll have to before he finds out some other way, if he hasn't already."

"Will he understand?"

"I've no idea," she said softly as she felt her stomach muscles clench. She wasn't at all sure that he wouldn't immediately head back to the city and out of her life. It shocked her to realize how painful that would be.

Wanting to delay her encounter with Brad as long as she could, she said, "You don't seem to be too shocked by what I do."

"I'm still taking it all in," Marie said, "but since I've gotten to know and like you it's difficult to be too judgmental."

"I think I'm still in shock," Abby said, "but that's not all bad. Part of me is repelled, and part is fascinated. I've grown to like you so much, and you seem so—I don't know—sane, that if you are able to do it without bad feelings, I want to accept it."

Leslie felt tears gathering behind her eyes. She had never expected these two wonderful women to be so open-minded.

"What's the weirdest thing you've done?" Abby asked, then quickly added, "I don't mean to pry, but I'm so curious by what goes on in places like yours."

Leslie pulled herself together and thought about an answer that wouldn't shock the women too badly. She'd done so many off-beat things that she wasn't ready to mention to Abby and Marie, then she remembered Easton. "Let's call him Mike. He paid me and before that first evening he told me exactly what he wanted and we set up a room for him."

"Set up a room?"

"That's how the place I work does things. We find out what fantasy the customer wants to live out, then create a location in one of the rooms of our building where it can happen."

"What did he want?"

"You asked for unusual. This was a first. We used a room we call the motel room, a sort of plain vanilla room we can dress up as the client wishes. In this case, we moved in a leather recliner with a goose-necked lamp to the foot of the chair." When Abby drew a breath, Leslie raised her hand, wanting to tell this story in her own way.

"He arrived first, then I walked in dressed as he had asked, in white blouse, a very short red skirt, mesh stockings, and a pair of red sandals with five-inch high heels. I think of them now as my whorehouse shoes and I've worn them with him several times since that first time."

"Come on, I'm dying here. What exactly did he want?" Marie asked.

Leslie grinned. "Mike arrived with a suitcase filled with all the equipment needed to give me a full-blown pedicure."

"He wanted to give you a pedicure? That's it? I don't get it. That's not sexy."

"For him it was the most erotic thing he could do. He had a thing for feet and, when we met to talk about what he wanted, he fell in love with my toes. So I sat in the lounge chair, leaned all the way back and wiggled my toes while he positioned the lamp to shine on my tootsies. He spread a towel over the foot of the chair and carefully positioned my feet on it, then laid out all his stuff on it. He'd asked for a large bowl of warm water so he soaked and massaged my feet for almost half an hour. Then he filed my toenails, used cuticle cream, and eventually painted them flaming red."

"That was it?"

"No. He spent almost fifteen minutes blowing on the polish to be sure it was dry, then spent another half an hour stroking himself while he played and sucked on my toes. Eventually he used my soles to rub himself until he came. Finally he washed my feet again, put all his stuff back in his suitcase and left."

Abby's eyes were wide and Marie's jaw hung open. "You're kidding."

"Nope."

"He paid you for that?"

"He paid very well, and has paid several times since. It's his fantasy and I don't judge him. He's totally happy, and well able to afford it."

"Okay," Abby said, "I think my mind is more blown by that story than by what you do."

"Mine, too," Marie said.

Chapter

18

Brad stood at the front window of his cottage and watched through the curtains as Leslie talked to Marie and Abby. He hoped the two women would be accepting. The three had become close and he hated the thought of Leslie losing two friends.

As soon as Suze arrived home she'd called him and told him about Leslie's occupation. "I'm not accusing her of anything, but I thought you should know, you being a cop and all." Brad had remained silent as Suze continued. "I know you're involved and this must be difficult for you, but you're entitled to the truth. She hasn't committed any crime here in Sound's End or I'd have her arrested on the spot." After a long silence, Suze had asked, "She didn't take money from you, did she?"

Brad had slammed down the receiver. What now? He had known all along what Leslie did, but she didn't know that he knew. God, he thought, this sounds like a bad soap opera or a political scandal. Who knew what and when? The main thing he needed to decide was how to react. In one way this was good news. He could now pry more openly into the goings-on at Club Fantasy, maybe find out the names of some of their prominent customers.

Okay, stop thinking like a cop, he told himself. *How are you going to do this without letting on that you knew all along?* Unless he could play this just right it would destroy something that had become very important to him. How would he have reacted if he hadn't already known? He took a deep breath and let it out slowly, trying to calm his panic. If this had happened out of the blue he'd have pitched a fit and run. But this wasn't then and he didn't want to run. He'd let her explain then accept her as she was. Would she believe his acceptance of her? He had to pull off an acting job unlike any he'd ever done before.

He watched her end her conversation, rise and cross the road to his cottage. She knocked and he opened the front door. "I'm sure Suze called you as soon as she got back into her house," Leslie said. Her body was stiff as if waiting for a blow.

"She did." He tightened his stomach muscles. "Was what we did just a business opportunity? Get in tight with a cop and it might do you some good in the future?" He hadn't planned those words, they had just slipped out.

"You can't think that," she said softly, her eyes filling.

His shoulders slumped as if all the air had run out of him. "No, I don't. I don't know what to think. I thought we had something going here. I told you my secrets and you seemed to understand. You held out on me." This was an almost intolerable balancing act. He had only told her some of his secrets.

"I know, but I couldn't tell you. What should I have said? 'Hi there, my name's Leslie and I'm a prostitute. Wanna go out with me?' Tell me, how should I have broached the subject?"

He paused, considering his next sentence. "There was no way, was there? I guess I understand that much." He wasn't being totally honest with her either. God, how tangled it was all getting.

"You understand why I didn't tell you or you understand what I do?"

"Both. Neither. I don't know." The entire conversation had taken place in the doorway. Now he stepped back.

Leslie brushed past him and moved into the living room. This was a moment she'd dreaded, but now that it was here she felt an immense weight lifting from her shoulders. Either he'd deal with it or he wouldn't and the decision was his. There was little she could do to affect it.

She watched him tunnel his fingers through his hair, destroying the neat wave across the top. She yearned to comb her fingers through it and ease the wave back into place. "I won't apologize for what I do," she said. "I'm not ashamed of it." Should she give her usual speech about the need to legalize prostitution, that it was a victimless crime, that her body was hers to use as she saw fit? There was no need. He wasn't stupid. He could figure all that out.

"I don't want an apology about your job, or about Club Fantasy, but you were dishonest with me."

"For that I am truly sorry. I hated lying, but I didn't see any other way. You're a cop, after all, my archenemy."

He smiled ruefully. "Yeah, and you're doing something totally illegal."

"It's illegal in New York, but totally legal in parts of Nevada. Does that make much sense?"

"It doesn't have to. On Fifty-Fourth Street, it's still illegal."

"I'm sure you know of people who are doing illegal activities but whom you use for your own purposes. What we do isn't hurting anyone so the police brass leave us alone. I know that my bosses have worked with the police on one or two occasions so maybe that has something to do with it, too."

"Maybe they've got a little black book with the names of people who wouldn't want that fact publicized."

"That's probably true. I can only repeat that what we do hurts no one."

"What's also true is that I am still a cop."

"I care about you," she said, her body waiting for the blow that she was sure would follow. I'm sorry, he'd say, and I'm going back to the city. We won't be seeing each other again.

"I care about you, too." He hadn't said it was over. She allowed her muscles to relax a tiny bit. As he scrubbed his hand over the back of his neck Leslie realized that she had no idea of where his head was. Now that there was a little ray of hope, she wasn't going to give him up without a fight. If necessary. "Can you tell me what you're feeling? I'm sort of out on a limb here."

She watched his shoulders rise and fall. "What we have is too important to me to toss away. I'm no kid and I've finally found a woman who makes me happy, who understands what I'm going through, who makes me feel like I can get past the nightmares. I think I'd like to get to know the woman who entertains men for money. Maybe we can get past this. I want to."

My God. This might work out after all. Could she dare hope that he'd accept her the way she was or, in the end, would he give her the "get out of the business and go straight" speech? Heartbeat still rapid, she said, "I want to as well. We could go feed the ducks at Soundings and you could think this through. The noise would make long silences more tolerable."

"I think we need to talk, or at least I need you to. How about the Italian place on Route 1?"

"Done."

Over dinner, for the second time that day, she went through her beginnings at Courtesans, Inc. She told him about Kayla, Cameron, and Erika without using any real names. "I won't discuss the names of my current employers or the place I work. I will call it 'The Club' but nothing more than that. I'm sorry. I won't lie, but I won't betray my friends."

"I understand that. Tell me what it's like to be a woman

who makes love with men for money. Is it still 'with' when you're getting paid?"

"Of course. I give pleasure, but I get pleasure, too." She spent the next half hour explaining her job, her feelings about legalized prostitution, the way she interacted with the men she entertained.

"What about being with me?" he asked. "And don't give me the usual platitudes. I don't want to hear that I've got the biggest or that I'm the most skillful. I would just like to know whether our lovemaking was different from what goes on when you're working."

"Brad, I care about you. I've known all along that you were a cop and I was what I was. Originally I wanted to be a friend, not a lover. What we became happened by accident. When I'm with you it's different. It's more"—she struggled with the words—"more personal. I give of myself to the men I'm with, but with you it's bigger. I've never said I love you to anyone. It's too important, and I'm not saying it to you now either. Love takes time, it takes really knowing each other, not a two-week summer romance. But what I feel is more serious than I care to admit." She sipped her wine. "At least I can be honest with you now and whatever we build from here on out will be based on honesty."

Brad looked at her over his wineglass. Unwittingly she'd made him feel like more of a rat than he already did. He was still lying to her and she was talking about the value of truth. Maybe he'd never have to tell her what his assignment was. Maybe she'd never find out. And maybe pigs could fly. All he could think of doing was rolling with it and hoping. "You told me that your place fulfills fantasies. Like what?"

"It varies from man to man. Do you have a fantasy?"

Brad blanched and his eyes dropped. "Phew. That's almost too personal. It's really difficult for a guy to discuss things like that."

She placed her hand over his on the tablecloth. "Don't I know it. I spend quite a bit of time getting men to spell out exactly what they want, but when they do it's dynamite."

He had some very active fantasies that involved both lingerie and anonymous sex, but he wasn't about to tell Leslie about them. "I don't think I'm ready for that just yet."

"That's fine. You can see, however, how it might excite some men to act them out. That's what we do."

He thought about how he'd have reacted had he not already known about Leslie's occupation. "I have one other problem with what you've just told me." He sipped his wine. "This is a bit embarrassing." She remained actively silent. That's exactly what she was, not speaking but intent, interested in whatever he had to say next. "I mean us, in bed."

"If you mean how are you in bed, compared with other men, just know this. I never, never compare any man to any other. Ever. Not you, not my customers, not anyone. Every man is wonderful in his own way, and you're fabulous—we're fabulous together. I hope you believe me on that."

Brad's grin was slow to materialize but now that the thought was out of his mouth, maybe they really could move on. "I do believe you."

She squeezed his hand. "Where do we go from here?" she said.

Deliberately misunderstanding her, he said, with a twinkle, "My place?"

He could see the relief in her entire body. "Your place it is. Maybe we should have dinner first, however. I'm suddenly starving."

While Leslie and Brad were having dinner together, Abby fed her children and sent them upstairs to play computer games. She sat in the living room deep in thought for almost an hour until the phone rang. That would be Damian. She'd debated whether to tell him about Leslie and had decided that he'd find out when he arrived anyway. Prostitution, at least the high-class kind that Leslie practiced, didn't seem so bad after she turned everything over in her mind. "Hi, honey," she said.

"How was your day?"

"We found out something really mind-blowing today." She proceeded to tell Damian about Leslie's business.

"She's a whore? Leslie?" Damian sounded totally shocked.

"I wouldn't put it quite that way. She explained her feelings on prostitution and I've done a lot of thinking. I wonder whether it's so bad."

Damian's voice got low and he accented each word. "I want you to listen to me very carefully. She's a whore and that's that. I don't want you to spend any time with that woman ever again."

"That's ridiculous, Damian. She's still the same person she was yesterday and she's become a good friend."

"Stay away from her," he growled, "and keep the kids away, too."

Abby was used to taking Damian's guidance on important issues, but not this. "I think you're wrong about this. She's a nice woman and I'm sorry but I don't want to stop seeing her."

"You heard me. I'm deadly serious. Not one minute with her."

"Thanks for the opinion, Damian. I'll think about what you said." Was she really going to disobey her husband? Disobey? Where had that word come from? It made Damian sound like her father, not her husband.

"Don't think about it, do it. I mean it."

He wasn't her keeper. "I'll talk to you tomorrow evening and I hope, by then, you'll have reconsidered." She put down the phone and ignored it when it rang again a moment later.

In his apartment in Hartford, Damian seethed. Leslie, that little slut. He wasn't good enough for her but that cop, who probably wouldn't make in ten years what he made in a month was. Slut. Whore. He could still feel her breasts in his hands and remembered how she'd pushed him away like some virtuous maiden. She'd pay. Oh yes, one way or the other, she'd pay.

Marie told Joe as soon as he arrived home. "How the hell about that," he said. "More power to her."

"You're not shocked?"

"Surprised, yes, but not shocked. She's a gorgeous sexy woman and I can certainly understand her having all the men she wants. Getting them to pay for it is another matter. She must be fabulous in bed."

Marie cuffed her husband on the shoulder. "Cut that out. No fair thinking of her naked."

"How did you know what I was thinking?" he asked, laughing.

"You get that look."

"I'll think about naked women all I want, but there's no one for me but you." He grabbed her around the waist and squeezed.

"Joe," Marie said, hugging her husband back, "have you ever . . . ?"

She couldn't get the question out of her mouth but he knew her too well. "Ever what? You mean been with a hooker?"

She ducked her chin against his chest. "Yeah."

"Before we were married, when I was in the service, I used to," he paused, then continued, "uh, indulge from time to time."

"Not since we were married?"

He lifted his right hand, two fingers extended. "Scouts honor. Since our marriage there's never been anyone for me but you."

"Have you been tempted?"

"Any man who says he's never looked at another woman with a little trace of lust is either dead, blind, or a total liar.

Sure I look at a sexy woman and think about sex. Then I come home to you and we fool around. I love you and would never cheat on you or lie to you. Period."

They hugged more tightly. "Thanks for being so honest."

Joe pinched her behind. "Now that we've been talking about sex, let's bounce around the bed later. Maybe I'll pretend you're a hooker and have to do my bidding or you won't get paid."

Marie wiggled her hips and let out a girlish giggle. "That sounds like quite an idea. I'll see you in the bedroom after the kids are out of the way."

"You don't sound too surprised," Suze said to Kevin after she told him the news.

"I guess I'm not. She moves like a dancer or performer of some sort and I never bought into that interior decorator story. Therefore, since she was lying about that, she had to be covering for something she didn't want us to know about. Ergo . . ."

"I wish you'd imparted some of your wisdom to me. Here I am having tolerated her presence in town and all the time she's a criminal."

Kevin swiped her opinions away. "Only in the strictest sense of the word. There's no victim here."

Suze looked disgusted. "You sound like her. Society is the victim. Hookers spread disease, have abortions, do drugs. We're being undermined, and it's degrading to women."

"I agree with you somewhat about the ten-dollar, stand-on-the-corner-and-give-blow-jobs-to-truckers, hookers but high-class prostitutes like her are clean and safe. Have you any idea what she makes?"

"That's beside the point," Suze said, her voice rising. "Don't defend her."

"From what I've read about Heidi Fleiss and her kind, I'll bet she makes several thousand dollars a night so she'd have to be drug free and very careful. That's hardly chump change. You've got to admit that, if you can afford it, women like her are much safer than picking up a girl at a bar."

Suze was suddenly wary. "You sound like you've been to *women like her.*" Her eyes flashed. "Have you?"

"Not yet," Kevin said, his eyes slowly turning dark as he glared at his wife, "but since I don't get any at home, I must admit that I've thought about it. Frankly I didn't imagine you'd care as long as no one on the town board knew about it." He turned and slammed the front door behind him. Moments later she heard his car start and him drive away. He'll be back, she thought, and I'm sure he didn't mean what he said. Now I just have to figure out how to get rid of Leslie before she totally pollutes everyone on Atlantic Beach.

Upstairs, Eliza heard the door slam. Her parents were at it again. She put on her earphones and pushed a heavy metal CD in her computer and turned the volume up. She clicked on the "Write Mail" icon on her screen and began typing.

Dear Dennis . . .

Chapter

19

Late the following morning Leslie sat on the beach with her Sudoku book, enjoying the warmth of the sun. She was surprised at how engrossing the puzzles were, so entertaining that she'd only read two of the books she had stacked beside her bed. They also occupied her mind so she didn't play the what-if game.

She and Brad had made soft, quiet love the preceding evening, then had spent the night together with no further discussion of her occupation. Around 2 A.M. Brad awoke shaking from another nightmare but Leslie managed to calm him and they both fell back to sleep quickly. He had gone back to his cottage early that morning, leaving Leslie with a slightly lighter heart.

"I knew you were my kind of people," a woman's voice behind her said.

Leslie looked up and saw Vicki, backlit by the bright morning sun one hand on an outthrust hip. "Good morning, Vicki."

"You devil," she said, plunking herself down on a tiny available corner of Leslie's towel. "You get paid for it. Real money."

She'd been able to predict Vicki's reaction pretty well. She really didn't want to discuss it but, short of being rude, she had little choice. "If you mean that you've heard that I'm a professional escort, yes, I get paid for it."

"It's amazing what men will do when under the influence of an erect dick."

She couldn't help but chuckle. "I wouldn't put it exactly that way."

Vicki's grin was slightly malicious. "I would. So much of what I've gotten throughout my life has been by leading a man around by his cock."

Leslie didn't particularly want to hear Vicki's views on men so she dropped her gaze to her puzzle. Totally ignoring Leslie's not-too-subtle request for silence, Vicki said, "Now I totally understand your support for my store. Any advice for me?"

"Not really," Leslie said not looking up. *Go away and keep your jaundiced view of men to yourself.*

Undaunted, Vicki continued, "What kind of stuff do you find men want? What kind of stuff do you think women will want to buy for their husbands?"

"I really couldn't say, Vicki. The men I entertain are not the type you'll be getting in your store."

Vicki's face clouded. "Are you putting the men here down? Are your *customers*," she sneered when she said the word, "better than mine?"

Sighing with exasperation, Leslie looked up and said, "Not better, Vicki, but different. The men I'm with have sufficient income to spend several thousand dollars for an evening of pleasure. I doubt that many folks around here, especially the ones who live here year-round, have that kind of disposable income."

Leslie watched Vicki's face soften. "On that, you're probably right, but men are men. Are they interested in toys?"

"Sure. Why wouldn't they be?"

"Right. Do you find many interested in bondage, hand-cuffs, whips, like that?"

She heaved a resigned sigh. "I do, but remember that many

of the men I entertain are doing things with me that they wouldn't do at home with their wives so your experience in the store might be quite different."

"You've probably been in stores like the one I want to open. There are a few in the city and I'm sure you've bought things from time to time. I'm going to send Trish over with some catalogs and Web site addresses. I'm sure you'd be a big help in deciding what to get."

She's a master manipulator, Leslie thought. "If you like," Leslie said, seeing no way out of it. "Why are you sending your daughter? Won't you be doing the ordering?"

"Eventually, but for now she'll be handling most of it. She needs to help make this a going business. After all, it's going to be hers someday."

Leslie barely avoided saying that the business would be hers in twenty or thirty years, if it lasted at all. "Sure, Vicki, send her over."

Without a please or a thank you, Vicki rose and walked back to her house.

Ten minutes later Trish walked over, a stack of booklets in her hand. "I'm so sorry to drag you into this, Leslie," she said as she dropped on the sand beside Leslie's towel. "My mom can be really pushy when given half a chance." Her laugh was sardonic. "When you give her no chance at all, if the truth be known. If this isn't something you want to do, I'll buzz off. Don't feel obligated just because she guilted you into it."

Leslie hadn't said more than five words to Vicki's daughter in the past two weeks but now she instinctively liked the young woman. "I'll be glad to help." She put her book down and skooched over so Trish could sit on one side of the spread towel. "What can I do for you?"

Trish dropped the pile of catalogs on the sand beside her. "This is really embarrassing," she said, pulling her knees up and lowering her chin.

"I'm not bothered at all." She wondered about the two

women, Vicki so overtly sexual, so "out there," and her daughter so quiet and introverted. Other contrasts were obvious. Vicki was never without makeup, always dressed to emphasize her shapely body, while Trish didn't even wear lipstick and dressed in shapeless shirts and pants. "Tell me what you need me for," Leslie said softly.

Leslie could almost feel Trish steel herself before she said, "Mom wants me to find out what we should stock in the store."

Leslie had spent many years dealing with reluctant clients and she was an expert at reading people. "You don't want to do this, do you?"

"What makes you think that?" Trish said, sitting straighter, her chin jutting forward. "I'm glad to help my mother with the emporium."

"Right. I'll ignore what I sense if that's the way you want to play it, but don't pretend. I'm too good at understanding people not to see things."

Trish's body drooped like a puppet with its strings suddenly cut and she rested her cheek on a bent knee. "You're right, I don't want to do this."

Leslie lifted the girl's head and watched tears pool in her eyes. Empathizing with the younger woman, she put her arm around Trish's shoulder. "Want to talk about it?"

"No." She shuddered. "Yes." She turned away. "I don't know."

"I'm a pretty good listener, if you want to talk."

"I can't talk to you."

Leslie stiffened. "Because of what I am?"

"Of course not," Trish said, eyes flashing. "Because we're so different. Look at you and look at me. You're so gorgeous and sure of yourself, and I'm so . . . so . . . so nothing. You couldn't possibly understand."

"First of all, you're not nothing. You're a lovely girl who needs some help to bring out what's lovely about her. I'm not going to lie to you and tell you how shy and ordinary I was as a kid." She cupped her hands a few inches from her breasts. "I was a 36D in high school and I was noticed by every overtesteroned boy who came within twenty feet of me. That's not the point, though. It took me years to learn that I'm not just a big pair of boobs and you're not just a shy, embarrassed girl with a mother like Vicki."

"I love my mother," Trish said quickly.

"Of course you do, but you resent her like hell, too. I know quite a bit about people and I think I can guess at the dynamic. She's a constant reminder of what you think you want to be. I'll bet she was like me as a kid, attracting men without even trying. Maybe having sex with them to prove something to herself." She let out a small snort. "Sorry," she said, stopping herself. "There I go, Leslie Morgan, amateur shrink. Forget what I just said and let's concentrate on you. Don't you want to be part of Vicki's store?"

She shook her head slowly. "No. Not really. She started this for me, at least partly, so I'd have a career."

"This store isn't going to become a career and I suspect that your mother started it at least as much for herself as for you."

"She can't do it alone."

"Probably true, but what most people do is hire help."

"She can't afford that. Not at the beginning."

"Then she'll have to stay open when she can be there and close when she can't."

"She needs me to keep the books and all. I've showed her a computer program she could use but she's helpless."

"I don't think she's nearly as helpless as she'd like people to believe, but that's neither here nor there. What would you do if you didn't join her?"

Trish's face brightened. "I've got some friends in Hartford who have an apartment. They want me to move in with them, but my mother won't hear of it."

"Could you support yourself?"

"That would be easy. My grades were pretty good and I could take classes at UConn part-time and find a job for the rest. I'd even flip burgers, but I don't want to work in her store, have her watching me all the time. I've got no space now, and in the store it will be worse."

"You've obviously thought about it, so do something about it."

"I can't. My mother gave up so much to have me and I owe her . . ."

Leslie hated to take sides in a family argument, but someone needed to help Trish see the other side of things. "Stop right there. I'm sure she loves you but you don't owe your mother anything for giving birth to you except your respect and consideration, and she has to earn even those. From the little I know of Vicki, she's not a bad person. She's a bit of a manipulator, and a little self-involved, but that's not a mortal sin. I think she's worried that you'll go off somewhere and never come back. Then she'd be alone and she'd miss you. There might be a compromise. Maybe you could work in the store one day over the weekend. You could do whatever book-keeping needs to be done then and you'd see each other at least once a week."

Trish swiped at the tearstains on her cheeks. "I guess I could do that."

"I could help you out with what to order and we could do a little surfing and see what's out there. That might mollify you mother enough so you could make a life of your own."

"I've already found several online stores with generous partnership plans but my mother wants your advice, as if I'm not well enough informed."

Leslie stood and dusted the seat of her bathing suit. She reached out her hand. "Let's give that a try. I've got my laptop all set up."

Trish extended her hand and let Leslie pull her to her feet.

She grabbed the pile of catalogs and, while Leslie got her puzzle book, Trish swept up the towel. "Okay."

Sitting at Leslie's dining room table, the two women looked through booklets and surfed the web while Trish made detailed notes. When they finally slumped back on the sofa Leslie said, "I think that should give you a pretty good start."

"I can't thank you enough, Leslie. You've got a great business sense."

"You're more than welcome."

When Trish stood up to leave she said, softly, "I wish I looked more like you. You always look so good."

Leslie decided to take another step. "I don't want to make you feel self-conscious, but a little makeup might make quite a bit of difference in your looks. I could give you a few tips, if you like."

Trish's face lit up. "Would you? I could never look like you, or my mother, but maybe . . . ." Her voice trailed off.

"Come on upstairs and let's see what I've got."

The next hour was a frenzy of makeup, hair styling, and clothing advice. As Leslie had expected, Trish's looks were greatly enhanced by the subtle use of cosmetics and when she used a curling iron on the top of her hair to give it some height and softness it enhanced her best feature, her large green eyes. When they pulled the back of her hair up and away from her face with a butterfly clip she looked sweeter, and subtly sexier, with a sort of muss-me look.

At around two they stopped for lunch, a pair of peanut butter on toast sandwiches and glasses of iced tea from the pitcher Leslie had learned to keep in the refrigerator at all times. Sated, they searched through Leslie's closet. Except in the bosom, they were of similar build so Trish tried on several of Leslie's blouses and skirts and both women were surprised to discover that she looked much lovelier with the right necklines and becoming colors.

"Trish," Leslie said when a new-looking young woman was ready to leave, "I certainly won't advise you to leave your mother in the lurch, but you have to do some serious thinking about what you want to do with the next phase of your life."

"I will." She hugged the older woman. "Thanks. I feel so much better, so much lighter."

"I'm glad," Leslie said and returned the embrace. "One more word. Don't go home with a chip on your shoulder. Your mother wants what she thinks is best for you and you can't blame her for that. Take some time before you confront her to decide what you really want and how best to approach things."

Trish left Leslie's house feeling like a new person. For the first time in a long time she felt strong. As she walked down Atlantic Beach Road she heard KJ's motorcycle as it pulled to a stop behind her. "Hey, Trish," KJ said, kicking down the stand. "Want to go for a ride with me?"

She turned to face him and almost laughed out loud at the startled look on KJ's face. "You look surprised."

"I am," KJ said with a grin. "You look—pretty good. Pretty damn good."

He'd noticed. She hadn't changed much. Trying on Leslie's clothes had been enlightening so, when she'd redressed she'd rolled up the legs on her shorts and put her shirt back on, tails tied beneath her breasts with an additional button open at the front. As she'd looked at herself in Leslie's mirror she'd giggled. "It looks like I have cleavage," she'd said.

"You do have cleavage," Leslie had said, grinning.

Now she walked with her shoulders back, spine straight. "Thanks." Her voice softened. "Do you really like?"

"Sure, but it makes me a little uncomfortable. I'm used to the old, comfortable you."

"Get un-used to the old me. I'm done being comfortable. This is the new me and I like it."

KJ's eyes kept roaming her body. "What led to this over-haul?"

Trish told KJ about Leslie, her occupation, her attitude, and her helpfulness. As she relived the morning she realized the depth of the changes inside her. Leslie hadn't done anything radical, just made her take a good look at herself away from her mother's shadow. She liked what she saw. Now all she had to do was keep this new self and find a way to convince her mother that she needed some freedom.

"That's just great," KJ said. "Leslie sounds like a nice woman."

"She is." She turned toward a stairway over the seawall. "I'm going to take a long walk on the beach. I need to think some things through. Want to walk with me?"

"Not just now," KJ said, seemingly lost in thought himself. "I have some thinking of my own to do." As Trish walked toward the beach, KJ quickly climbed on his bike and roared away.

Trish arrived home several hours later to find her mother sitting in the living room watching a rerun of an adventure series. As Trish entered the room, Vicki stared at her. "What the hell have you done with yourself?" Vicki asked.

"Leslie gave me a few tips about my looks," she said, taking in her mother's shocked expression. With trepidation, she said, "What do you think?" She pirouetted slowly.

Vicki seemed unable to speak for a moment. "Where's my little girl?"

"Come on, Mom, it isn't that drastic. Don't go all drama queen on me."

"I'm not. You just look so grown up."

Grown up wasn't the reaction Trish had anticipated. "I'm a big girl now, Mom. I am all grown up and ready for the world."

Vicki held her hand over her heart. "Darling, you look lovely. I never anticipated. . . ."

"Thanks." Wanting to change the subject and not ready to confront her indecision, Trish continued, "Leslie and I surfed the Web and I've got lots of notes on suppliers." She pulled a sheaf of folded papers from her jeans pocket. "Want to go over them with me?"

"Sure." Vicki patted the sofa beside her and the two women put their heads together and made copious notes. After about an hour, Vicki said, "I hope you realize now how much I need you in this."

"I do, Mom. I truly do but I haven't made up my mind about what I want. Maybe I could help you out on the weekends even if I wasn't here during the week. I could keep the books and do some ordering then."

"I need you to keep the store open when I can't be there."

"Hire someone or close the store when you can't be around. That's what real businesses do." She started feeling the walls closing in. "Don't force me to make difficult decisions."

Vicki slumped against the sofa cushions. "It's okay, Trish. I understand. Your desires are important to you and I respect that. I was so hoping, after all these years of supporting you, that I could . . ."

"Mom, please. I've heard this song so many times I can even sing the lyrics. Let it go. I've got a lot of thinking to do, so stop smothering me."

Vicki looked shocked. "Is that what you think I'm doing? Smothering you?"

"You think you know what's right for me and I sympathize with that. It's time, however, for me to make some decisions about what's right for me." She stood, leaving the papers on the coffee table, and walked toward the stairs. "Look all that information over again and make some decisions. It's your store after all. I'm going to my room."

As she climbed, Trish heard her mother mutter, "Leslie. I should never have trusted her."

Chapter
20

By the following day it seemed as if everyone in the town had heard that they had a professional prostitute in their midst. Leslie had breakfast at the Wayfarer and was surprised that she saw curiosity in the stares of the other patrons, not universal condemnation. Several women turned away with a huff and one couple glared at her, then quickly put money on their table to pay the check and left, but many assessed her, then gave her a slight smile. Two women at a nearby booth grinned, leaned forward, and talked conspiratorially then gave her a little wave and a thumbs-up.

When the waitress arrived to take her order she said, "You're her, aren't you?"

Deciding not to misunderstand she said, "Yes."

Expecting a rebuke, she was surprised when the waitress slid into the booth opposite her. "I know this is really out of line but I need some advice. My name's Sandy. You know what men like and my husband seems to be pretty bored with our, you know, sex life." She ducked her head and stared at her hands in her lap. "I want to do something to liven things up."

Eyes widening in shock, Leslie took a calming breath. The young woman had waited on her before and seemed pleasant enough, probably in her early thirties, slightly thick in the waist, brown hair pulled back in a ponytail, deep brown eyes with short stubby lashes, and no makeup. Her fingernails were bitten to the quick. "You really want my advice?"

"Sure. You know men, don't you?"

"I guess. Tell me a little about your marriage," Leslie said gently.

"Doug and I have been together for nine years, married for six. We have three kids, Erin is five, Maureen is three, and the baby, Scott, is nine months. We love each other but we're bored and tired. If we make love at all it's a real quickie. He falls asleep and I'm . . . you know . . . left hanging."

"I assume your husband works?"

"He's in construction and he works six days a week."

Leslie reached across the table and took Sandy's cold, clammy hand. "It's okay. I'm sure you both still care a lot about each other."

"We do, but I'm so scared, scared that he'll go somewhere else."

"I understand. He'll go to someone like me."

"I'm sorry. That sounds terrible but I don't know what to do. I read all the women's magazines but I can't greet him when he comes home in a teddy and high heels."

"Of course you can't. Let me ask a different question. Where are your children while you work?"

She looked startled and said, quickly, "My mom takes care of them." She glanced around at her customers and when they didn't appear to need her Sandy seemed content to remain for a bit longer.

"It seems to me that you and your husband need to get some time for yourselves. Let me guess. You two get home, do chores, take care of the kids, and by the time you get to bed you're too exhausted for much. Right?"

Leslie watched tears pool in Sandy's eyes. "That's exactly it."

"Okay. Here's what you need to do. Ask your mom to keep the kids one evening this weekend. You can beg, offer to pay her, ask for the evening's baby-sitting as a birthday present, whatever it takes. Then you and Doug go out. Be Sandy and Doug instead of Mommy and Daddy for one entire evening. Have dinner together, with some wine. Hold hands. Talk. Really talk, and not about the kids—about some of the things you used to talk about before. Then go home to an empty house and have at it. Remember what you two used to do on dates before the kids were born?" When Sandy's eyes softened, Leslie continued, "If that works the way I think it will, suggest to your mom that rather than a present for any occasion, you want time alone with your husband."

Sandy smiled a watery smile. "That sounds like a wonderful idea. I'll do just what you said. Thank you so much."

"This is my next-to-last week here so do it this weekend. Then you can report back and let me know how it went. And if it's not against your beliefs, use birth control so you can look forward to a little more freedom sometime in the future."

Sandy slid out of the booth and gave her a quick hug and kiss on the cheek. She quickly took her order and then, each time she returned to the table, she thanked Leslie again. As she finished her breakfast, Leslie said, "Stop thanking me and do it. Make a phone call to Mom. You might even set it up as a surprise for Doug."

"I will, and thanks again."

As she drove back to Atlantic Beach Leslie was amazed at the turn of events. She had been afraid she might have to cut her vacation short because of the attitude of the people around, but she'd been wrong. The reaction seemed much more mixed than she could have hoped.

It rained almost continuously for the next three days and by the beginning of the weekend everyone had a bad case of cabin fever. She and Brad had seen each other every evening but, although everything seemed like before, Leslie sensed that there was a fine veil between them. They worked out most afternoons and saw a movie in a multiplex on Route 1 one evening. The Yankees were on a road trip so they watched night games and made long, quiet love each evening. Leslie noticed that, more and more often, Brad slept through the night without dreaming.

One morning they shared breakfast at the Wayfarer and, when Sandy walked over, she winked at Leslie. "Saturday," she whispered, leaning close to Leslie's ear. "Doug's thrilled. Last evening was great just thinking about getting the kids out of the house."

On Friday they went to a small out of the way seafood restaurant with great shrimp scampi and ate themselves silly. They rented a recent award-winning movie and watched it, holding hands, until the final credits. "That wasn't a great movie," Brad said as he pulled the DVD from the player.

Leslie laughed loudly. "You should have said something sooner and we could both have avoided the final hour of misery. I was bored silly."

"I thought you were enjoying it."

"And I thought you were. Oh well, now we have a zero on the zero to ten rating scale. Just about anything's got to be better."

"I've watched a few worse ones." There was a long silence and Leslie sensed that Brad was deep in thought.

Brad had thought a lot about how to broach the subject he'd been sent here to investigate, or whether to do it at all. Who were her customers: governmental officials, police brass, judges? "I have something on my mind," Brad said. "I've been trying not to talk about your"—he blew out a breath—"your job and I'm finding my curiosity is getting in the way of my enjoyment of you."

"In what way?"

"I hate myself for thinking this way but I keep wondering

whether you've ever done what we do with other men, how you do your fantasy thing, what famous people you've been with, like that."

"I won't discuss the people I've been with, especially with you."

He bristled. "Especially with me? You mean because I'm a cop? You have to know that I won't let my job interfere with yours."

Leslie put her hand on Brad's arm. "Not because you're a cop but because you're important to me. I don't want you thinking that I've been with this celebrity or that when we're together. I don't want you wondering whether I've done what we're doing with Brad Pitt or Derek Jeter. I want you thinking only about us."

"You can't blame me for being curious."

"Of course I can't. I'd love to impress you with the names of some of the folks you know of, but I won't."

Brad decided this was the end of it. He didn't want to pry anymore, and she wouldn't give up names easily, if at all. "Okay. Enough of that. I'm also curious about how you do the fantasy thing."

Leslie leaned back on the sofa and tucked her legs beneath her. They were treading on dangerous ground and she had no idea how much of this she wanted to tell him. He'd dealt with her job in the abstract, but how would he react to the reality of it? Much as she hated the idea, she'd better find out before this went much further. "I believe that most, if not all, men have sexual fantasies. Many wouldn't want to act them out, but a goodly number would, and some of them have the money to make that happen. That's what we do."

"How do you make it happen? What's your club like?"

"We have a four-story brownstone in the city with rooms devoted to different types of fantasies. We have a western room where a guy can be the sheriff and make love to the saloon madam, or he can accept the gratitude of the grateful rancher's daughter, or have his way with his prisoner."

"I wouldn't have thought those were common fantasies. Is that one used a lot?"

"More than I would have imagined. I guess lots of men have macho fantasies. We also have a medical suite. Lots of guys, and women too, have dreamed about some doctor doing deliciously unspeakable things to their body during an exam. We have several all-purpose rooms that can be rearranged into motel rooms, bedrooms, and even a pirate's bedroom on a ship. We have a dungeon for those who want to play with heavier stuff. We use costumes and sound effects and we have a full photography setup for those who want movies of the evening to take home. You'd be surprised at how many men want videos to help relive the experiences."

"You guys take pictures? I wouldn't think people, especially famous ones, would take a chance of something like that becoming public."

She watched him become intent on what she was saying. She wondered what would happen if she let something about a customer slip. Could she trust him? She hoped so, but for now she'd be very, very careful. It wasn't just her safety that was involved. "We never do any photography without the customer's permission and they get the only copy. No one would dream of taking advantage. Never have, and never will. Don't get your cop instincts in a turmoil."

"Okay. Enough said."

"I hope so because if I can't trust you to keep quiet about an accidental slip of the tongue, we'd better stop this thing we've got going right now."

She watched him consider for a minute, then he said, "I want us to explore what we've got, as you put it, without reservation." He'd obviously made an internal decision. "I will promise you I won't use anything you might reveal in any way without getting your okay first. Will that do?"

"I suppose it will have to." She shook her head slowly. "What are we getting ourselves into, Brad? I feel sort of like you're a Hatfield and I'm a McCoy. Can we make this work? Can we trust each other?"

"God, I hope so." He kissed her thoroughly. "Let's change the subject. I'm still curious about how you do what you do. How do you go about finding out what a guy wants?"

"Some men know exactly and that's the most difficult kind for us to deal with. They have their internal movie so carefully programmed that deviations are difficult. We can use cosmetics, wigs, and outfits, but it will never be exactly what the guy's been imagining. Our customer is warned, then he takes his chances. If it's really a disaster we will refund his money, of course."

"Okay, tell me about an unusual one you've been part of. No names, of course."

"Do you really want to hear about my job? You're poking at it like a sore tooth and it scares me."

"It scares me, too, but if I can't get comfortable with this, our relationship can't go much further. I guess I'm sort of testing myself."

"I understand, but what if you can't live with the things you hear?"

He scrubbed the back of his neck again. "Then there's no future for us. I hate that thought, Leslie. I've come to really care for you but it's better we find out now, rather than later."

Leslie's long deep sigh was the only sound in the room for several minutes, then she said, "Okay. You're right. I've known since I met you that we have a long way to go to reconcile your career and mine." She put her feet onto the coffee table. "I've done just about everything. Most are pretty ordinary, but sometimes we have to be really creative. For example, we rearranged the dungeon into a gym using some of Rock's workout stuff. Rock's our live-in bouncer. Anyway, we've had several people who wanted to play on equipment with a beautiful naked woman.

"I've been a cheerleader with a guy who always envied the captain of the football team, a World War II spy captured by a soldier who can take advantage of my powerlessness. That's a pretty common one. Prison guard, gang initiation, like that. Power is a very potent fantasy."

Brad uncrossed and recrossed his legs. "How about anonymous sex?"

"That's a very common one too. Having sex with someone you'll never see again means you don't have to worry about consequences of any kind."

"How can you make that one come true?"

Leslie slowly smiled at him. "In my years of doing what I do, I've gotten pretty good at reading people's body language. I'm treading on dangerous ground here, but is that one of yours?"

Brad shifted in his seat. She saw all the signs. "You do pick up on things, and this is really embarrassing."

"Of course it is. The question is, is it delicious embarrassment or truly upsetting? Some discomfort can enhance a fantasy."

Again he shifted in his seat. "I'm not sure I want to go here."

"If you don't I certainly don't." She knew he did but he had to do it in his own time.

"Okay, I'll admit that anonymous sex has always intrigued me."

"Does it make you feel better to know that many others share your dreams?"

"Yes, but it's still embarrassing."

"Of course it is." She reached over and gently touched the bulge in the front of his shorts. "It's exciting, too." She withdrew her hand.

His "Yes" was hoarse and his breathing quickened.

"Want to play?"

"How can you . . . ?"

"Leave that up to me. Do you want to play?"

When he nodded, she stood. "Just stay here, then come up-stairs when I call you. And go along with whatever's happening. It will be worth your while."

She watched his Adam's apple bob as he swallowed hard. Then he nodded again.

Upstairs she thought quickly and, having created scenarios like this many times over the years, she decided that one of the spare bedrooms would serve her purposes nicely. Inside the blue room she pulled the blinds and drapes closed so, when she turned out the lights, the room would be as dark as she could make it. She moved a few straight chairs from other rooms and, using their backs and one empty wall, she formed a small enclosure with a narrow opening facing the room's door. She took a few moments to put on a slightly heavier dose of a different scent so she'd smell unfamiliar and used a strong, minty mouthwash so she'd taste new and fresh. After only about fifteen minutes she called, "Come on up. First door on the right at the top of the stairs."

She heard his heavy footsteps on the wooden stairs and held a flashlight pointed at the door to momentarily blind him and hide her new identity. "I'm not sure this elevator is working properly," she said and, as Brad entered the room, she turned off the flashlight and tossed it on the bed. "I pushed the button but nothing happened." She bounced hard against him. "There it goes again." She bumped him again. Then suddenly the light went out and it became almost totally black in here.

"Shit," she hissed. "I think we're stuck in here." She raised her voice slightly. "Help. Let us out of here." Had she been back at Club Fantasy she'd have recorded a man's voice giving some sort of message about how long it would take to get someone to fix the elevator, but she wasn't able to. "I think he said there was a brown-out and we'll be stuck here for quite a while.

"I guess we'd better introduce ourselves. I'm Carolynne." During the long pause she wondered whether Brad would be able to let go sufficiently to play along.

Finally he said, "Of course. Carolynne. With an 'e.' I'm Brad. Brad DeVane."

Her voice trembled as she said, "It's nice to meet you but I have to tell you that I'm terribly claustrophobic. Will you hold my hand? It might help."

Brad touched the backs of the chairs and the wall, orienting himself. "It's pretty small in here."

"Thanks," she said dryly. "That's just what I needed to hear."

"I'm sorry. Here," he said, fumbling for her hand, "hold on."

"That's better." She pressed against him, then clung to his arm and bounced. "Sorry. When it lurches like that it scares me to death."

His arm slowly snaked around her waist. "Don't worry. You're safe. Nothing can harm us." She felt him slowly adapting to the artificial, yet sensual situation.

"I wish I were that sure. I worry that the car will fall and we'll be crushed."

"Nonsense. That never happens. The power will be out for as long as it has to be, but we're safe."

She clung harder to his arm. "My mind knows that you're right, but my psyche is still terrified." She slid her arms around his neck and, keeping her voice small and making it quake, said, "If you kiss me it might help me forget where we are."

"Carolynne," he sighed and his lips found hers in the darkness. She felt him let go of Leslie and accept Carolynne. He played with her mouth, tasting and nibbling, exploring with caressing strokes of his tongue. His light kisses strayed across her cheek and found the sensitive hollow below her ear. She shivered as his tongue flicked over her flesh, then his teeth found her tender lobe and bit down lightly. She moved closer in the dark, melding her body to his.

She'd quickly changed her clothes so he'd have to guess

how to proceed. She now wore a slick, silk blouse and full cotton skirt, stockings with elastic tops and high heels. She wore no underwear.

Leslie felt his hands slide over the silk at her back. "Carolynne." His breath was hot in her ear. "I've never felt you like this before."

"We've never met before." She wrapped her arms around his waist, trying with every movement to keep the illusion alive. Unbuttoning his shirt, she kissed his chest, then licked and nipped along his collarbone. In her high-heeled shoes she was almost as tall as he was, so his erection pressed blatantly against her pubic bone. She tilted her pelvis so her body stroked his hardness. "Do you think it will take them long to get the elevator started again?"

"Long enough," he murmured. His hands weren't still. He slid them to her breasts and felt their heaviness. "You're not wearing anything beneath your blouse."

As she said, "I'm not wearing any panties either," she felt his cock twitch. She pulled his shirt off, then unzipped his slacks and pushed them to the floor. Then she slowly kissed and licked her way down his chest as she helped him remove his briefs. Her mouth found his erection and she licked the length of him.

"God, Carolynne, do that."

She slowly drew him into her mouth and cupped his balls with her fingers. She scratched along the tender skin between his balls and anus and felt his knees tremble. "I want to fuck you," he said, slowly sliding down until he knelt on the floor.

In the pitch darkness, within the confines of the enclosed space, he fondled her stocking-covered feet, then slid up her legs as she quivered beneath his touch. He gasped with pleasure when his fingers found the border and the top of her hose, then the soft, tender skin above. When he found her opening she was soaking wet.

He lay on the floor and she quickly covered his cock with a

condom, then he pulled her on top of him, slowly lowering her body as his cock penetrated. Sitting on his rigid staff she was in heaven. She levered herself up, then let her body drop onto him over and over. She clenched her muscles so her vaginal canal squeezed him inside her. It might be his fantasy, but she was loving this mysterious encounter as much as he was.

He bucked and, with a long, deep half moan, half sigh, came. His fingers found her clit and he rubbed her until she too climaxed. Together they lay on the floor, totally exhausted. It was a long time before he spoke. Pulling her still fully clothed body close, he said, "I get it." Then she could tell by his deep breathing that he'd fallen asleep.

Later they woke and moved to her bed. "That was amazing. For long periods of time I forgot who you were. Is that dreadful?"

"It's exactly what I intended. That's what I do for a living, assume other identities and give men what they most desire in a woman." She took a deep breath. "That's part of why I did this. If we're going to have any future, you have to be able to deal with who I am."

"That's a tall order," he said, holding her tightly, "but you're worth the effort. I'm not sure how I'll deal with it, but I want to try."

"Me, too."

Later, as she replayed the wonderful fantasy they'd shared she remembered him saying "Carolynne, with an 'e.' " How had he known about the "e" ? Lucky guess? It must have been. The following morning she realized that he'd slept dreamlessly and smiled.

Chapter

21

Saturday morning Leslie heard a knock on the door that faced the ocean and as she crossed the living room saw KJ through the screen. Oh Lord, she told herself, remembering his frequent assessing glances at the barbeque. She prepared herself to fend off his advances now that he knew what she did for a living. "Good morning, KJ," she said cheerfully, keeping the mood light, yet blocking the door so he couldn't enter. Neither of them would be able to stand the gossip if anyone knew they'd been in the cottage alone together.

"I think I need to talk to you."

His expression was dark and very serious. She stepped out on the concrete patio that topped the seawall. This area was out of direct view of Atlantic Beach Road. "What's up, KJ?" she said, keeping her voice impersonal.

Looking at his sandal-clad feet, he said, "Would you walk down the beach with me? I don't want to take any chance that my mother might see us."

"KJ, you're a very nice young man, but . . ."

He interrupted. "It's not about me, but about my sister. I'm worried about her."

It might be a ploy, Leslie thought, but we'll be in plain sight of all the houses along the beach so she closed the door behind her and they walked down the seven steps to the sand. She could certainly fend off a teenaged boy if she had to. "Okay, what do you want, KJ?"

They'd walked for several hundred feet before KJ said, "I heard what you are, and that's fine with me."

"Great," she said dryly.

"As you can gather my mother pitched a fit, and is still pitching it. I've heard her on the phone talking to several people about you and what a bad influence you are to the neighborhood."

Leslie's shoulders rose and fell. "Sadly, that doesn't surprise me."

"I want you to know that I think it's fantastic. I'll bet you're very good at what you do." He continued, "Eliza has heard, too, and when we talked about it late last evening she let something slip. I don't know what to do about it."

Maybe this wasn't going to be what she feared. Leslie kept silent, letting KJ gather his thoughts as they walked. "She got her own computer for Christmas and now that she can do things in private she told me she's been chatting with lots of guys on the Net. She put up some information and her school picture on one of those personal pages Web sites. You know the ones."

"Where you can meet other teens online and talk about movies and music, boys and sex?"

"Yeah. She's been spending more and more time there. There's one older guy in particular that she's been e-mailing. She sends him pictures and she told me he thinks she's a real beauty and wanted to see more of her." He stopped, bent down, and picked up a rock and threw it into the gentle waves. "She told me that a few of her girlfriends had a photo session with a digital camera and no clothes. She said she was going to send him one of those pictures." He kicked a small pile of sand. "I'm really scared that she's in over her head. I'm old enough to know better, but she's just a kid. I don't know that much about stalkers on the Net, but I've seen some TV things about molesters who pick up girls that way then arrange to meet them." His eyes finally met Leslie's. "I'm really scared."

He had every right to be worried. What he'd told her was really scary. "I can understand that and I think you might have reason to be frightened. Have you told your mother or father?"

"Eliza would kill me. And anyway, Suze is on a rampage about you and I know she'd freak if I said anything about this. I just can't tell her. My dad is never around. He and my mom fight all the time now so he stays away. I didn't know who to tell, but I thought you might understand. Maybe Brad could check this guy out. He's a cop after all. I don't know what to do." His head dropped and from the quaver in his voice, Leslie knew he was making a strong effort not to cry.

Leslie felt every ounce of the weight KJ had just dumped on her shoulders. "How about I talk to your mom about it?" That was the responsible thing to do although she dreaded even the thought of it.

"You?" KJ said, incredulous. "She'd never listen and you mustn't tell her." His voice rose in desperation. "Promise! Promise me you won't say anything to her or to my dad."

She held up her hand to make him stop ranting. "I promise. Do you think I could talk to Eliza?" What the hell would she say?

"I'm not sure she'd listen to you any better than to my mom but you could try. In secret, of course."

"I'd like to talk to Brad first. He might be able to help me get Eliza to understand how dangerous this all is." Maybe he'd share some of the load she was suddenly carrying.

"I guess that would be okay," KJ said, brightening. "I know guys aren't supposed to care about stuff like family and all, but she's my sister and she's only fifteen. She's not old enough to know any better."

"I think she knows but right now she's choosing not to. I'll talk with Brad and we'll see what we can figure out."

"Thanks, Leslie. I knew you'd be able to help." He turned and took a few steps down the beach. "I'm just going to keep walking for awhile. I don't want any chance of my mom seeing us together."

Leslie watched him walk away, then turned and headed for Brad's cottage. Inside, she told him what KJ had told her and asked for his opinion.

Brad was silent for awhile, then said, "Under most circumstances I'd tell you to butt out, but this is too serious to ignore. Granted, the number of people on the Net is huge and the number of predators is not that large, but the odds aren't what's important here. She should know better than to send pictures like that to anyone, much less someone she doesn't know at all."

"We don't *know* she's in any trouble, Brad." She could hope.

"No, we don't. Did KJ say whether Suze knows what's going on?"

"He said she didn't. I don't meant to speak ill, but Suze seems to be a pretty hands-off mother."

"And Kevin?"

"I don't know much about him but he and Suze seem to be on the outs right now so he might be too wrapped up in his own problems to be sensitive to what's going with Eliza."

"Parents sometimes think kids can raise themselves once they're teens. I've seen that much too much. Like you, I hate to butt in. Do you have any relationship with the kid?"

"Not much. I've seen her around and bumped into her at the buffet, but not much more than that. You?"

"Not even that much."

"I'm a bit of a buttinsky, so I suppose I could just invite my-self over when she's home alone. I certainly don't want to run into Suze while I'm talking to her daughter about sex. God, what the hell can I say? She probably thinks that she knows everything. At her age I know I did."

Brad slowly shook his head. "I don't have an idea in hell as to how to broach the subject. Did KJ say you couldn't use his name?"

"No. Maybe the 'Your brother's worried about you' line might work." She certainly hoped so.

"You brother's worried about you," Leslie said to Eliza that afternoon. She'd rung the doorbell, knowing that Suze would be in town at a meeting and had heard steps running down the stairs through the door. Totally puzzled by Leslie's reason for being there, Eliza had invited her into the kitchen.

"Why?" she asked, eyes wide. "What does he care about me?"

"He's worried about some of the people you're visiting with on the Internet."

"He told you about that?" She stormed across the room. "He's such a shit. What I told him was in confidence."

"You frightened him."

"Why is it his business?" she snapped. "More than that, why is it any business of yours?"

"KJ talked to me this morning and shared his concerns. I'm worried, too."

Eliza's face was contorted in anger. "Well, just forget it. Whatever he said, it was just his way of trying to get into your pants. That seems to be pretty easy. All you need is money."

That one hurt, but Leslie pressed on. "Listen, Eliza, right now you feel totally superior and like you understand everything about the world. Let me assure you, you don't. I remember myself at your age and I, too, thought I was hot shit and knew it all."

"Don't give me that past history crap," she spat. "I've heard it all and it's bullshit. You're not anything like me and never were."

"Let me tell you a few things about me as a teen. I was always well developed and guys always wanted a piece of me. For the most part I let them and now I have nothing left to give to a man I really care about." God. Who was she to advocate saving her virginity?

"Virginity is crap. All the girls in my school have already done it."

"Are you sure? Everyone says they've done it; it's a status thing. I'll bet you that many of them are as curious as you are."

"I'm not curious." Leslie could tell by Eliza's face that she was dying to ask a few questions.

"Sure you are. Have you ever done it?"

"Of course I have. I'm no kid."

Leslie remained silent, her querulous expression obvious. Eliza's lips remained pressed tightly together. "So you're really knowledgeable about sex," Leslie said, "and you know enough to stay away from guys who lead you on to try, as you put it, to get into your pants. You only do it when it's right for you, with guys you know and trust."

"Of course," she huffed.

Leslie wanted to pound some sense into Eliza but that wouldn't help anything. How to get through to her? "Okay, why don't you tell me what you're doing on the computer?"

"I'm talking to my friends, that's all."

Leslie sensed there was more. "School friends?"

"Friends I've made online. They like to talk to me so we write and chat. They don't judge me. They tell me what a beautiful person I am from my letters."

"You are beautiful," Leslie said.

"Bullshit. I've got a mirror. The guys I meet online know that looks are meaningless in true, deep relationships and that's what I have."

"How do you know that the people you meet are what they say they are?"

"Come on. I trust them and they trust me."

"What if they're not worthy of your trust? You should choose the people you trust carefully and that takes time."

"Of course they're trustworthy," she snarled. "You don't know jack."

"Actually I know a lot more than you might think."

"Because you're a hooker."

Leslie didn't flinch. "Because I do what I do, yes. I've met all kinds and I know that all kinds of people are out there. Good ones, and not so good ones."

"That stuff in the papers about girls who get in trouble with men they meet online is bull. I don't get that anyway. What would a man want from me?"

"You can't be that naive, Eliza. There are men who want to have sex with young girls." Leslie watched curiosity slowly take hold.

"Why?"

"I don't know all the answers. Maybe some of these men want to be the first, maybe they want to feel superior, maybe it's a power thing. Some of them want to prove to themselves that they can attract a beautiful, innocent young woman like you. There are zillions of reasons. Women like you want to feel grown up, able to attract mature men who may be as attractive as their pictures or may be short, fat, and as ugly as their thoughts. They may have no respect for themselves or others." Leslie paused, then said, "This is a conversation you should be having with your mother. She's the best source of information."

Eliza suddenly looked panic-stricken. "Don't you dare tell her. Swear!"

"I won't tell her unless you tell me I can." Leslie took a breath and continued. "Eliza, listen to me. I don't know whether you've had sex yet or not, but let me just tell you a few things from someone who's *been there, done that*. Life seems endless and it seems like it's going to be forever until you're truly old enough to go out on your own, but it's not that far in the future at all. It's only around the corner. I certainly can't preach about keeping yourself pure until you find the right guy, but I can say this. Respect yourself and your body. Only give yourself to the boy, or man, who respects you and lets you make your own decisions. Don't make love because some guy makes you feel mature; make love because someone makes you feel special inside. Don't make love because some guy says he'll love you more if you do. Make love because it seems the rightest thing you could possibly do at that moment whether it's with a guy in your school or someone you meet outside. There's a world of difference between having intercourse and making love."

When Eliza remained silent and appeared to be listening, Leslie continued, "Most important, Eliza, and please hear these words when you're the most tempted. When you decide that the moment is right, make sure that he uses a condom. If he doesn't have one, use the one that you're going to keep in your purse, just in case. If he refuses to wear it, don't have sex no matter how much you want to. That guy is only interested in himself. Bareback sex is never safe. Ever. Please."

"Yeah, right. Do your johns always use condoms?"

"Always."

"You're shitting me."

"I'm not at all. I insist on it as do all the women who work with me. No condom, no intercourse. The end."

"You talk about respect but you sell yourself. How can you talk to me about respect?" she snapped.

"Every time I make love with a man it's my choice. He pays me, yes, but I can take it or leave it. Have you ever seen the movie *Pretty Woman*? In it, Julia Roberts is a prostitute, but she and her friend have a deal. 'I say who, I say when, and I say how much.' If you believe that about yourself, then you're part of the way toward being a grown-up."

Eliza stared at Leslie as she continued, "Men you meet on the Net might be wonderful people but the odds are against it.

Think really hard about the kind of man who would want to have a relationship with a fifteen-year-old highschool student."

"I've found that kind of guy. He's older, very mature, and he likes and respects me. He wouldn't do anything I didn't want."

"So he's older. How much?"

"He's really old. He's thirty-two."

Old? I'm thirty-four. "That is pretty old, but he went to the Web site looking for a teenaged girl. What could he have wanted? What could he possibly have in common with a girl of your age? You can't like the same music, the same TV shows. You don't have the same background, the same collection of experiences. You probably like to do things at 2 A.M. He's probably already long asleep."

"We share lots of things."

This sounded like a man to worry about. What would a thirty-two-year-old man want from a fifteen-year-old, except the obvious? "Do you share, or do you each talk. While he's talking about his life, his likes and stuff, are you really hearing, or are you just thinking about what you're going to say next? Ask a few questions about your favorite games or movie stars. Do you really connect?"

"Of course we do."

"Does he know how old you really are?"

"Sure. He says I'm a beautiful and mature person."

"What do you know about him?"

"He works on Wall Street. He's a very important stockbroker. He lives in a penthouse on Park Avenue and he's very rich. He tells me about the important people he knows and the fancy places he goes to. Manhattan places, not diners like Sound's End."

"I don't mean to be insulting, but if he's so rich and successful, why you? He obviously can have any woman he wants. Why a fifteen-year-old?"

"Don't be like that. He's lonely and he likes women who are young and don't have a lot of preconceived ideas about things. He likes introducing me to new things."

There seemed to be no way to talk sense to the girl. "Eliza, I'm afraid there's nothing I can say that will change your mind about things, but I can ask you to think about what I've said. Think long and hard about who you're talking with and what he's really, really like."

When Eliza didn't react, Leslie said, "One more request. If you ever decide to meet personally with someone you've met online, tell KJ, or one of your school friends all the details about your rendezvous in case of trouble. Listen to them and value their opinions. Then think about it again, and yet again. It's a dangerous world out there and you're not yet equipped to deal with the weirdos. Even I'm not sometimes."

"Have you had any weirdos?"

"On occasion some man gets out of line, but where I work, there's a two-hundred-pound bouncer who can take care of me if I get into difficulty. You don't have that luxury."

Eliza's face broke into a tiny smile. "Maybe he could come with me if I ever meet Dennis."

Dennis. It was somehow scarier now that the guy had a name. Leslie grinned. "I only wish he could."

They heard a car pull into the driveway. "Shit," Eliza said, "that's my mom. She's early."

"Okay," Leslie said, making her way quickly to the front door, "I'm out of here. Just think about what I've said. Deal?"

"Okay, just get out of here. Mom will go ballistic if she sees you."

But it was too late. Suze was already talking as she walked into the kitchen through the back door. "Eliza? You home? This is a disaster. It seems there's nothing I can do to force Leslie to go back where she came from, and Vicki's store looks like a *fait accompli*."

Leslie had her hand on the doorknob when Suze stormed

into the living room. "I had a meeting with—" Suze's face reddened. "What the hell is she doing here, Eliza?"

"Calm down, Mom, before you have a coronary. She's leaving."

"What was she doing here?"

"We were just talking and she's leaving now."

"Suze," Leslie said. "Eliza and I were talking about some very serious things, things that you and she should be talking about."

"What do you know about how I talk to my daughter?" she shrieked. "Get the hell out of here!"

"Eliza, talk to her. She's your mother and—"

"I'm her mother and you're," Suze sputtered, "you're what you are. Don't you dare go near my daughter again."

"Eliza," Leslie said as she opened the front door. "Tell her. And remember what I said about respect and trust."

"What would you know about respect and trust," Suze said. "You're a whore, and nothing more. You've conned everyone else around here, but not me. I've known there was something not right about you from the first."

"I'm leaving," Leslie said as she walked out, "but please Suze, despite what you might think of me, Eliza's in trouble and she needs you. Talk to her." As Suze slammed the door behind her, Leslie heard Eliza running up the stairs.

"What should I have done?" she asked Brad several minutes later as they sat in his living room. "First KJ then Eliza confided in me and I promised I wouldn't tell anyone. I didn't feel I could tell Suze but I hate the way I left things. I'm really worried about Eliza. She's got a specific online friend named Dennis who is filling her head with bullshit and, like most teenaged girls, she's insecure and sure this guy is her real friend. She's discovering sex and she wants to try. Curiosity and hormones make a powerful cocktail."

"You speak as if you know how she feels."

"The way she feels isn't so different from the way most of

us felt at that age. It's just that some have more patience and more sense than others. I had neither, and so I had lots of dates and lots of backseat sex. I've learned since then to have respect for myself." She chuckled ruefully. "That sounds funny coming from a prostitute, but it's true. Unfortunately, since I do what I do it's difficult for me to explain to kids like Eliza."

"I think you've done all you could. You gave Suze enough to go on. If she's got any brains, she'll attempt to find out what you and Eliza were talking about."

"I wish I thought she could get past her preoccupation with Vicki and me. I'm really frightened for Eliza's safety."

Chapter
22

Wednesday afternoon Leslie got a call from Marcy. Leslie told her friend about her conversations with Brad and that he seemed to be getting comfortable with her job. "Are you sure you can trust him?" Marcy asked.

"As sure as I can be. I think we have a future and I have to go for it. I haven't mentioned the club by name nor have I mentioned the names of any of you guys or our clients, and I don't intend to. That's a subject we'll just bypass. After all, he wouldn't tell me about his criminal investigations."

"You know best, but it's a little worrisome for me, too. Club Fantasy has a lot to lose, not to mention jail time for the principals at least. If you and he continue your relationship, will you also continue to work? Full time?"

"I don't know," she said, "but whatever happens, I'll be careful." The conversation veered off in other directions including catching Leslie up on the status of both Marcy's pregnancy and her twin sister Jenna's.

Finally, Marcy got serious. "I've got to talk a little business, Leslie. I don't mean to bug you but several of your regulars have called to make dates for September. What should I tell them? Are you coming back? You'll leave a lot of disappointed folks, including Jenna and me, of course, if you don't."

"I've had a wonderful time these past weeks and indolence has a lot to recommend it, but I think I'm ready to come back to work. I miss it, the guys, the fun, the entertainment. Let's do this. Book me for September, beginning after Labor Day, and if I change my mind about working from then on I'll honor those commitments anyway. I'll know more after a week or so back."

"What about Brad? How will he feel about your going back to work?"

"That's something we'll have to deal with. I am who I am and I don't intend to change it. I wouldn't expect him to give up the force if I asked him to so why should I be any different."

"True enough. I've one other piece of business. Simon called." Simon was one of Leslie's regular customers, one who wanted only phone sex. "He wants to call you sometime this week. I told him you were on vacation but he asked me to ask if you'd be willing to suspend your vacation for one phone call. He misses you."

She'd never met Simon Patterson and that wasn't even his real name. He'd teased once that he named himself after Simon Templar, the Saint. "I'm certainly no saint," he'd said, "but I like to think I'm urbane and clever the way he was in those old TV shows." To further shield his identity he sent anonymous money orders every time he wanted a phone call.

"Sure, what the hell," Leslie said, considering the five hundred dollars she'd make for a half an hour on the phone. "It's nice money and he's such a sweetheart. Suggest that I call him tomorrow evening about seven-thirty." She knew the phone he used was one of those prepaid, untraceable ones. "That should work for him."

"Will do. I'll take charge of your calendar for next month but I won't make any dates for October until you give me the go-ahead. That will give you an out if you want to take it."

"Great, and thanks for being so understanding, Marcy."

"Of course."

As she hung up she found herself both dreading talking to Brad and looking forward to talking dirty with Simon.

She hadn't considered phone sex for her first several years in the business until one evening Marcy approached her, asking whether she'd be willing to give it a try. "I've no idea what phone-sex women say," Leslie had answered. "What do men want?"

"Why don't you call one of the phone sex hotlines"—she'd grinned and said,—"and I do mean hot, and see what they say and do."

"I'm not a man. The woman at the other end of the line needs to respond to a man's voice."

"I know and I thought about that. What if I lent Zack to you for a few hours. Not to keep, mind you. He's all mine but I'm sure he'd agree. He could make the call and you could listen in on an extension and see what happens. Let me do a little scouting and find out who's the best."

She'd listened and discovered that talking dirty over the phone was little different from talking dirty in person, something she did often with her clients. Her naturally low, sexy voice was a particular asset. From then on, several men called her on a regular basis to listen to her voice and participate in their shared fantasies.

Early the following evening Brad and Leslie had dinner together and, over coffee, Leslie explained that she had a date that evening for phone sex with a client and that she wanted privacy. "It's a very intimate thing," she explained. "Can you deal with that?"

Brad thought for several minutes. "I guess this is where the rubber meets the road. Do I love the idea? No. I have always had very provincial ideas about relationships but over the past week I've had to do a lot of rearranging in my brain."

"And . . ."

"And it's your life and your career." He took her hand across the table. "Obviously there are going to be things about my job that I can't talk about with you, and I don't want to share what you do either."

"That's just what I told my friend Marcy recently. She asked whether I could trust you and I said that I could. Absolutely."

"You can, and vice versa. I don't have to like it, but I'll deal with it. Will you come to my place afterward?"

Leslie felt lighter than she'd felt in weeks. "Of course." It just might work and she wanted it to desperately. She loved him. Very much. She'd realized that several days before but had been denying it to herself ever since. It was much too fast. They'd need time to really get to know each other. If they could get past this evening they might just have that time.

At seven-thirty she dialed Simon's number and heard his warm voice. "Hi, Carolynne with an 'e.' " The *with an "e"* part had become a sort of trademark with her. Something about Brad and that name nagged at her, but she ignored it.

"Hello, Simon. How are you?" They always began with a short bit of small talk.

"Fine. Lonely. I haven't spoken to you in too long. Where have you been?"

His voice sounded like that of an older man, but she'd decided early on that it was pointless to try to guess things about her phone sex partners. "I'm on vacation in a fancy hotel with a beautifully landscaped hot tub. Want to fool around in it with me?"

"I'd love to. Tell me what it looks like?"

She'd learned early on that Simon liked to play the scene in exotic places so she'd decided on this slightly pagan setting. "It's outdoors, set into a grassy area with tall trees all around. There are flowers of every color and description, with heavy scents to occupy the senses. It's dusk and the sun is setting. I can see the golds and pinks through the branches of the trees. There are bees humming, flying from flower to flower, trying to finish up before nightfall. Can you see it?"

"I certainly can. We've never visited this particular spot before. Tell me about the tub."

"It's old-fashioned, wooden, with benches at various heights inside. It's sunk into the ground so when you're in it you're at ground level so you can smell the newly mown grass and thread your fingers through it. The air is cooling down, now that the sun is dropping behind the trees. There's a mist rising from the heated water."

"Are you sitting in the tub?"

"Not yet. I'm just leaving my bungalow. There's no one else around. It's totally private. I'm wearing my bikini, but I'm thinking about how wonderful the hot water would feel on my naked body." As Leslie spoke, she began to slip away, but not before she thought about the totally phoney world she was creating, not unlike the one Dennis was creating for Eliza. Hers was totally benign and she hoped Eliza's was as well.

"It sounds so beautiful. May I join you?"

"Not quite yet." She loved putting him off, and he seemed to enjoy it, too. "I want to get comfortable first. I think I'll take off the top of my bathing suit before I climb into the tub." She paused. "I have it off now and I'm climbing in. The heat makes my body languid and I stretch out, draping my arms on the grass beside the tub. I'm leaning my head back and closing my eyes."

"Excuse me if I'm disturbing you."

"You're not." She wanted him to start things so she could discover how he wanted to play this evening. He might want to be aggressive or passive, and she needed to find out.

"Good. My name is Simon and yours?"

"I'm Carolynne. Spelled with an 'e' at the end."

"Good evening, Carolynne with an 'e' at the end. Mind if I join you in the tub?"

"Not at all. I'm always eager for company. If you want, you can take off your briefs and enjoy the water all over your body. It's a beautiful body, so muscular. I especially love your shoulders, well-defined like a basketball player's."

"Thanks for the compliment. I have to admit that I watched you as you walked across the grass. You've got the most gorgeous legs, and great breasts. And I love a woman with long blond hair."

Long blond hair. That was the persona she'd adopted for him for the moment. Originally he'd liked black hair, but about three months ago he'd shifted. She'd learned to play very loose, and pick up on every nuance. "Come in here and join me," she purred.

"I'm going to do just that. Let me pull off my briefs. It's difficult when I'm so aroused."

"Such a big cock. I noticed it through your shorts. Come on in here and maybe you'll let me touch it."

"I'd like that." He paused, his breathing loud in her ear, then continued, "It's hot in this water."

"You'll get used to it quickly. I have. Sit here beside me."

"Mmm, you're right. The water's perfect."

"I'm taking your hand. Would you like to touch my breasts?"

"I would." He let out a long half moan, half sigh. "You feel so good. Your breasts fill my hand and float lightly on my palms."

"I'm sliding my fingers up your thigh beneath the bubbling water. Can you feel me?"

"I can. I love it when you touch me."

Leslie lay on her bed, the phone cradled against her ear. She'd removed her shorts and her fingers played in her pussy. "You're so hard. Have you been thinking of making love with me?"

"I've thought of little else, Carolynne. My cock's getting harder just thinking of pushing it into you."

"My pussy's wet. I can touch it and feel the difference between the water and my own slippery wetness. Want to feel me?"

She could hear his harsh breathing. "Oh yes. I want to slide my fingers into you. You feel so tight around me."

"Let me climb out and lay on the grass so you can feel all of me."

"That way I can push my face between your beautiful legs."

"Please, lick me. I love what your talented tongue can do to me. Lick and suck me." She sighed audibly. "Yes, like that." Her fingers rubbed her clit. It had taken her a while to get into the phone sex thing but now it excited her, probably almost as much as her clients. "Just like that." She sighed, then, knowing exactly what he liked, she added, "There's someone watching us. She's tall, a brunette, with long, flowing hair down to her waist. She's opening the door to her bungalow and coming out here."

"Will she join us?"

"If you want her to."

"I do."

"Good. She's wearing a tiny white bikini that makes her deep tan look even darker. Wait, she's taking off the top. She's got large breasts, white where the sun hasn't touched them. They have deep brown nipples in the center of dark areolas. She's taking off the bottom of her bikini too, so you can see the white area where it was, surrounding her neat, black pubic hair. She's coming over."

"Is she getting in the tub?"

"She's sitting on one of the benches and reaching out to cup your balls while you bend over me. Does it feel good?"

"Oh yes," he sighed. "Maybe she'll squeeze them."

"She is doing that now, but don't stop licking me, too."

"I won't. Your scent is so exotic and you taste so wonderful."

"I want you to fill me, too."

"Let me stand up. I think if I stand on this bench I can just reach your sweet snatch. I can play with your clit with my cock, rubbing it up and down."

"And the brunette can slide her fingers between your ass

cheeks. Bend over a little so she can reach your anus. She's rubbing it and it's wet from the water in the tub. She's pushing her finger in just a little bit. Does that feel good?"

"Oh yes. I'm going to push myself into you now."

"As you do, she's pushing her finger into your ass. As you pump into me, she's pumping into you."

"That feels so good. Am I pleasing you too?"

Her fingers knew exactly where to touch. "You feel perfect. Push your cock in deeper now."

"I'm doing just that." He was panting now.

"Can you feel both your cock inside of me and her finger inside of you? Are you as close to coming as I am?"

"Oh, yes." She pictured him with his fingers wrapped around his cock, pumping as they were in the fantasy. "Oh, God. This feels so good." His sharp gasp told her that he'd climaxed.

She pushed herself over the edge. "Right now, baby. Right . . . now!"

They lay hundreds of miles apart, panting, hearts pounding, for several minutes. Then he said, "As always, darling, you were fabulous."

"Simon, you can always get to me. I'm going to have to clean up when we hang up."

"Me too. I'm going to do that and I'll talk to you next month."

"Good night, Simon. I enjoyed our time together, as I always do."

"Me too. Good night." He hung up.

Later that evening she met Brad in his cottage. They sat together and watched the end of the ball game, then cuddled together in his bed, never mentioning the way she'd spent the early evening. That seemed to work for both of them.

Chapter
23

The Labor Day weekend First Friday barbecue two days later was a gigantic success. Someone counted and at the high point of the meal there were forty-seven people, not including the small gang of children. With Marie's help Leslie had actually found a recipe for orzo salad with dried cranberries and walnuts and, although it had involved almost no cooking, Leslie was proud of herself for making it successfully. She brought it to the salad table and was delighted by the words of praise from the neighbors, who all realized what a feat it was.

She and Brad had been sliding along, not talking about the following Monday, when each would head back to the city. Leslie was pretty sure that their relationship couldn't continue and she didn't want to spoil their last days together with discussions about the future.

Leslie had asked KJ several times whether he had any new information about Eliza's computer friend but he seemed not to know anything. Eliza had told neither Suze nor Kevin anything and spent every day in her room.

Suze was oblivious, still waging a seemingly one-woman war against Vicki's store, devoting all her energies to preventing the emporium from opening at all, much less the week after Labor Day. Somehow, her hatred of Leslie and her occupation had been redirected toward having a sex shop, as she called it, in *her* town. Leslie had taken to reading the local newspaper, published on Wednesday and Saturday, and over the past few issues, the letters to the editor had shown a slow turn in favor of the emporium. It had become a live-and-let-live issue with several letters touting the new business the shop would bring to Sound's End. Suze, however, remained obdurate, focusing all her energies on her campaign.

Vicki had taken out a tasteful, full-page advertisement in the previous Wednesday's paper inviting everyone in town to visit during the Grand Opening Week. Over burgers and portions of Leslie's salad, Trish had confided in her that her mother had decided to eliminate the heavier "whips and chains" department, at least for the moment. "I think your mom has made a wise decision," Leslie said.

"Me, too. Actually she's backed off quite a bit."

"Have you talked to her about your future?"

"Several times," Trish said slowly. "It always ends up the same way. She agrees to think about how to get along without me, and I agree to think about whether I can stick around for a few months until the business is off the ground."

"Would that be so terrible?"

"I suppose not," Trish said, "but it's like quicksand. If I stand still too long I'll sink."

Leslie grinned. "It's said that you can float on quicksand if you just relax."

Trish threw her hands up in mock surrender. "I give up," she said, laughing.

"Maybe you two could agree on a timetable."

"I'm not sure I can trust her to abide by any agreement we reach."

"That's not a very nice way to feel, is it?"

"No, I guess it isn't."

Later, when she went over to the ice chest to get another

soda, Leslie saw KJ and Eliza obviously arguing, gesturing wildly, yet keeping their voices low. Finally Eliza stomped off into her house while KJ stalked off down the beach.

Damian finally showed up after seven, filled his plate and beckoned to Abby. They walked back to their porch and sat on the steps to eat, not joining the usual crowd at their table. Leslie noticed that, while he and Abby talked quietly, he kept glancing over at her, then glaring. There's one person who hated her because of her job, she realized.

She watched them talking and hoped Abby would finally relax and feel better. Abby had been in a terrible mood all week. Her husband hadn't appeared at all the previous weekend and Abby had been quite closed-mouthed about it. "He had to work," was all she'd said and no one had pressed her further. Leslie had spent that afternoon helping Abby pack many of her children's things for their return to Hartford. Mark and Tammy had been told to help with their own stuff in return for missing the first few days of school but their progress was slowed since they kept begging to spend "one last hour at the beach," so Leslie had offered to help to free the children to play with Phillip and Stacy. She and Abby talked amiably but it was obvious that Abby was fuming. "When are you leaving?" Leslie had asked.

"Damian will be here this evening and we'll get everything organized, then we'll leave Monday morning. It's not a long drive but Damian wants to miss the Monday evening traffic."

Not looking at Abby as she put clothing in a box, Leslie asked, "Is everything okay?"

"Everything's fine," Abby said stiffly. "Damian's just busy, that's all."

Deciding to drop the subject, she said, "Are you looking forward to getting back home?"

She heard Abby's long sigh. "I don't have nearly as many friends in Hartford as I have here. I've come to feel really close to Marie, you, Brad, even Suze and Vicki. It's lonely for me back home. The kids are both in school and Damian's gone all day. There's nothing much for me to do there."

"Have you ever thought of getting a part-time job?"

"Damian doesn't want me to do anything like that. He says he's quite capable of supporting his family."

"What about some volunteer work? There must be lots of places that would leap at the chance of having someone with your abilities."

"What abilities? What could I do?"

"You're well organized and great with people. I'm sure you could find something."

"I don't think Damian would like that. He likes to know where I am and what I'm doing at all times."

Leslie recognized the "yeah but" syndrome, as her friend Marcy called it. Occasionally, when one of them talked with a prospective client and suggested slight deviations from the customer's rigid ideas, every suggestion was met with, "Yeah but that wouldn't work because . . ." There was no point in continuing such a conversation and Marcy usually declined the business. Now Leslie realized that talking with Abby was meeting with the same resistance so she gave up.

Around nine, when the crowd thinned to just the locals, Leslie went back to her cottage to wash and put away the bowl from her salad. *I made something that everyone liked*, she thought. *What a kick.*

She heard the beach-side door close quietly and wondered whether Brad had decided to come over early. He'd said he had a few phone calls to make and that she should come over to his place in about an hour. "Did you finish your business early?" she called.

Getting no response, she said, "I thought I was going over to your place."

When she heard only light footsteps she glanced around and saw Damian standing in the kitchen doorway. "Well, hello, Damian," she said. Puzzled she turned back to the sink and continued washing her bowl. "Did you enjoy your dinner?"

"So I'm not good enough for you. Slut," he snarled.

She whirled and saw his face, contorted in anger. Leslie didn't need advanced radar to know that she was in trouble. She looked at him and saw that his jaw was rigid, his hands fisted at this sides. Her mind raced but she couldn't think of anything to say.

"When Abby told me I couldn't believe it, but then I realized what had happened. You're a whore and wouldn't let me touch you without some cash changing hands." He reached into his pocket, pulled out a handful of bills and threw them onto the kitchen table. "Am I good enough for you now?" His voice was tight, his shoulders hunched, his eyes slitted. He began to unbutton his short-sleeved dress shirt. "I'm sure that will buy me a few minutes of your precious time."

Keep calm, she told herself. She'd dealt with angry men before. "Damian, don't do this. Despite what you've heard about what I do for a living, it's not like this."

He pulled his shirt off to reveal his furry chest. Damian wasn't a particularly large man, but he was muscular and powerful looking. Leslie's thoughts bounced in her head as she tried to think of words to defuse the situation. "Damian, listen. Abby's my friend. She's right outside helping clean up. You really don't want her to know about this, do you?" She wondered whether Damian was hearing anything through the red haze of his fury.

"I don't give a crap what she thinks," he snarled. "She knows what I do on the side and she puts up with it since I give her and the kids a good home. Otherwise I do what I want, and right now I want you. You're bought and paid for now so it's my turn."

Leslie now knew she was in deep trouble. She didn't think she was going to be able to dissuade Damian from what he had in mind with just words. She was in her kitchen with lots of knives and other sharp implements, but she hesitated to cause a scandal for herself and for Abby and her children. She backed up against the sink. "Damian, think about this. You don't mean what you're doing."

"I certainly do. After all, what has Brad got that I don't? I'm pretty good-looking and I keep myself in shape. There are dozens of women who will testify that I'm damned good in bed." He rubbed his crotch. "And this is one fine piece of equipment. Come on, whore, you're bought and paid for. Let's do this."

He unfastened his belt and pulled it from the waistband of his slacks, then unbuttoned and unzipped himself. "Damian, don't make me scream."

"Scream all you like. With the noise of the waves and the wind no one will hear you."

There was a light in his eyes, a feral gleam that told her that all her talking wasn't going to get her anywhere. Slowly she reached behind her and grasped the heavy ceramic bowl she'd been washing. Would it be heavy enough?

Damian toed off his shoes, dropped his slacks and kicked them aside. Through his briefs, Leslie could see his rampant erection. As he stalked close enough to press his body against hers she felt the edge of the sink dig into her spine. She didn't want to hurt him and, in a moment of lucidity, she realized how it might look. He could say that she led him on then wanted money. He'd paid her and she'd refused to honor their agreement. After all, he was a lawyer and would be an expert at spinning things to his own advantage.

What would Brad think, and Abby, and everyone else on Atlantic Beach Road? Then his mouth covered hers, his tongue driving, forcing its way into her mouth. His fingers tangled in her hair while his other hand found the front of her shirt and pulled. Funny, she thought in some small part of her mind, I make this fantasy happen often and clip seams so shirts rip off cleanly as they do in movies. In reality, shirts didn't tear nearly that easily.

She felt the neckband of her shirt dig into the back of her neck and finally the material gave way and the garment split partway down the front. "Damian," she shouted, finally realizing that she would have to resort to more than talk. Now terrified, her heart pounding, her breath rasping in her ears she screamed. "Damian, stop! Help!" she kept screaming. "This is rape! Rape!" She hoped the use of the word rape would bring him to his senses, but it didn't.

She took a deep breath and screamed as loudly as she could. "Help! Stop this!" Not knowing whether she'd been heard, she closed her fingers around the lip of the bowl and raised it over Damian's head. "Stop! Help!" Knowing that she had no other choice she brought the bowl down on his head, breaking it and causing his knees to buckle. Since a piece of her shirt was still tangled in his fingers he pulled her down on top of him. She felt a sharp pain where the shards of ceramic slashed through the heel of one hand as she tried to keep herself from falling.

"Damian!" Abby screamed. "Leslie! My God! What's going on?"

Unable to speak coherently, Leslie untangled Damian's fingers from the front of her ripped shirt and rolled onto the tile. As she lay, trying to catch her breath, she heard Abby screaming for help and Damian's rasping breath beside her.

Suddenly Brad's arms were around her, cradling her in his lap. She felt a cloth being pressed against her bloody hand. "Brad," she said, her throat raw from screaming, tears flowing down her face.

As she opened her eyes she saw that the kitchen was now full of people: Suze and Kevin, Marie and Joe along with Vicki, Trish, and KJ, all crowded into the small room. "What the hell happened here?" Suze shouted, quieting the other voices. "I should have known," she said, glaring at Leslie.

"She was the victim here, Suze," Abby said. "Are you okay, Leslie?"

"I'm all right." She looked down at her hand. "Just a few cuts and bruises." He moved her leg and her hip hurt like hell.

"Oh, Leslie, I'm so sorry," Abby said, in tears.

"You have nothing to be sorry for," Leslie said. "This is all on Damian."

"Not all of it," Suze said. "After all, she's the whore and she probably started it."

"I doubt she started anything. I saw the end of it and Damian was ripping her clothes off."

"You have no idea how it started," Suze snapped. "I'm calling the police."

"I would think before you do that," Brad said, his calm, authoritative voice de-escalating the situation. "I think it's pretty obvious what happened here."

"She asked for it. She's been asking for it ever since she got here."

"Suze, shut up!" Marie snapped. "Leslie hasn't been asking for anything and everyone but you knows it. Look at her and look at Damian. He's the one who's undressed, with a piece of her shirt still in his hand. She's the one bleeding from both her hand and her neck, where his yanking shredded her shirt and the back of her neck. Get the hell off your self-righteous horse and think for a minute." Joe put his arm around his wife's shoulders and squeezed briefly in a show of support.

"You look at the money on the table," Suze hissed. "He obviously paid her and she wouldn't put out."

"Suze, I don't care if he gave her the moon and stars, if she didn't want him, it's still rape." While she spoke, Marie efficiently filled a bowl with warm water and soaked several kitchen towels. She handed one to Brad, who carefully washed Leslie's palm.

"There's no rape here. Damian's Abby's husband, not some piece of trash," Suze said.

For the first time Abby spoke. "Actually he's a piece of trash anyway. He might be my husband right now, but not for long."

Damian pulled himself to a standing position and yanked on his pants. "This isn't what you think, Abby. Really."

"You have no idea what I think. I think you're a shit, a cheat, a liar, and a shit." She grabbed Suze's camera from her pocket and there were more than a dozen flashes. "My divorce attorney will get these and I think you'll give me whatever I want."

"Abby, be reasonable. It isn't the way it looks. We had an arrangement. She promised me that, for the right price . . ."

"Damian," Brad said, his voice low and threatening, "stop right there. Leslie's not in business here. She's been with no one but me, and I will swear to that. You couldn't have any arrangement. You haven't even been here in two weeks."

"We made plans on the phone. I was to bring the money . . ." Damian snatched up the bills he'd thrown on the table. "See?" He brandished the handful of bills. "Then she changed her mind."

"I don't believe a word of it," Brad said, "but let's just say for the sake of argument that she did. Any woman has the right to say no and it's pretty obvious from everything we see here that you wouldn't take no for an answer. That's rape."

Damian had put his shirt and pants back on and was fastening the last of his buttons. "You would say that. You've been fucking the whore for weeks."

Leslie could feel all of Brad's muscles tense so she put her hand in his. "It's okay, Brad. Really it is."

"Say all you want, Brad, but we all know what she is," Suze said.

"She's not like that." Leslie recognized KJ's voice.

"Of course she's not," Trish echoed. Leslie looked at the two young people standing just inside the door, then at Vicki's horrified face.

Suze turned to her son in the doorway. "Shut up, KJ, and go home."

"No. I won't. Leslie's only done good stuff and you've no right to talk to her that way."

Leslie struggled to a sitting position. Her entire body felt battered and her neck and hand hurt like hell. "It's okay, KJ," she said softly, "you don't have to defend me."

"I don't have to, but I will. I think you're a good guy"—he glared at his mother—"as opposed to some. You've only tried to help with Eliza and everything."

"Your mother is trying to do the right things," Leslie said. She didn't want to reveal any of the conversation she'd had with Eliza.

Suze was livid. "Don't you dare defend me, and stay out of our business, Leslie." She grabbed KJ by the arm and pulled him from the room. "Stay far out!"

Kevin followed his wife, then turned at the door. "I agree with KJ and I'll talk to Suze. None of this was your fault." He closed the screen door behind him.

During the conversation, Marie had dashed across the street and returned with a first aid kit. "What are we going to do about Damian, Brad?" Abby asked, opening a dressing and covering the abrasion on the back of Leslie's neck. "Should we call the police?"

Damian stood quietly in the corner of the kitchen. For a moment it appeared that Damian was going to play it tough, then thought better of it. He quickly decided to try to smooth everything over. Trying to look contrite and not quite succeeding, he said, "I don't know what came over me and I don't know what I can do to make amends." Slowly he turned to Leslie, then crouched beside her. "I'm so sorry, Leslie. I had a few drinks before I drove out here and I guess they hit me harder than I realized."

"Abby?" Brad said, getting to his feet. "We can sweep this under the rug if you want. It's really up to you and Leslie."

"He won't be any good to me in jail," Abby said. "Are you okay, Leslie? Did he hurt you?"

Her hand throbbed and her neck was abraded, but all in all she was okay. "A few bumps and bruises but I'm okay with whatever you want to do. I don't need to see him in jail." Maybe in hell but she realized from the look on Abby's face that her wish would probably come true.

Damian looked at his wife lovingly. "I'm really sorry, darling, and I'll make this all up to you. We'll talk this all out at home."

Leslie's head whirled as Abby slapped Damian across the face, the sound loud in the quiet room. "Bullshit. There's no 'home' for us," she said, sounding calm and more furious than she'd ever sounded. "Go back to Hartford and get your things out of the house there. I'll pack your stuff here. Move to your apartment. And don't be in the house when I get back Monday evening."

"The kids . . ."

"I'll tell them that we're going to be living apart and I'll put as good a spin on it as I can. I hope you'll be part of their lives and see them as often as possible. We can work out finances as time passes but I know," she said, waving the camera, "that you'll be generous."

Abby turned to Brad, now standing, still holding Leslie in his arms. "Brad, I want to thank you for not getting the police involved in this. It wouldn't have gotten us anywhere and nothing like this will ever happen again."

"I'm sure of that. And if, by any chance it does," Brad said to Damian, "Abby will know where to get in touch with me and this 'happening' will be brought up again. Are we clear on that?"

"Of course, Brad," Damian said quietly. "Leslie, I don't expect you to forgive me but thank you for at least not pressing charges."

Leslie remained silent as Damian walked toward the door.

Brad turned slowly as he passed and like lightning his right hand flashed out. His punch landed squarely on Damian's jaw, knocking him to the floor. "Remember that too, Damian, just in case you're ever tempted to assault a lady again." He rubbed his scraped knuckles. "Now do as your wife said."

Chapter

24

Leslie got a little sleep that night thanks to an over-the-counter product that both eased the pain of her injuries and relaxed her enough for exhaustion to take over. Brad spent the night holding her. As dawn broke, Leslie awoke and, as Brad rebandaged her hand and put antibiotic ointment on the back of her neck they talked about the previous evening again. They both agreed that there was nothing to be gained by prosecuting Damian. It would still be a case of his word against hers, and with her occupation, proving an attempted rape would be difficult and pointless. Much as she wanted to put the bastard in jail it would only hurt Abby and her children to have him prosecuted. She vowed to make every effort to deal with her fury.

Her return to New York on Monday was never far from Leslie's mind, yet both she and Brad deliberately avoided any discussion of the future. She felt like a coward not broaching the subject but she just couldn't. A cop and a hooker. Much as she wanted it to, it could never work. Even Romeo and Juliet died at the end of the play.

Something had been nagging at her since their elevator fantasy and over midmorning coffee she broached the topic to

Brad. "Remember that evening we played in our pretend elevator?"

"Hell, yes," Brad said, a broad smile lighting his face, showing his chipped tooth. "That was wonderful in so many ways."

"Remember the name I chose, Carolynne? Why did you say that you knew that it was spelled with an 'e?' "

Brad abruptly straightened and his face went white. "Did I say that?" he sputtered.

Seeing his reaction, small things he had said seemed to come together. Although she hadn't focused on it at the time she now realized that he'd known too much. She replayed snippets of their conversation the night she told him about her job.

"I don't want an apology about your job, or about Club Fantasy . . ."

"On Fifty-fourth Street, it's still illegal."

Why hadn't she put it together before now? Maybe she hadn't wanted to. "Yes, you did say that. You knew about Club Fantasy by name and you knew where it was located, too."

Brad's body language said it all. He had known about her before they'd met. She'd been had. "Oh God, Brad. You knew about me before I arrived, didn't you? This has all been an illusion. You were planted here for some cop-ish reason."

He scrubbed at his face with his palm then rubbed the back of his neck, gathering his thoughts. "Damn, Leslie, I was hoping you'd never find out." He tried to take her hand but she yanked it away. "Okay, yes, I was sent here to see what information I could glean about Club Fantasy and its clients."

Leslie's body went rigid and she turned her face away. "Oh," was all she could think to say. She thought she was so smart, so worldly, able to tell a scam in a potential customer but she'd fallen into this with both big feet. No wonder Brad didn't want to talk about the future. There was none. The pain was almost too much for her to deal with. Her throat closed and hot tears made her eyes burn.

Brad cupped her chin and turned her face so she had to look

into his eyes. "At first I didn't care much whether the assignment worked or not. I took it because it gave me a few weeks away from the city, which I will now admit I needed badly. I didn't think much about you as a person, you were just a source, a woman who worked for a brothel.

"I never imagined that you'd be so perfect and that I'd— well—become so fond of you. I didn't understand your business or your morality but it all crystalized that night in that silly elevator. Oh, I liked you a lot but that evening I finally understood your humanity and your business. Much to my surprise, I find that I agree with you about what you do. Although I can't imagine myself doing it, I now know it's right for you and, more importantly, it's right for your customers and doesn't hurt anyone."

"Why didn't you tell me sooner that you knew about me?"

He pressed his forehead against hers. "I knew how you'd react and I was scared shitless. I still am. I've found something very precious and I'm terrified of losing you."

He looked so sincere, and he obviously knew he wasn't going to get any information from her so he had no reason to say what he was saying. Maybe he really cared. But he was such a good con man. "Brad, you lied to me. Over and over. Mostly sins of omission but you lied."

She watched his shoulders slump. "I know," he whispered, and she felt the heat of his breath on her cheek. "There isn't any way for me to tell you how sorry I am."

Could she ever believe him? Would she ever trust him again? She wanted to so badly. "I need a little time to digest this. I lied to you in the beginning, too, but I didn't know you then. I couldn't lie to you now."

"You had a difficult time trying to find a way to tell me about yourself, and I couldn't find a way to tell you. We both started out with big secrets. In a way you were luckier than I was. Your truth was revealed early on. Mine festered inside of me until I couldn't find a way to be honest."

Leslie leaned back. She had to think. Without trust, there was no possibility of a relationship. "Why don't you go back to your place for a few hours? You didn't get much sleep and I need a little space."

"Do you think you can forgive me? Can we find things to build on back in the real world?"

"I don't know right now. It's all too new and I'm too scrambled. Give me some time to think about this rationally."

"Don't be too rational." Brad kissed her thoroughly. "Think about how I feel about you. Think about the fact that I'm in love with you."

"Don't complicate things, Brad."

"I don't find loving you a complication."

She huffed out a breath. "Neither do I." She pushed him toward the door.

He kissed her again on the porch. "I'm going to go to the fitness center and work out. I need to pound on something and a punching bag is much safer than beating Damian to a pulp. I'll see you later and we'll talk."

By early afternoon, after a nap and several pain relievers, Leslie felt considerably better, at least physically. She slathered herself with sunscreen and headed out to join Trish, Vicki, Marie, Joe, Kevin, and Abby who sat in beach chairs on the parking area behind the seawall watching heavy surf pound the sand. She wasn't sure she wanted to deal with all the questions she thought she'd get from everyone but she didn't want to let Damian keep her hiding in her cottage.

The tide was only halfway in but due to an offshore storm white-capped waves were almost touching the wall. She hadn't seen the water this angry since she'd been here, but somehow it seemed to fit everyone's mood.

"Come join us," Marie said. "We're trying not to spend the entire afternoon rehashing last evening. How are you feeling?"

Leslie's hand still throbbed where she'd cut it on the bowl, and her neck was a little stiff, but in general she was fine. "I'm okay."

"Did you get any sleep?" Joe asked.

"I did, and I'm really all right. It happened and that's that." She looked at Abby who had deep circles beneath her eyes. "Abby, are you okay?"

"Actually, I'm better than I thought I would be. I was just starting to tell everyone that it's like the other shoe dropped." Her sigh was long and deep. "I guess I've known for a while that Damian wasn't a very nice man and that he cheated on me and the kids but now there's no doubt and it's over."

"Did he leave?"

"I don't think he even went back to the cottage. I called the house in Hartford this morning and got the answering machine. Marie suggested a few steps I needed to take, so we drove into town first thing this morning and found a branch of our bank. I transferred cash from our savings account to a new one I opened in only my name, just in case."

"Do you think he'd be nasty enough to do anything like what you're thinking?" Leslie asked.

Vicki answered. "I stopped over right after they got back and helped Abby download those photos she took and put them on a CD. Marie and I each have a copy, and Abby opened a safety deposit box and put another copy in there. He'll have bigger problems than he can imagine if he tries anything."

"Vicki's been great," Abby said, taking her hand. "I don't think I would have thought of it but making copies of the photos was a very wise thing to do."

"You helped her with her computer?" Trish said. "That's interesting."

"It wasn't anything much," Vicki said, seeming to realize that her "I know nothing about computers" line had just been discredited. Trish glared at her mother, then looked away.

"Good work, Vicki," Kevin said. "That way Damian won't

be able to screw Abby ever again." He grinned. "Pardon the quite deliberate *double entendre*."

"Way to go, Vicki," Leslie said. "Now we all need to move on."

"Have you told the children, Abby?"

"Not yet. I want them to enjoy their last few days here, but I will. I think they probably sense that things haven't been going well the past few weeks. Kids are very wise."

"They know more than you can imagine," Leslie said, thinking about Eliza.

"Has anything like that ever happened where you work?" Joe asked.

"No. We have a great guy who lives in the building where I work. He's our bouncer and discourages anything like last evening but it doesn't mean I haven't thought about it. It's a little scary, and a bit ironic. I've never had any trouble with my customers, but here . . ."

"I'm so sorry," Abby said again.

Joe answered. "It wasn't your job to watch your husband. In the end, this whole thing might have done you a service, helping you accept things. I think it's best if we drop the subject and let last evening be history."

After everyone voiced their agreement, Marie asked, "Where's Brad?"

"He's working out this afternoon but I assume he'll be around later." She didn't want to say more since she was still trying to adjust to the fact that he'd been sent to spy on her and had known all along who she was.

Marie turned to Vicki. "We haven't seen you around in quite a while. How's the store coming along?"

"I'm opening in two weeks." She hesitated, then looked at Leslie. "I know you don't want to talk about last evening, but I can't stop thinking about one aspect of this whole mess." She hesitated again. "Do you think having a store like mine makes something like that more likely? I know Brad and Suze believe it will bring an unsavory element into town."

"You're certainly sounding more open-minded than you have been," Marie said.

Leslie watched Trish stare at her mother, open-mouthed. "I know," Vicki said. "I was just wondering."

"Damian's being here had nothing to do with your store, Vicki," Leslie said, "but I don't know the deeper answer to your question."

"I can't get it out of my mind. I want my store to attract all kinds of customers and secretly I want to annoy Suze, too, but I certainly don't want anybody to get hurt."

Trish leaned over and squeezed her mother's arm. "Of course you don't."

"Suze has gone off the deep end about your emporium," Marie said, "but lingerie is a far cry from spanking videos and handcuffs. It's your store and you have to make decisions about what merchandise it will carry, but maybe you could think about toning it down a bit. This is a family town, after all."

"Actually I already have considered that."

"Mother, maybe we need to talk," Trish said, and the two women wandered back to her house while the group's conversation moved on to other topics.

About an hour later, KJ hurried over, appearing very disturbed. "Leslie, can I talk to you for a minute?"

"Sure. What's the matter?"

"I need to talk to you in private."

He was obviously quite upset so Leslie stood and walked beside him toward her cottage. "Okay, what's going on?" she asked softly.

"Eliza's in trouble. She's gone."

Leslie stopped in her tracks at the foot of the stairs to her porch. "What do you mean, gone?"

To Leslie's shock, she saw tears trickling down KJ's cheeks. "She's left to meet one of the guys she's been meeting online. Somebody named Dennis."

Leslie tried to calm her whirling thoughts. "Dennis?" That was the name Eliza had mentioned to her when they'd talked.

"She didn't tell us how far things had gone with him. She told me last evening that he'd sent her money for the train fare and a cab to somewhere where they could be together." He grabbed her upper arm. "That's what we were fighting about at the barbecue. She told me she was thinking about going into the city to meet him. I got really angry but then she laughed and said she'd consider what I'd said. I think she was just agreeing to get away from me."

"He sent her money?" She couldn't focus so she dropped onto her top step.

KJ sat beside her. "She told me that he's sent her cash several times. She said it was so she could buy herself pretty things to wear when they got together. I was up early this morning and I heard a car in the driveway. I looked out the window and saw her get into a cab and drive away. I don't know what to do."

Leslie's brain was tumbling. "What about Suze and your father? Do they know about this online person? Didn't Suze ask her what we'd discussed that afternoon I talked to her?"

"They don't know jack about either one of us. They're so involved in their own things that they pay no attention. I could grow another head and they wouldn't notice. The only thing that penetrated about your visit was that you'd been in our house."

KJ continued, "Eliza was furious at me, yelled at me for telling you about her *friend*. I gather that Suze sent Eliza to her room without asking her anything. Some punishment. That's where her computer is and she probably cried to Dennis about how mean and uncaring her mother is."

"She left hours ago. Why did you wait to tell anyone?"

"I don't know. I didn't have anyone but you to tell and you had your own problems. I kept hoping she'd come back or that she was with someone here. That was until I found her note. She'd put it under my motorcycle helmet. I just found it a few minutes ago." He pulled a crumpled piece of paper from his pocket.

> *KJ,*
>
>   *I'm finally going to do it. Dennis has been asking me to meet him in the city and I'm going. He's paying for my train ticket and we're having dinner in a fancy restaurant. Don't tell Mom or Dad and cover for me if you need to. Be back late tonight.*
> *E.*

"That's all I know and I'm scared to death."

This is all my fault, Leslie thought. *She's willing to sell herself because I do. I was too chicken and too involved in my own problems to talk to Suze or Kevin. Shit, shit, shit.* "We have to tell your folks, KJ. This is one secret you can't keep. It's just too dangerous."

KJ's head dropped. "I know, but I can't do it myself. Can you help me?"

What am I getting myself into? Leslie asked herself, but she had to help. "Where are your folks?"

"Dad's playing tennis but Suze is in the house."

Without another word, the two walked toward the Murdock house. With Leslie right behind him, KJ walked into the kitchen and called, "Suze?"

"I'm working, KJ."

His voice quavering, KJ called, "I need to talk to you."

"I'm in the middle of something. Whatever it is, handle it yourself."

"I need to talk to you right now!"

"KJ, honey, I'm really busy."

It was time to get serious so Leslie said, "It's important, Suze."

She heard movement, then Suze burst into the kitchen. "What the hell is *she* doing here?"

"Suze," Leslie said, "KJ has something he needs to talk to you about."

"What the hell are you, his nanny? Some nanny." She turned to KJ. "What's this all about."

"Eliza's gone."

Suze waved the idea away. "Of course she's gone. She's spending the day with Chris. She left me a note."

"She's not with Chris," KJ said, softly.

"Show her the note, KJ," Leslie said and KJ handed the piece of paper to his mother.

Suze read it quickly, then her eyes widened and she dropped into a kitchen chair. "What's this all about? Leslie, you had something to do with this."

"No, Suze, I didn't. This has been going on since long before I arrived."

KJ was in tears again. "It's not Leslie's fault. She tried to talk some sense into Eliza a while ago and I thought it had worked. Don't blame her."

"Eliza told you about this," she said, waving the note, "and you didn't tell me? I should have known."

"I didn't know that she'd actually do something like this. You have every right to be angry with me, Suze, but she'd told me things in confidence. Remember that afternoon? I all but demanded that you ask her what was going on, but you were so involved in your war with me that you ignored it." When Suze looked stricken, she continued, "I'm sorry, Suze. Blame isn't important."

Leslie quickly explained what KJ had told her and what she and Eliza had talked about. "It's been going on since soon after she got her own computer last Christmas."

She stared at the note. "He sent her money?"

"Don't you get the mail, Suze? Haven't you noticed letters for her?"

"A few," Suze moaned, "but I just gave them to her. I knew about the teen bulletin boards she'd joined and I thought she just had a few pen pals."

"Suze," KJ said, "people on the Web send e-mails not letters." He sat at the table and dropped his head into his hands.

"Look," Leslie said, "there's enough blame to go around. For now, our first priority is to find Eliza."

"Leslie?" Brad's voice called. "I just got back and Marie said she saw you go into Suze's house. She thought you and KJ seemed upset." He opened the screened back door and strode into the kitchen.

Forgetting their earlier argument, she hugged him, then briefly summed up what she'd learned about Eliza's plans. "The cops have had lots of experience with online"—he stopped himself and Leslie was sure he had been about to say pedophiles but in deference to Suze he continued—"scams involving kids. What more can you tell me?"

"There's not much more," KJ said. "Mom, I'll go upstairs and check on her computer and see whether I can find out where she's gone."

"Good idea," Brad said. "I'll be up later to help. Suze, I want to call my precinct and get the word out about Eliza. It's probably like looking for a needle in a haystack but it's worth a shot."

"Please," Suze said, now in tears, "do whatever you can." Brad walked into the backyard and paced while he used his cell phone to make a few calls. Suze grabbed her phone from her pocket, dialed, and, while Leslie tried to ignore it, Suze had a screaming match with her husband.

Brad walked back into the kitchen and said, "I'd like to join KJ and look at Eliza's computer. I might be able to get some clues from that."

"Of course." Suze, looking dazed, led Brad up the stairs.

Neither Brad nor KJ had any luck with Eliza's computer, but Brad forwarded some e-mail headers to computer experts at the NYPD to see what they could learn. The police were very interested in apprehending guys like Dennis so they were quickly deeply involved.

KJ stayed in his room, but, with Leslie and Brad following, Suze walked slowly out to the blacktop and told the group what had happened. Everyone wanted to help but there was little to do for the rest of the afternoon but wait and pray that Eliza wasn't in any trouble she couldn't get herself out of. The group sat together and tried to think of things to talk about.

Kevin arrived home about half an hour later and he and Suze went into the house for a short while. When they returned, holding each other with one hand and a cell phone in the other, hoping for a call, they both looked as if they had been crying.

Brad spent the remainder of the afternoon on the phone but, from his body language as he paced back and forth, his cell phone against his ear, they all knew he was getting nowhere.

Chapter
25

Around six, Abby went back to her house to feed her children, and a little later, although no one was hungry, Leslie went back to her cottage to make a pot of coffee. As she spooned beans into the grinder she jumped as she heard the beach-side door close. Someone came up behind her. It couldn't be Damian again, could it?

"Leslie?" a small voice said. She whirled and saw Eliza, face splotchy from crying, eye makeup smeared all over her face. "Help me?" She looked like a little girl, even with her lovely short-sleeved blouse, short leather skirt, and high boots. Leslie realized that she'd never seen her wearing anything but a T-shirt with a snappy, totally self-involved saying on it with tight shorts or jeans.

Leslie opened her arms and the girl walked into them. "Oh God," Eliza said, gulping air, her face buried in Leslie's shoulder. "Everyone knows what I did, don't they?"

Leslie's heart was beating rapidly as she wrapped her trembling arms around the child. "Yes and they're worried sick. How did you get here without anyone seeing you?"

Shaking all over, Eliza explained, "I took a cab from the train station. The driver dropped me at the bend in the road. I walked along the beach and came up that way."

Leslie hugged the miserable girl still more tightly then held her away from her. She looked like hell. "Are you okay?"

Eliza struggled to speak through her tears. "Yes. Thanks to you."

"We need to tell your folks you're here. They're frantic."

"They can wait a few more minutes." She gulped for air and grabbed Leslie's hands. "Please. I need to talk to you first."

She couldn't keep from agreeing. Eliza was all right and everyone would know that soon enough. "I hate to prolong their agony."

Eliza's arms snaked around her waist and she clung like a frightened baby. "Please?"

"All right, but only for a few moments. Tell me what happened."

Eliza dropped, exhausted, into a kitchen chair. "I heard about last evening, with you and Damian. It scared the shit out of me. Someone wanted me to have dinner with him this evening and I knew that if I didn't do it soon I'd chicken out."

"Maybe your heart knew something your brain didn't want to admit. When you think about chickening out of something, you should realize there's something really bad going on." Enough preaching, she told herself.

"I know, but I couldn't stay a baby all my life. Dennis, the guy I met online, kept telling me how grown up I was, how grown up and mature I seemed. He kept saying I was beautiful and I started to believe him."

"Eliza, you're lovely."

"That's not beautiful the way I want to be. Beautiful like you."

"Everyone has his or her own kind of beauty." God, I sound like Dr. Phil.

"That's what grown-ups tell you instead of just saying, 'You're a dog.'"

Leslie cupped her chin and gazed at her. "You're going to be a lovely looking woman."

"Stop handing me bullshit." She stopped, then said, "Sorry, Leslie. You're the only one I can talk to. Don't be mad at me."

"I'm not angry, yet. Tell me about this morning."

"Dennis has invited me to come to the city, that's New York City not Hartford, several times so late last night I accepted. He said we could do stuff, then have a fancy dinner. Then he'd take me to the train and I'd come home. You know he's sent me money to get clothes so I'd look pretty." She stood. "I got these a few weeks ago." She smoothed her leather skirt and sat back down. "He'd even give me cab fare to get to the train station and then back here later."

Terrified of what she'd find out, Leslie asked, "Tell me what happened between you and Dennis."

Eliza rested her head against her arms on the table so Leslie had to listen closely to hear what she was saying. "I was so stupid. So stupid."

"What did you do?" She waited, then said, "Eliza, tell me. Whatever it was, we can fix it. It's important that you tell me." She wondered whether Suze and Kevin would consider the morning-after pill.

Eventually, when Eliza started to talk, the words came tumbling out. "I met him at Grand Central late this morning and we walked up Fifth Avenue and then around Central Park. I've never been there before and he told me about all the buildings and stuff. There were long silences, too, because other than the sightseeing, we didn't seem to have much to talk about. He had his camera and took lots of pictures and movies of me, then showed them to me on the tiny screen. He asked me whether I wanted to see them on the hi-def TV at his place before we went to an early dinner. I'm not totally dumb. I knew what that really meant and I was scared, but I said yes."

She stopped talking so Leslie said, gently, "You went to his place?"

"We got a taxi and, in the cab I thought about what you had told me about respect for myself and love and all. I got more and more nervous. He talked to me and told me it was okay, that nothing was going to happen that I didn't want but I didn't believe him. I knew he wanted to make love to me and part of me wanted it, too. But part of me was really scared and it didn't feel like love at all. Finally the cab stopped in front of his building. He got out and reached in to take my arm to help me out. I realized that I didn't want to do what he wanted, so I pulled away and told the driver to take me back to the train station. I looked back and he was just standing there, looking surprised. We weren't even on Park Avenue. I was afraid he'd follow me so I hid in a ladies' room at the train station for a few hours, then got a train to Old Saybrook and came here."

Maybe I did some good after all, Leslie thought, elated. "So nothing really happened."

Weeping, Eliza said, "Nothing happened. Except to my soul. I'll never be the same."

Leslie again enfolded Eliza in her arms and the two women clung together, each knowing what a close call the girl had had. "Probably not. You'll be wiser and more mature having learned a very valuable lesson without paying the kind of tuition you might have had to pay."

Snuffling, Eliza pulled away and found a box of tissues on the counter. She blew her nose loudly and tried to wipe the makeup off her face. "I must look a fright."

"I've seen you look better but you'll be the best thing your folks and everyone else out there have seen in a long time. Let's go outside and tell everyone you're all right. Okay?"

"My mom and dad will kill me. I'll be grounded for the rest of my life."

"I've no idea how your parents will react but you have to

admit they might have good reason to want this lesson to stick."

"I guess." Eliza slowly put the tissues in the garbage and finally nodded. "Let's go."

The group had moved their chairs closer to the roadway to avoid the spray from the waves that crashed against the seawall and splattered salt water into already-large puddles. The entire Atlantic Beach enclave sat in a circle talking quietly as Leslie and Eliza emerged from the house. Abby was the first to see them. "Eliza, my God, you're back," she squeaked and jumped up.

Everyone ran over and they all talked at once. As Suze approached, Eliza flinched and took a step backward. "You are never going out of the house again, except to school, young lady."

Kevin closed the distance between them and enfolded Eliza in a hug. "Oh, baby, we're so happy to see you. Where were you?"

"Oh, Daddy," Eliza said, then burst into tears. She pulled away from her father, reached out and took Leslie's hand.

"Get away from her," Suze shrieked, pulling at her daughter's shoulder. "She's the one who put those ideas in your head."

"What do either of you care?" Eliza yelled. "You don't give a damn about me. Leslie's the one who saved me."

Having heard the commotion, KJ ran out of his house and hugged his sister. Then he stepped back and put his hand on Eliza's shoulder. "Don't pay any attention to either of them," he said. "Are you okay?"

Face quivering from a combination of tears and rage, she nodded.

"Did anything happen?" he said softly.

She shook her head.

"Okay." He turned on his parents. "Nothing happened, so just go away."

"I don't believe nothing happened," Suze said. "You get into the house, young lady, and we'll talk about this when I've calmed down."

"Baby, it's okay," Kevin said. "You can tell us. You don't have to lie about it. We can deal with whatever you did."

More angry now, Eliza said, "I didn't *do* anything. Nothing happened and I'm not going into that house. Not right now." She turned to Leslie. "Can I stay with you tonight, Leslie? Please?"

Leslie didn't want to be in the middle of this, but Eliza needed her help. "Eliza, your parents are the ones you should be with. You need to talk to each other."

Eliza glared at her parents. "Yeah. Sure. My mother is freaked and my father doesn't believe me. Fat lot of good they'll do me."

"Sure," Suze snarled. "Like to like. Stay with her if you want." She turned her back on her husband and her children and started to walk toward her house.

"Suze!" Marie shouted to make herself heard. "You're an idiot and you're making the biggest mistake of your life."

Everyone stopped talking and looked at the older woman. "Eliza's your daughter and, except for a few recent mistakes, she's a good kid, and so is KJ. You're throwing away your chance to make this better. Let her tell you what did or didn't happen and try to figure a way to move on. And stop blaming Leslie for your mistakes."

"I didn't make mistakes," Suze said, turning back.

"How many times have we asked about Eliza and you didn't really know where she was? How many hours did she spend on the computer without anyone knowing what she was doing? When is that last time your family did something just for fun? Together!" Marie was obviously getting angrier and angrier but she lowered her voice and looked at Eliza. "What did you mean when you said Leslie had saved you?"

"We talked a few weeks ago and she said some things that made me think. That's all."

"Think about what, honey?" Kevin asked.

"About me, and my values. About my virginity, about love and the difference between making love and having sex."

"So you really didn't do anything?" Kevin said.

Eliza shook her head.

"Suze, it's your move," Marie snapped. "It would seem that Leslie had the conversation with your daughter that you should have had many times. I wouldn't be so quick to condemn her or her occupation."

"You're right, Marie," Kevin said totally shaken.

"And where have you been? You're her father and for the last few months you've been nowhere to be seen. You've left both Eliza and KJ to fend for themselves. They're not children, but they're not fully grown yet either. They need parents."

Kevin hung his head. "I guess you're right. I've been so wrapped up in myself and my problems that I forgot there was anyone else out there who might need me."

"Suze?"

Suze's jaw was rigid, her teeth clenched, her arms tightly crossed beneath her breasts. "Stay with Leslie if you want, Eliza."

"I'd rather she talked to you, Suze," Leslie said, "but I'll do what Eliza wishes for tonight." She put a supportive arm around the girl's shoulders. "Can you at least tell your daughter that you care about her?"

"Of course I care about her," Suze said. "She knows that."

"Does she?" Leslie said. "When did you last tell her that? More importantly, when did you show her last?"

"I don't have to tell her or show her. Parents love their children. She just knows it."

"I'm afraid not, Suze," Leslie said.

"Come on, Eliza," Suze said, facing her daughter. "You know I care about you."

When Eliza remained silent, Suze said, "Eliza, tell her."

"I can't because I don't know anything of the sort." Eliza's voice rose as she spoke. "You care about your job as mayor, but not about me. Not at all. You don't care about any of us, not me, not KJ, and not Daddy."

"Of course I do," Suze said, sounding desperate.

"Suze, you can't keep saying of course I do," Joe said gently. "Leslie and Marie are right. You have to show kids, talk to them, ask what they're doing and about their friends. Maybe it's time you got more involved with them and less with the town."

"I hate it when you're right, Joe," Kevin said, "but maybe you are. I've been trying to remember when we last did something together as a family and I can't recall anything within the past year. Suze?"

Suze unfolded her arms. "I can't either," she whispered.

"How about you all sit and talk for a few minutes, Suze?" Leslie said. "Maybe just you, Kevin, KJ, and Eliza. You can sit here or use my living room if you want neutral territory."

"That's a good idea, Leslie," Marie said. "Now that we know Eliza's safe, Joe and I'll go back home and talk to our children." Marie hugged Eliza and the couple headed back to their house. "I'm glad you're okay, darling. We all love you."

"Trish and I have some talking to do, too," Vicki said, "so we'll be on our way." She draped her arm over her daughter's shoulder and, with Trish's arm around her waist, they walked companionably toward their house.

"I need to hug my children," Abby said and left.

"Eliza," Brad said. He'd remained silent and off to the side of the group while Eliza talked. "If it's okay with you and your folks I'd like to talk to you tomorrow about the guy who invited you to the city. He's not a nice man and I think the police would like to chat with him."

"He didn't really do anything," Eliza said.

"I'm glad of that, but I think we all know that he wanted to. He might try things with other girls so we need to try to put a stop to it. It can certainly wait until tomorrow."

Eliza nodded, then the four Murdocks pulled chairs together and began a quiet conversation. As Leslie watched, she wondered how much good this powwow could do. Granted, Kevin leaned forward, his elbows propped on his knees, but Suze sat back, arms folded.

Brad took Leslie's hand and together they walked back to Leslie's cottage. "Do you think they'll make it?" he asked.

"They've got quite a ways to go. They've made a few big mistakes, but I think they've got a chance."

As they entered the living room, Brad turned Leslie to face him. "Do we have a chance?"

Leslie took in a deep breath and smiled. "We've made a few mistakes ourselves, but I think we just might make it."

Brad's lips were on hers. They'd date back in the city and see whether a cop and a prostitute have a chance. She believed that if any two people could, they'd make it work.

Epilogue

The sky was deep blue, with high, wispy clouds and the ocean off of Atlantic Beach was mirror flat. Brad, wearing a short-sleeved, collared, pale blue knit shirt stood on the blacktop behind the seawall, beside a justice of the peace. The remainder of the enclave sat in lawn chairs then stood as Leslie, looking radiant in a yellow summer dress, walked out of the Rogers Cottage, followed by Eliza and Trish in matching dresses of pale blue.

It had been an eventful year. Vicki's store had started slowly, but was now a moderate success. Trish had helped get it up and running then had moved to Hartford, returning each weekend to help with the ordering and bookkeeping. She had also taken several courses at the local state college and was planning to go full time this semester. Vicki stood in the crowd, gazing affectionately at her daughter, holding hands with a bookish looking man who, Trish reported, seemed to be seeing her pretty regularly.

Abby had returned to Atlantic Beach for the summer, with Mark and Tammy, now a year older and a little more mature. Damian, now officially divorced, had arranged for the cottage for them and visited his children frequently. Abby had gleefully told everyone that, when school began in the fall, she was beginning a new, part-time job as a librarian.

Marie and Joe had begun Martinelli Catering and were working diligently almost every weekend. That didn't preclude either the First Friday cookout or the magnificent spread they had prepared for today. The day before, when Leslie and Brad had arrived, Marie had whispered that she was thinking of running for the town board in the fall.

From what Leslie had gathered from her phone conversations with Marie, Suze hadn't changed very much. Right after Eliza's return, Suze had vowed to withdraw from the mayoral race and devote her time to her children but in the end the temptation to remain "queen of the town," as Marie put it, had been too great. Suze was still Suze and probably wouldn't change all that much.

Kevin, however, had gotten much closer to both his children and, with his help and some long heart-to-heart talks, both seemed to be on the right path. KJ had graduated from high school with surprisingly good grades and was enrolled in the local community college. To everyone's surprise he'd even gotten a small scholarship from the local Lion's Club. Eliza still spent time on her computer but had learned a valuable lesson. She'd phoned Leslie several times since last Labor Day, admitting that she still linked up with guys on the Net but took everything everyone said with a large boulder of salt. Whether she was still a virgin or not was a mystery, but Leslie was pretty sure she'd at least make love for the right reasons.

She and Brad had returned to the city together after that awful weekend and had spent more and more time together. Leslie cut back her hours at Club Fantasy so that during the winter she entertained only two evenings a week. Brad had gnashed his now-perfect teeth at first, but held his tongue and learned to deal with Leslie's evenings out, confident in her love for him. He had decided not to go back onto the streets and had accepted an assignment with a group of other forensic computer experts specializing in apprehending online preda-tors. He'd helped to crack several difficult cases and was mak-ing quite a name for himself.

In June Brad and Leslie had decided to try to have a baby. She knew that Brad wouldn't have asked her to give up her job for any reason, which made it easier for her to do just that. Although she had always been doubly careful with her clients, she didn't want there to be any question whose baby it was. She now spent two evenings a week having phone sex with clients but otherwise was monogamous. She found she loved having time to herself but, if the home pregnancy test she'd taken that morning was accurate, she'd have plenty to do by the following spring.

In addition, although it had taken some convincing, primar-ily by Eliza, Leslie had begun to put together a book about teens and sex, aimed at both the young people and their par-ents. The first several chapters had been enthusiastically re-ceived by several agents. Boredom wouldn't be a problem.

As Leslie walked slowly toward her soon-to-be husband she considered the previous, eventful summer. One year ago she and Brad had met here and fallen in love. Now they would make it official. They'd had a party to celebrate the impend-ing wedding in a large hotel in Midtown, with many of her friends and his in attendance. It was a strange gathering, in-cluding cops, and prostitutes and their families, but for their sakes everyone tried not to think about the occupation of the people eating hors d'oeuvres beside them.

Leslie walked to Brad, took his arm and handed her bou-quet to Eliza. She's turned out to be quite a woman, Leslie thought, then added, for a teen.

"We are gathered together . . ."

As Leslie beamed at Brad a slight breeze ruffled their hair. It was a perfect day all around.

Dear Reader,

I know you enjoyed *Hot Summer Nights* and I hope you loved the people as much as I did. When I finish writing a book I always miss the characters and sometimes I have the joy of bringing them back for guest appearances in future stories. I've done so here.

If you want to learn about Erika and the opening of Courtesans, Inc., read *The Price of Pleasure*. *Club Fantasy* and *Night after Night* cover the lives of first Jenna and then Marcy, the twins you met briefly here, while both of them get deeply involved in the business of fantasy fulfillment. My other two recent books, *Never Enough* and *The Secret Lives of Housewives* have entirely different casts. In future books I never know who's going to turn up for a cameo role, so I'll just keep writing and I hope you'll keep reading. Of course, if there's someone in particular you'd like to meet again, please let me know.

I've got a lot of books being published over the next few years so check on my Web site (*www.joanelloyd.com*) frequently to keep up with what's happening. The site also contains sexual advice, stories, questions from visitors, and lots more. Click over and stay a while.

I always love to hear from folks who've read my books so in case you want to write, here's how to get in touch. My e-mail address is *Joan@JoanELloyd.com* and I usually answer my mail at least once a week. You can certainly send a letter to me via snail mail at PO Box 221, Yorktown Heights, NY 10598, but those letters take quite a bit longer for me to answer. I look forward to hearing from you.